LEONORA ROSS

The Suncatchers

First edition

ISBN: 978-1-7778909-4-0

Editing by Jill French
Cover art by Siski Kalla

This book was professionally typeset on Reedsy.
Find out more at reedsy.com

For O.G.—my sun

There is a sun, a light that for want
of another word I can only call yellow, pale sulphur yellow, pale golden
citron. How lovely yellow is!

—Vincent van Gogh

Acknowledgement

To my brilliant editor and indispensable helping hand, Jill French, as well as my amazingly talented cover designer, Siski Kalla: thank you for your hard work and belief in *The Suncatchers*. And to the loves in my life—couldn't do it without you!

1

All over the Roeterseiland Campus, in the Canal District of Amsterdam, there was the exciting buzz of when young energy connected and everything and everyone appeared interesting. It was the start of the academic school year. The seasoned operators were hanging around with confident smiles and blasé looks. Most of the newcomers bore the look of, where the hell should I be going now, mixed with uncertainty about what lay ahead for the year—for the next couple of years—for the rest of their lives.

Luka was between enjoying a fantastic time and dealing with chaotic turbulence, in a mix of being new to the campus but familiar with campus life. She was five days into her three-year geography course at the Faculty of Social and Behavioural Sciences, and all was going well, even if she felt she needed to keep touching wood.

Her father had already prepped her on what to expect, in his typical professor style. Not that she didn't appreciate his guidance. Ruben taught environmental geography at the faculty she now attended, so it made sense that he would want to help her ease into it. Maybe, on a subconscious level, he also wanted to compensate for the fact that she'd practically been raised by one parent—him. In fairness, it was hardly her mom's fault for being a concert pianist who was constantly touring. It was what it was, and she wasn't worse off, in honesty.

Luka wove through throngs of students moving up and down stairs and in and out of lecture halls. A guy who was looking at his phone, bumped into her and mumbled, I'm sorry, without taking his eyes off the screen, the look she gave him totally lost. Yes, that really showed him. Being passive aggressive served zero purpose in life. She felt annoyed with what she regarded as a weakness.

Her last class for the day, and for the week, was done. Tonight's dinner was her responsibility. She lived with her parents. The three of them took turns cooking, although it was mostly between herself and her father. She sent him a text:

I'm done for the day, Papa.

Good. Meet you at the station at 5:30 p.m.

Okay. I'm heading off to the market. Chicken with Greek salad, okay?

Perfect. Could you get something for dessert, please?

Sure. See you in a little bit.

Yes, later, Lukie.

She slung her backpack over her shoulders and secured the straps in the front, smiling at her dad and his sweet tooth.

It was an approximate 1.5km walk from the campus to the Albert Cuyp Market. There were other markets closer to Amsterdam Central Station, but not all were open on weekdays, and she liked a particular supplier of fresh chicken at this one. If she took a brisk walk, it was less than fifteen minutes to get there.

Amsterdam Central Station was a 2.8km walk from the

market, and from there, she and her father would take a twenty-minute train ride to Haarlem where they lived. There was plenty of time if she didn't get distracted at the market.

Luka walked along Toronto Bridge, looking at the water traffic on the Amstel river. As she took in the sights of the city she loved, she thought Amsterdam an abundant metropolis of people and culture. It made her proud to think how it embraced all nationalities, and despite being a brilliant, innovative place, it was typically, modestly, Dutch.

There were still plenty of tourists walking around, although now much fewer than during the summer. They were also easy to spot, ducking out of the way of speeding bicyclists. Bewildered looks came from both those on foot and those brave enough to ride. Luka grinned. In Amsterdam (and the rest of the Netherlands for that matter) bikes ruled, and the locals were kings and queens on their chariots, showing little tolerance for anyone slowing them down.

A mild and sunny September day drew people out, to sit on restaurant and café patios, to enjoy a cup of coffee, a glass of wine, or a beer. There was a laid-back Friday-afternoon city vibe.

The Albert Cuyp Market she headed toward was a spectacularly busy attraction—it was the busiest market in Amsterdam and stretched for several blocks on Albert Cuypstraat, between Ferdinand Bolstraat and Van Woustraat in De Pijp, a neighbourhood in the Oude Zuid district.

When she'd managed to manoeuvre herself through the slow-moving crowds to the stall she was looking for, she bought a few pieces of chicken breast and asked the vendor to wrap them in additional paper before she put them in a reusable bag she'd brought in her backpack. At a cheese vendor, she bought fresh feta cheese and put it in the bag with the chicken. She bought three sweet crêpes, one for herself and two for her father—for dessert.

She inspected some green peppers, cucumbers, tomatoes, and a red-leafed lettuce at a greengrocer's. When she reached for the last bag of arugula, a man standing next to her did the same and their hands touched. Both apologized awkwardly.

He gave her a crooked smile and waved. "Please go ahead, you look like you need it more than I do."

She lifted her brow and reached for the arugula again.

"My mother always tells my brother and me how important green vegetables are. Of course, she's also taught us to always be courteous to a lady, even when it meant that we'd have to go without our greens for the day," he said.

She looked up into humorous grey-blue eyes and saw a jaw-droppingly handsome face. He had dirty blond hair that was slightly windblown, but it somehow fitted the scene. He came across as confident, but not annoyingly so—a relief. She decided: not a corporate type. Something scientific perhaps, or tech. It was hard to tell for sure.

"Your mother sounds like a wise woman." Luka paid for the vegetables and put them in another reusable bag, then turned toward the stranger and said, "Well, thank you for the sacrifice, I'm sure your mother would be proud of you. Perhaps if you come a little earlier next time, you might have better luck. Goodbye."

"That's it? No more silly chit chat and bantering over vegetables?"

"I have what I need, what more could I possibly want?" She held up her bags with a triumphant smile.

"I thought perhaps you would want to have coffee with me,

to tell me a little about that shrewd nature of yours."

"I can't, sorry. I'm meeting someone." She checked the time on her wristwatch.

"Is it a man?"

"Yes, it's a man."

"Is he special?"

"Yes, he's very special."

He shook his head. "Lucky guy. That's too bad—for me that is. First losing out on an essential part of my daily diet, then losing out on what could potentially have been a life-altering experience—for both of us."

She chuckled and started walking away. He called after her, "My name's Espen De Cleene, in case you were wondering."

"I wasn't," she called over her shoulder, but she stopped and turned anyway and said, "Luka Bakker. Take care, Espen De Cleene. I hope you find all the arugula and accompanying life-altering experiences you so desperately seek."

He laughed and gave a final wave. She wondered if she shouldn't have given him her phone number. When she turned to look, he'd already disappeared among the masses. Luka felt a pang of regret.

At Amsterdam Central Station she waited for her father on the platform from where they took the train to Haarlem.

She lifted her hand as she saw him approaching. "Hoi, Papa!"

"Hoi!" They kissed on the cheek and Ruben asked, "How was the day?" He took one of the grocery bags from her and peeked inside.

"Not too bad. I'm glad the week's over though, my mind feels stretched. How was yours?"

"Your mind should always feel stretched, my love. I've been doing this long enough now, so my week wasn't as mind-bending as yours. The first week's always a bit disorienting for students, but next week should be better."

The train arrived and they got on, found seats and sat down.

Ruben looked at her and said, "What's that mysterious little smile all about?"

"I'm just thinking about something. It's nothing."

She didn't elaborate but looked out the window, and Ruben could see her rueful smile in the reflection.

2

"I'm sorry, Miss, but we're sold out on that title. Why don't you try Books Brothers? Another option would be Stadsboekwinkel," the shop assistant said.

"Thank you."

Luka walked a couple of blocks west, down Herengracht toward Stadsboekwinkel—City Bookstore—but they too, didn't have good news for her. Great, she'd already been to three other bookstores and the university's library was also a blank. She was looking for a book that was on their supplementary reading list for school, but apparently everyone else in Amsterdam was also interested in reading it.

There was a light drizzle, and it was cold. The spray was blowing in her face, and she could feel her hair getting damp underneath the cap of her raincoat. Last chance: Books Brothers, then she'd give up the search and go home. It was already past four and they closed at five. She'd texted her father to say he should go on home, rather than wait for her at the station.

Once inside the bookstore, she searched for a member of staff.

"Excuse me, please. I'm looking for *Gambling Away Our Planet*." Luka crossed her fingers.

The shop assistant did a search. "Yes, Miss, we do have one left in stock. It's in the science section."

Success at last!

As she was paging through the book a man came and stood next to her. He was looking on the shelf and when he saw the book she was holding, "Aha, I guess that's the last one," he said.

"Excuse me?"

"The book you're holding—do you know if that's the last copy?"

"I've been told it is, unfortunately. I've been all over town and finally got a hold of it, sorry."

He was tall with dark-blond hair, and she thought his face could stop traffic. There was something familiar about him. She tried to place him.

"Have we met before?" Luka asked as she studied his face.

"No. I'm positive I would have remembered you." He gave her a big smile.

"That wasn't a come-on line," she added quickly.

"I wouldn't have complained if it were."

Luka went back to scanning through the book.

"Is it for work or for pleasure?" he asked.

"Excuse me?"

"The book."

"It's supplementary for school."

"Ah, then you need it more than I do."

It felt like déjà vu. Her mind was back at Albert Cuyp Market, and she saw Espen De Cleene's smiling face before her. That's who he reminded her of. She realized he was watching her with an amused smile, because she'd been staring at him again.

She hesitated before asking, "I don't mean to sound too forward, but are you by any chance related to a man by the name of Espen De Cleene?"

The question clearly caught him by surprise, and he stood looking at her for a moment, then he reached into the pocket of his jacket for his phone. After searching for something, he turned it for her to see. "You mean this guy?"

For a second, she was numb with disbelief and shock. She nodded. "Yes, that's him."

He gave a little sniff which could have meant anything. "He's my brother. Are you … a friend?"

"No, we met at Albert Cuyp Market a few months ago. Just a brief chat. I only know his name." He nodded and she asked cautiously, "Is he dating anyone?"

"No, he isn't." He seemed disappointed to disclose this fact.

She took a pen and sticky note from her backpack, wrote down her name and number, and handed it to him. "I don't usually do this, but will you please give this to him?"

He read the name and looked at her. "Luka Bakker."

"Tell him if he wants to, he may give me a call. If he's not interested, he may throw my number away."

"May I call you, if he doesn't want to?"

"Let's stick with the plan, shall we?"

He chuckled. "Fantastic luck I have, meet a great girl, but she wants to go out with my brother. I'll see him later, he's at a study group tonight. We live together, so I'll make sure he gets this, Luka. I'm Sebastian—Bas—by the way."

Luka liked him. He had a modest, private way about him. Not a big talker—as if he held on to words, rolling them around in his mouth and swallowing them.

They shook hands, and she said, "Pleased to meet you, Bas.

And thank you. I have to go. Enjoy your weekend."

"The same to you. Goodbye Luka. And enjoy the book," he added as she walked off.

She kept her phone by her side all evening, but he didn't call. Later she lay awake in bed, counting the minutes and wondering if he was going to call at all.

Her phone rang at 2:15 a.m. She'd fallen asleep and it made her jump. She answered in her calmest sleepy voice, but her heart was pounding in her ears, "Hallo?"

"Hallo, Luka Bakker. I'm not prone to believing in fate and all that airy-fairy stuff, but I'm beginning to think perhaps I've been wrong all along. When and where can I see you?"

She paused for a moment to collect herself. "Can you come to Haarlem tomorrow morning and meet me for coffee?"

"You live in Haarlem?"

"Yes." She gave him the name of the restaurant.

"Great, what time?"

"Let's make it for ten. I'll be generous and let you catch up on sleep, since it seems as if you're a creature of the night."

He chuckled. "I only just got the message from my brother. He'd either forgotten to give it to me, or he was deliberately withholding it—my bet's on the latter. And I'll never be able to wait until ten, can we make it eight thirty?"

"Let's do nine."

"Are you a natural contrarian or just not a morning person?"

"Both. See you tomorrow Espen—well, it's already tomorrow. See you at nine." She visualized his smile.

"See you in a few hours. Sleep well, Luka."

She hardly slept at all.

* * *

Espen was waiting at the coffee house when Luka walked in. She hung her coat and scarf on a hook by the door. He had a broad smile as he stood up. When she extended her hand to shake his, he took it but kissed her on the cheek.

She ordered a cup of coffee and he a second cup. Each scanned the other's face. Luka thought it was a surreal moment—two strangers sitting across a table, knowing they were going to learn things about one another. Their start was awkward, both acutely aware the very first thing said would confirm one of two things: either it was a good idea to get up early after a night of lying awake in bed (because they were so blown away over the fact that such a bizarre coincidence had brought them together again). Or, it would shatter the illusion and, after a cup of coffee and some small talk, they would say goodbye and politely move on.

He looked outside saying, "I haven't been to Haarlem in a while, I'd nearly forgotten how much I like it." Then he looked at Luka and grinned. "So, what happened to your special guy? Did you grow tired of him?"

"No, he's still around." She sipped on her coffee, smiling inwardly.

"You mean you're still seeing him?" His eyebrows twitched into a frown.

Was he shocked, surprised, or laughing at her? It was hard to tell, but she found the situation amusing.

"Of course I'm still seeing him, I love him. Besides, it's hard not to see him since we live together."

"Does he know where you are at the moment?"

Now he sounded surprised. "He knows where I am."

"And he's okay with that? I mean, you were the one who gave me your number. It wasn't as if I pursued you."

Luka chuckled. "Relax, he's my father, and I still live at home with my parents."

He looked at her with slanted eyes. "You are shrewd, you know that? But that's a relief. For a moment I had visions of a jealous boyfriend knocking on my door. I'm not much of a fighter, and Bas isn't either."

"No jealous boyfriend, just a lovable, slightly overprotective, father. He's harmless, don't worry. I'm his only child, he has the right."

"Are you a daddy's girl? You still live at home."

"Both my parents and I are close. Do you disapprove of the fact that I live at home still?"

"I couldn't wait to be out on my own. Don't you feel like spreading your wings?"

"Sure I want to, but people have different objectives."

"What made you decide to give your number to Bas? He says hi, by the way. How did you even know?" He changed the subject.

"There was something—the resemblance," she said, "I just had to know. Pretty mad odds, wouldn't you say? And I like your brother, he's sweet."

"Bas is a good guy. So, you remembered me, and just had to know … and here we are." His gaze roamed her face.

"And here we are," she repeated.

"Does this live up to the expectations?"

"So far I haven't felt the need to run away screaming."

Espen gave her a great smile. "Me neither. Tell me about yourself, Luka. Are you studying? Are you working?"

"I'm studying geography at the University of Amsterdam."

"Great, which campus?'

"Roeterseiland. My dad's there too. He teaches environmental geography, which is what I study."

"An earth science girl. Interesting."

"Guess I am. What do you do?"

"I'm also at UvA—Science Park. I'm doing my master's in marine biology, in oceans and climate."

"So, you want to save the oceans of the world," she said and smiled with pursed lips.

"Yup. I'd like to do everything I can to help—they need a lot of help."

"Are you a zealot? Do you attend rallies where protesters walk through the streets, blocking traffic, and chanting, 'the Earth shall have justice'?"

He chuckled. "I haven't attended any of those—not recently anyway. But I suppose you could say I am. I believe in the work I do."

"Bas mentioned that you live together."

"Yes, we have a flat in De Pijp, the old part. My parents bought it years ago and it's a great location. Did Bas mention what he does?"

Luka shook her head. "He's in his final year of biomolecular science at AIMMS—Amsterdam Institute of Molecules, Medicines and Systems at Vrije Universiteit. He's a smart guy, my little brother, although not so little. We're only a year apart."

"I expect you think yourself smart also. I nearly did molecular cell bio myself but decided on geographic information science instead, also at Vrije. Thought it would be more beneficial to my future career. I want to become a cartographer, and ideally, to specialize in nautical work."

"You expect I think I'm smart also." He laughed. "So, not a geographer, but a mapmaker. Why that?" Espen leaned forward on his forearms and scanned her face.

Luka stared at the slight cleft in his chin, and it drew her gaze up to his mouth. The vibrations of his voice so close sent strange sensations through her.

"I suppose it's the element of fiction, blended with painstaking precision. I'll get to sail the far oceans in my mind with the beautiful charts I'll create."

"You have everything neatly mapped out, don't you?"

"Is that a question or an observation?" He didn't answer, but she could see the laughter in his eyes. "Are your parents in Amsterdam?" She switched topics.

"No, they're in Den Haag. They are both doctors." He took a sip of coffee and asked, "You mentioned your father, but what does your mom do?"

"She's a classical musician."

"Cool."

"My mom travels a lot, so it's mostly my father and I at home."

"You don't get lonely out here in Haarlem?"

"It's hardly a one-horse town."

"Tell me what you do for entertainment in the pulsating city of Haarlem."

"I go to the theatre. I go to bookshops and out to dinner and the movies with friends. I do have a life."

Although not a terribly exciting one. She decided he needn't know.

"Of course," Espen said. "I am sure you are the glue that holds everyone together."

"I don't know what that means. When's your birthday?"

2

She changed the subject again.

"Getting to that already. I guess this means you do want to see me again," he said with a sly smile.

"Just tell me."

"September sixteenth. Why do you ask?"

"A Virgo, then. How old are you?"

"Is that a question or an observation, Luka? I'm twenty-four."

"A person's star sign can tell a lot about them."

"And you think by knowing my birthday, you will gain insight into the innermost recesses of my heart and mind, all based on some generalized description of my personality type. I don't believe in all that astrology stuff. It's not real science." He shook his head, scooping up a drop of coffee that was running down the outside of his cup with his index finger and licking it off.

He had beautiful hands.

"A lot of people believe that astrology is a natural science," she pushed back.

"It has no scientific validity, there's no scientific method. Besides, I think some people read way too much into how the stars rule their lives."

"Perhaps," she said, "but you know a scientific theory isn't an absolute truth either, because it doesn't take future discoveries into account. And someone could easily disprove your theoretical labour of love. In the end it seems our ideas are more subjective than we would like to believe, and one person's brilliant idea is often nothing but BS to another person."

Espen shrugged with an amused grin and Luka continued, "Why can't people believe in the power that the planets and stars wield over us? Even you can't deny there's something to be said for people who are born under the same star sign."

"When's your birthday, Luka?"

"March fourteenth."

"A Pisces with strong opinions. Now that's refuting an argument. How old are you?"

"I'm twenty-one. For someone who doesn't believe in astrology, you seem to know a lot about star signs. And Pisces do have strong opinions, they just don't shove them down other people's throats."

"As we Virgos do, right?" he laughed and said, "You have a birthday coming up in two months, then." He sat back in his chair and folded his arms. "You know what, you may just be the freshest little Pisces that swam into my ocean, Luka Bakker."

"You certainly don't limit yourself, do you?" she said with an ironic smile.

He appeared unaffected by her remark. "Never when I can help it, no." He contemplated for a moment, then took her hand in his. "Bas and I are going skiing in Bavaria this coming weekend. Why don't you come along with us? We have family on our mother's side who have a cottage in Mittenwald. It's quite big, there's plenty of room. Only our two cousins, Hugo and Klaus, will be there, and they won't mind at all."

"I don't know … it feels like jumping ahead of ourselves. We haven't even concluded whether *this* was a good idea." Luka was skeptical.

"You know as well as I do, this was the best damn idea ever." He interlaced his fingers with hers and their eyes locked, she couldn't look away. "C'mon, be daring, it will be fun," he insisted. "It's beautiful there, and the skiing's fantastic. It can be our second date. We'll have plenty of time to get to know each other, and if you're a terrible skier, we'll just shake hands and wish each other well on our separate journeys."

"Perhaps you should first speak to your cousins and find out if they would really be okay with it."

"Does that mean you will go?"

"Find out first. I don't want to get my hopes up, about kicking your but on the alpine slopes of Germany, and then it was for nothing."

He burst out laughing. "Oh, they will be okay with it. We'll leave just before 12 p.m. on Friday, that way we should still be able to get some night skiing in. Don't worry, you have plenty of time to get your airline and train tickets. It's going to be great; you can trust me Luka."

* * *

When Luka told her parents that she'd been invited to ski with Espen and his brother in Mittenwald for the weekend, and that she'd accepted, Evi was ecstatic about the news. Her mother was more open-minded and free-spirited by nature than her more reserved father.

When she told her father Espen was studying marine biology, Ruben was thrilled since anyone who worked to save the Earth and its creatures ranked high in his opinion—his exact words. Luka smiled at his predictability. She was in many ways like him, although she sometimes wished she could be more free-spirited, like her mom.

She walked around for the rest of the day, thinking about her date with Espen. How strange that their paths had crossed again. He was definitely a go-getter, and she liked his energy.

She chuckled at the thought.

But he didn't seem crazy about the fact that she still lived with her parents. For someone who was such an independent person himself, would that put him off?

Luka lay in bed that night and found herself thinking about Bas, the brother who had passed on her phone number to Espen De Cleene, who wanted to save the oceans.

3

Mittenwald was a gorgeous mountain village in the Bavarian Alps, close to the Austrian border. The cottage was big, as Espen had said it would be. Luka was relieved to have her own room. She didn't know what Espen had told his cousins, but he obviously must have mentioned that they weren't *there* yet.

It was beautiful beyond words skiing in the Oberammergau. The men were superb skiers and, unsurprisingly, immediately made it a competition between themselves, racing down the slope, calling out challenges to each other. Espen and Bas glanced in Luka's direction to see if she'd noticed. Of course she had; it was impossible to ignore such an obvious display of male bravado.

When she put the skis on she felt intimidated at first—it had been a while since she'd skied—but she was no slouch, and she wasn't going to show she was scared. After a couple of runs, the guys were encouraging her and that made her feel good.

She tried not to stare at Espen in a too obvious way, although she caught herself a couple of times. He had an all-or-nothing kind of vibe, and it was sexy. Bas was less of a show-off, but a strong, confident skier. Luka observed, with an inward smile, how it didn't sit easy with Espen's competitive nature when his brother won a race and gave him a smirk.

Luka's newfound confidence in her skiing abilities was soon put to the test.

Espen asked, "Do you feel up to trying the black line? Don't worry, I'll ski with you."

"Sure." She sounded much more self-assured than she felt and looking down the steep slope she tried not to let him see she was terrified. But after a couple of this-surely-is-it moments, she was flying down the mountain with confidence.

Bas caught up with her at one point and said, "You're a great skier."

"Thanks." She smiled broadly at the compliment.

Her moment of triumph was shattered when another skier lost his left ski and screaming, came crashing into her. A harrowing moment, but later, reliving it in her mind, it seemed quite comical—almost like something out of a Peter Sellers movie. Her dad would have appreciated the analogy, not necessarily her predicament.

Espen was clearly shaken by the event. She'd never seen anyone cover a horizontal stretch of ski slope so fast, except for the man who'd knocked her to the ground.

"Are you okay?" Espen asked with wide eyes.

His concern was sweet, but she didn't like that it turned all the attention on her.

"I'm fine, really—just a bump on my shin." A huge, throbbing bump. "Hey, luckily, it's not a front tooth. My bruised ego's the worst of it," she reassured all the concerned men hovering around her.

The embarrassed man, who'd done a summersault over her,

later bought her and the guys each a mug of beer at the lodge to compensate for the consternation he'd caused.

They all raised their mugs in "*Gesundheit!*"

Espen held her gaze as he said with a wide smile, "To the best second date ever."

Luka had to agree. Aside from her inaugural Bavarian skiing fiasco, she was having a great time.

After everyone else had gone to bed, Espen, who shared a room with Bas, came to her bedroom. "Would you mind if I cuddle with you tonight?"

She hesitated for a moment, and said, "Okay, but no funny business."

He climbed into bed with her, scooted closer but left a little bit of space between them.

"I promise. Tell me more about yourself."

Luka was glad for the slight distance between their bodies because it made it easier to talk. Even still, she could feel the energy oozing out of him.

"What do you want to know?"

"What were you like in school? Did you also map everything out so meticulously?" he asked with that hint of laughter in his voice.

"No, I was a rebel," she said dryly. "My parents didn't know how to deal with me. It was only later that the light finally went on in my head, and I'd discovered the amazing world of order and discipline."

He chuckled, "Lucky for that light in your head."

"I like things where I can manage them. But you've already figured that out, haven't you?"

"Yes, I've figured it out. I like that about you. You are determined, I've seen it today when we were skiing. But what drives you, Luka? What makes you want to go out there and do things?"

"I don't know. Not all of us are rock stars. Some of us are just fans, showing up for the concert."

"I think you underestimate yourself."

"Maybe, but I doubt it. Have you always known you wanted to make a difference? To save the planet?"

"I've always disliked apathy, I suppose. We must stand for something important in life that will make a positive, lasting difference, whether it's big or small."

"And that's why you're going to change the world and convert humankind into responsible users instead of abusers. I wouldn't put all my hope in people if I were you. You are one person, and the Earth's bigger than you think. There are a lot of people to convert."

"If we don't believe that every person's actions can be turned into a positive outcome, we're screwed as a species, Luka."

"Aren't we already?" she asked.

They lay quiet for a moment, and then he asked the question she'd been dreading, "Have you been in a relationship before?"

"Nothing serious. Have you?"

The dark accentuated the uncertainty in her voice. Or was it insecurity? Either way, it didn't sound confident. Her answer was vague, but she didn't want to tell him she'd become aware that men were interested in her—some time during her first year of university—but those who'd pursued her and had gotten somewhere, hadn't impressed her much.

She was looking for something much more than a physical thrill. Something with substance that would lift her up and elevate her soul. None of the men she'd gone out with, had done that.

That wasn't to say she was disinterested in sex, but again, it would be more meaningful with someone with whom she could connect on an emotional level. And for that reason, she found relationships, or the attempts at them, draining. She had until then.

On the other hand, she was terrified that Espen would say yes, he had been in a serious relationship, and that it had been this great love he can't get over. She didn't want to think of him having a past, loving another woman. These possessive feelings surprised her.

"Not anything for the annals," he said. "You're not opposed to it—a relationship—are you?"

"No, not really, although my dad keeps telling me how I have the rest of my life ahead of me, every time I look at a man."

"I happen to agree with him. But I also think it's good to have an open mind in the present."

She sniggered. "Because like my father, you have my best interests at heart."

"Of course."

"Right."

"Where'd you learn to ski so well, anyway?" He changed the subject.

"I've been places, Mr. Hot Shot. My mom's an excellent skier. She had me take lessons when I was small, and then she planned lovely skiing vacations for us across Europe. My mom has an electrifying energy about her. It's intoxicating. I'm nothing like her," she said thoughtfully.

"That's not true. You're a geodynamo," he said, and the word sounded stunning in the darkness around them.

She sniffed. "So, I'm molten iron and nickel swirling around inside the Earth's core?"

"It's true. You have that self-sustaining energy inside you. When it's released, it becomes magnetic energy, and it holds everything around you, together. You are a force unto yourself, Luka," he said as he scooted closer, so their bodies formed a spoon.

She could feel his breath in the base of her neck when he moved her hair out of the way. He put his arm around her waist and took her hand in his.

A geodynamo. That was just about the most exquisite thing anyone had ever called her.

"Why don't we get some sleep," he said.

"Good idea."

Softly he said, "I'm happy you're here with me, Luka."

"Yes, me too," she replied.

He planted a kiss in her neck.

Luka woke up during the night and turned around to watch Espen sleep. He was a good sleeper and a great bed partner. He hardly moved and his face was relaxed and beautiful in sleep. She wondered what his dreams were about, this man who'd appeared out of nowhere, only to disappear in an instant. And now he has miraculously reappeared in her life.

The moonlight coming through the window provided enough light for her to study his features and she listened to his slow and steady breathing. She took her time until her eyelids became heavy, and she fell asleep again.

* * *

At Amsterdam Central Station, Espen and Bas walked with her to the platform where she'd take the train to Haarlem.

Espen pulled her to him. "We've concluded the second date now; may I at least get a kiss?"

Bas asked, surprised, "You two haven't even kissed yet? What have you been doing in bed then?"

Luka laughed and said, "Not kissing."

And then Espen kissed her. It was a slow and wonderful kiss. The kind of kiss that made her want to stay there on the busy platform with thousands of people pushing and pulling around them. She liked the way he held her, how their mouths felt locked together. She liked the taste of his chemistry.

Luka peeped around Espen and wondered why Bas had turned and looked away.

When Espen let go of her, he said, "Wow, imagine what our third date will be like."

As the train sped away, she could only see him for a few seconds before he was out of view. Espen, standing there, watching her.

* * *

"I'm glad you had a good time, Lukie," her father said.

"Perhaps when I'm back from tour, you can invite Espen over, Luka. Papa and I would love to meet him." Evi said.

She was leaving for a month-long tour to first Germany, then Denmark, the next day.

"Sure, Mama, we'll do that."

"You look happy, Lukie. That's good. Just keep an open mind, it's still early days," Ruben cautioned.

Luka kissed him on the cheek. "Don't worry, Papa, nothing bad is going to happen to me."

Espen called her when she was in bed. "Hallo," she said. Her happy voice sounded ridiculous in her own ears.

"Hallo. I thought I'd just check in quickly before bed and thank you again for the weekend. I had a great time."

"I had a great time too, thanks for everything."

There was a pause, then he said, "I also wanted to tell you ... I know this is early and a bit strange, and really not something ordinary—"

"Just get to the point," she interrupted, but smiled at his awkwardness.

"I'm in love with you."

"When did you decide this? Was it when I did the splits on a forty-five degree angle, with skis on, or when you rubbed my hairy leg with an egg-sized bump on it?" She tried to make light of the situation, but his bold confession was a surprise.

He chuckled. "No, although both were equally endearing moments I'll cherish forever. It was way before then, when you'd taken the last bag of arugula at Albert Cuyp Market and told me better luck next time. I knew then and there I'd love you for eternity."

"You'd offered it to me, I didn't take it. Is that the reason why you'd pursued me so fiercely?"

"I knew you'd come after me, it was written in the stars."

"You're blowing smoke now. I thought you didn't believe in all that airy-fairy stuff, but as they say, all's well that ends well."

"Does that mean you feel the same?" His voice had a hopeful hint.

She paused for a few seconds. "Yes." She could visualize his smile.

"Good, now let me go, I need my beauty sleep. Goodnight, Luka. I'll be dreaming of you."

"Goodnight, Espen."

4

The spring semester was in full swing. Luka was enjoying school, but the workload was heavy and required that students do a lot of self-study, as they'd been told would be the case. Her days were still predominately occupied with going to classes and she had little time in between to spend with Espen, who himself was busy with his thesis. They compensated with her staying over at his and Bas's flat a day or two out of the week, but she felt awkward having him over at her parents' house just yet.

Espen had not met either of her parents, and Luka hadn't told him her musician mom was, in fact, a beloved Dutch institution. Everyone in the Netherlands and across Europe, whether classical music fans or not, knew of Evi Gaal.

The opportunity arose when Evi was home from her Denmark tour and scheduled to perform for one week only, at the Royal Concertgebouw—Royal Concert Hall. Besides wanting to see her mother perform, she thought it would be a great evening out for her and Espen. Her father had already declined an invitation to join them. He had work to do and would attend the Friday evening performance instead.

Luka called Espen on his cell. "Hallo."

"Hallo. This is a pleasant surprise. You normally ignore

me until it's dark enough and you can seduce me with your witchy female ways."

She sniggered and said, "How would you like to go to a performance at the Royal Concertgebouw?"

"Excellent. Who's performing what?"

"Evi Gaal is performing this week with the Royal Concertgebouw Orchestra, and I was wondering if you'd be interested. They're performing Mozart's Piano Concerto No 11, and I can get us tickets, but will have to let them know today."

"Evi Gaal. How are you even able to get those? Don't they usually sell out months in advance?"

"Yes, but I have a connection. Are you game? The tickets are for Thursday evening."

"That would be great, thanks Luke. Our first cultural experience together, I can't wait."

"Get used to it, it's in my blood. Bye, I have to run."

"Luke, wait!"

"Hm?"

"I don't really have anything more to say. I just like hearing your voice."

"Speak to you later." She hung up with a grin.

* * *

The Royal Concertgebouw, situated in front of the Rijksmuseum on Museumplein, was one of the most beautiful cultural landmarks in the city with its signature golden harp shining like a beacon on top of the building. The entrance followed through a modern glass extension, into a spacious room suited for receptions. Straight ahead, past this area was the cloakroom, and then the Grote Zaal—main hall—the home base for the Royal Concertgebouw Orchestra. The finishings and decorations inside the building were astonishing.

They'd agreed to meet each other at the entrance to the concert hall at six. As Espen helped her take her coat off, wrapping his arm around her waist, he said, "You look lovely."

Luka wore a black turtleneck dress with stockings and high heels, and her hair was up in an elegant bun.

"Thank you," she replied. "You look lovely too. Very 007 in your tuxedo."

He chuckled. "I don't think James Bond has ever been called lovely before. It's good to be here again, I can never get over how spectacular this place is." Espen looked around.

"Have you been to a performance inside the Grote Zaal before?" she asked.

"No, I've only ever been to the Kleine Zaal, you know the small room? And that was a few years back, and I have to say, it was impressive."

"Then be prepared to be even more amazed. The acoustics will blow your mind," she said, hooking her arm in with his. "But let's have a coffee first."

After their coffee, people started moving gradually toward the Grote Zaal. Inside, the vast hall was filled with 1,974 red plush chairs. Gold leaf ornaments adorned the elegant white walls, and an enormous pipe organ drew the eye to the back of the stage.

Espen was surprised how close their seats were to the front.

Luka said, "This section's the dress circle. It's the first section below the balcony, and it has a front view of the stage and the orchestra. More importantly, it has a perfect view of the piano where Evi will be sitting. You'll almost be able to hear her tap the peddle with her foot, we're so close."

Looking up and around, he said, "No kidding. Geez, you definitely have good connections. These must be the best seats in the house."

"They are."

"You know a lot about all this, don't you?" He eyed her.

"Yes, I do." She didn't elaborate but smiled secretively.

One by one, the musicians arrived. They tuned their instruments and warmed up.

There was an abated energy in the air. Men looked neat in their tuxedos, and ladies looked elegant in their evening dresses.

Espen asked, "Are you excited to see Evi Gaal perform?"

"Yes, I'm always excited to see her perform. She's incredible."

"You've seen her live before?"

"Uh-huh." She nodded as she stared ahead to where the grand piano stood in the middle of the stage—turned so that the pianist would be facing stage left—and said, almost more to herself than to him, "As a little girl, I used to love falling asleep listening to her playing Chopin's Nocturnes ..."

"You are a rare and cultured orchid. Do you play the piano yourself?"

"Of course. My mom would never have let me grow up with such a gap in my education. But I had the best teacher ever." He squeezed her hand.

The lights dimmed and the concertmaster stood up, bowed, and asked for silence. Then he signalled to the oboe player to play the key, A. The orchestra followed. When the instruments had been tuned, Evi Gaal entered the stage looking sophisticated in a long, grey satin dress. There was a thundering applause as her home audience acknowledged her.

She bowed graciously and sat down. The conductor entered the stage, took a bow and turned to face the orchestra. The magic had begun.

Espen turned his head occasionally to watch Luka. Her face glowed and she moved her body gently in unison with the pianist on stage. She looked at him briefly and smiled a wide, happy smile. She mouthed, "Are you enjoying yourself?" He mouthed back with a grin, "Are you kidding, I'm loving this".

The encore lasted for several minutes. Evi and the conductor, left and re-entered the stage a couple of times as people stood applauding. She was a courteous artist who never appeared haughty and always expressed deep appreciation to her audience for their support.

When people finally started leaving in dribs and drabs, talking about the experience, Luka said to Espen, "There's someone I'd like you to meet. Come with me."

She took him by the hand, and he followed her to the backstage area.

"There are a lot of people still hanging around here; I didn't expect that," said Espen as he curiously looked around.

Luka knocked on a door and said, "It's me."

A woman's voice said, "Come in."

Luka looked at a puzzled Espen behind her as she opened the door.

"Sweetheart, you've made it. What did you think?" said Evi Gaal, as she rose from her seat to greet them while Espen stood there, stunned.

"You were wonderful, as always." And the two women hugged affectionately. Then Evi turned to Espen, and said, "Finally. I cannot tell you how eager I've been to meet you, Espen. Luka has told us only wonderful things about you."

She held his outstretched hand in a motherly way.

He couldn't hide his surprise. "She has?"

Luka intervened. "Espen, I'd like for you to meet Evi Gaal—my mother."

"Your mother?" Espen was dumbstruck. He stared at the two women standing next to each other, and they could see in his eyes how he made the connection.

Luka was her mother's spitting image. He gave Evi a sheepish smile and said, "It's a pleasure to meet you, Ms. Gaal." Turning to Luka he said softly, "You've got some explaining to do." Luka pulled a face and shrugged.

"Please call me Evi. Did you enjoy the performance, Espen?"

"I did Ms. Gaal … Evi. You were wonderful."

"Thank you. The Royal Concertgebouw Orchestra is a boon to our nation. They make me sound much better than I am." She gave him a mischievous wink and turned to Luka. "Sweetheart, I'm so sorry, but I need to speak to some people before I leave. Shall I meet you here in say, forty minutes?"

"Of course. Espen and I will have a coffee,"

"Why don't you come by on Sunday evening for dinner, Espen?" Evi said.

"I would love that, thank you, Evi. Have a good evening, and congratulations on a great performance."

"Goodnight, Espen."

"I'll see you in a while, Mama." Luka kissed her mother on the cheek.

Sitting down with their coffee, Espen raised his eyebrows and said, "She's your mother? Why didn't you tell me this sooner?"

Luka gave a guilty little laugh. "I wanted you to meet her first. It would have been so different if I'd told you ahead of time. You would have been all freaked out. This way, you were completely natural with her. She hates it when people act unnaturally."

"Well, you've taken care of that. You do have a shrewd mind, Luke. Wow, I can't believe it—Evi Gaal is your mom." He shook his head.

"Yes, but fame aside, she's also just a human being and an amazing and deeply caring person when you get to know her. I want you to like each other for who you are."

"I think you're amazing." He kissed her. "I was hoping you'd stay over at the flat tonight. You look so pretty, and I would have liked to relieve you from the constraints of that dress and ensemble, but I guess under the circumstances it's not meant to be." He took her hand in his and played with her fingers.

"Tempting, but I can't." Luka watched their interwoven hands for a moment, with a little frown. Then she looked up at him and said, "It's not that easy dealing with her fame sometimes, Espen. I don't see her that much. Her touring schedule is hectic. I've had to learn from early on to take the moments I can get.

"We don't go out much either when she's here. People adore her and they're curious about her private life and she's too polite to turn them away. Folks mean well, but there's no real quality time for my dad and me to connect with her in public, so we have to do it at home."

He nodded his understanding and she added, "We can still see each other on Saturday and do something fun, and maybe you can stay over at our place. That would be another first. We can then make it a Sunday brunch with my parents, instead of dinner. You'll finally meet my dad." When she saw the worried look in his eyes, she said, "Don't worry, I have no deep secrets to reveal about him. He's a complete unknown—outside of the academic field, that is." Espen gave her a doubtful look.

5

Espen and Bas's flat was in De Pijp, a vibrant, artsy neighbourhood also known as the Latin Quarter, in the south of
Amsterdam. They lived in Oude Pijp—Old Pijp—just three
blocks away from the Albert Cuyp Market, and a short walk
from the city centre. For Espen, it was only a 5.7km bike
ride to the campus at the Science Park of UvA. Bas studied at
Vrije Universiteit, that was only a 4km bike ride away. Their
location was unbeatable.

Even though there were plenty of neat restaurants, pubs and
coffee houses in the neighbourhood, the flat was the preferred
hangout spot, and since Luka and Espen had started dating
five months ago, she'd been spending more time there.

Espen and Bas's parents had bought the flat when the boys
were still little. The brothers kept it clean and tidy (Espen's
side a fraction more so than Bas's). Like most European
flats, it had only one bathroom, but with a tub shower
combination—not just the standard tall shower—something
that Luka liked, since she loved taking bubble baths. The
kitchen was small with a dining area next to it where they
had meals and often sat and worked.

There were two bedrooms next to each other and each had
windows (as did the living room) with views of leafy old elm

trees that brought a sense of calm to the spaces inside. Both rooms had a double bed and a desk.

Above Espen's desk hung a big, framed oceanic scene with the quote, "Individually we are one drop. Together, we are an ocean" by Ryūnosuke Akutagawa.

When she'd peeped into Bas's room during her first visit and had seen René Descartes's famous quote: *"cogito, ergo sum"*—I think, therefore I am—in a photo frame above his desk, she couldn't help but smile at the contrast in personality between the two brothers.

Luka's conclusion when she'd first seen the flat, was that it provided functional living space, although she wouldn't go so far as describing it as uninviting—it was, by all accounts, a cool flat. Her opinion of it being cool, was highly influenced by one piece of furniture that stole the whole show: Oude Oom—Old Uncle—a grey three-seater leather sofa that stood against the long wall in the living room. The leather was faded, and the interior not quite as plush anymore, but it only gave Oude Oom more character, and anyone who came to the flat was immediately drawn to plop down on it. Although they sort of had to scoot their bottom this way and that to avoid a stray spring poking their derrière. The guys put soft blankets on the seats to ease the discomfort.

Luka felt that one of the advantages—or negative side effects in some cases—of dating someone, was that their friends became your friends, or they were at least the people you had to hang out with for the sake of your relationship. And since Luka hung out at Espen and Bas's flat more, Bas and Espen's best friend, Constantijn, known as Stijn to his family and friends, became her friends.

Espen didn't mind this, but she knew he felt a little left

out when the three of them did something fun without him (usually when he was busy and couldn't join them). She thought it strange though, that Espen, who wasn't generally possessive sometimes became that way because of her close friendship with his brother. Perhaps it was sibling rivalry.

Unlike his brother, who was goal-driven and intense, Bas was a mellow guy who liked to point out life's ironies. More than that, he was her soft place, her comfort pillow, and aside from Espen, Bas was her favourite confidant. They had an easy connection, because he was so effortless, and Luka felt she didn't need to explain anything to him; not like with Espen at times. He was perceptive but often withheld his opinions—something she particularly enjoyed about their friendship, since she was like that in many ways.

When she came over for a visit and Espen had to work on his thesis, she liked hanging out with Bas in his room—him lying propped up against pillows on his bed, her swivelling from side to side in his desk chair—as they drank coffee and talked about everything under the sun.

The door to the bedroom always stayed open and there was nothing untoward about their behaviour and conversations, but Espen displayed signs of jealousy, like suddenly wanting to give her a hug or flopping down next to his brother on the bed and asking what they were talking about. Luka found it amusing at best and ignored it. Bas had a look she couldn't always decipher.

Stijn was her goofy angel. Although she didn't confide in him the way she did with Bas, Luka grew to adore him. He loved wearing T-shirts with retro slogans—his favourite was one of a bushy-haired Einstein with $E = mc^2$ written beneath. His neck-length wavy blond hair and scrawny build made you think he'd stepped out of a 70s peace march.

But Stijn's appearance and demeanour were deceptive—he studied statistical mathematics and had already received an invitation to start his PhD at the University of Amsterdam for the coming academic year. He had a super intellect and was—perhaps as a result—an offbeat character and wholly authentic. His family had wealth, but he was kind and down-to-earth.

Due to his sweet nature, Stijn was also an easy target for Espen and Bas's quick-witted comments.

It was June and the school year was nearly over. Luka and Bas were both preparing for their final exams, and Espen was wrapping up his master's thesis.

Stijn was over for a visit and apparently didn't have the same level of concern over his studies. It also didn't seem to bother him that Espen, Luka and Bas were engaged in their studies. They tolerated the distraction and appointed him as barista of the coffee. He happily obliged.

As he was pouring the coffee, Stijn lamented over his weakness for preposterously beautiful women. "It's a curse," he sighed.

"It's not a curse, you aim too high, and you're constantly setting yourself up for disappointment," Espen responded.

Stijn shrugged. "It's part of living dangerously."

"There's a fine line between living dangerously and being a self-torturing idiot," said Espen.

Bas said, "I certainly don't mind the beautiful women you bring along Stijn. Don't stop on my account."

"I'm flattered my presence is of some use to you," Stijn replied.

Luka usually sided with Stijn when Espen and Bas teamed

up against him.

"Stijn can't help being a hopeless romantic," she said.

Bas and Espen sniggered.

"Why do you always take his side?" Espen asked.

"Because Stijn's sweet. Some friends you are. Don't pick on him just because he's delightfully quirky."

"Thank you, Luka," Stijn said.

"A quirk is a matter of a personality trait. A quark, on the other hand, is a constituent of matter inside a molecule, and would better explain the otherwise unfathomable innerworkings of Stijn's brain," said Espen.

Bas burst out laughing, "Ha-ha! Good one."

"Thank you for giving us that mediocre lesson on subatomic particles Professor De Cleene. I would suggest you stick to the biosphere and plight of sea turtles in future to avoid stumbling over the dark quarks in your own brain," Stijn replied. He turned his attention to Luka who sat making summary notes, smiling. "You know what you should do, Luka?"

"No, what should I do?" she asked without looking up.

"You should hook up with one of the luxury yacht makers. They often employ their own cartographers."

Espen didn't share his enthusiasm. "Are you serious? Their clients are elitists who pollute the oceans."

"I am serious. It would be a great opportunity for Luka. And the pay is great—much better than most other places."

"Money isn't everything in this life, Stijn. I know you see it differently, coming from the privileged world you do, but Luka understands what the big picture's all about."

"Exactly!" exclaimed Stijn.

Luka stopped writing. "Do I?" she asked Espen with an ironic frown. "Before you two argue any further over my future career, could I please just get through these exams?" She held up her cup to indicate to Stijn that she'd like a refill. "I still have two more years to go, and when I get to that crossroad, I will make the decision that would be most beneficial to me. And you don't have to decide what I will or will not do, okay?" She tapped her pen as she looked at Espen again.

Bas smiled. "Well put, Lukie."

"Just let me know when you get there. I can ask my dad to make a few calls for you," Stijn added, handing Luka her coffee.

"Drop it, Stijn," Espen said and changed the subject when he saw the look on Luka's face. "Where's Fraja, by the way?" he asked Stijn.

Fraja was a gorgeous Danish girl Stijn had been seeing for about a month—practically a record in his dating stats. When Stijn had introduced her to them, Espen had looked at his friend, and just rolled his eyes knowingly. Bas's eyes had nearly popped out of his head and Luka had stifled a giggle and told Stijn what he longed to hear, namely that his new woman was stunning.

Fraja was a sweet girl with a laid-back disposition, and it was impossible not to like her. If she did have one clear ambition, it was to experience as much of the "world full of interesting points of view" as possible.

She'd told them, "For me, sitting in a lecture hall all day, is much too inhibiting, both mentally and physically. But I do enjoy the Amsterdam culture—for the time being anyway."

Espen had said to his friend, in private, "You're hoping that you're going to convince her to plant her roots in Dutch soil, but that's as likely as Fraja developing a love for lecture halls.

You're living in a fool's paradise."

Stijn had replied, "You never give any of my women enough credit."

Stijn looked at Espen now and blew out a slow breath. "Fraja's off philosophizing somewhere with some guy she'd met at Flick a Bean." (This was a marijuana coffee shop Stijn and Bas liked to go to.) "She says he understands her deepest self, something that I apparently could never do." Again, he sighed. "I thought we were soulmates. But now she wants a guy whose sole purpose in life, is to be a professional philosopher. I mean, if she wants me to be more philosophical, I can do that," Stijn took a sip of his coffee. "What I need is a stable woman like Luka."

"We all do," said Bas.

Espen said, "The women you hang out with, prefer to hang out in pot houses, philosophizing about things that can't be changed in the world, even though in an ideal world, we'd all like for that to happen."

"Ha, that's rich, coming from you, Mr. I Can Change The Whole World. Isn't talking about things we can't change, sometimes part of acceptance; part of the healing process?" Luka asked.

"What healing is there in talking about how unfair life is, or about the fact that we're all going to die at some point, or people's innate selfish natures that do others in and whose choices are destroying the world we're living in? Some things are bigger than us, Luka, but we're accountable to someone, all of us. Just sitting around and agonizing over it while you're filling your mind with dope, won't affect change," Espen said.

"That's a cynical way of looking at it," she said.

"Perhaps, but it's honest," he replied.

"That's really what this is all about, Lukie—his objection to people using weed. Don't read more into it," Bas said.

"Apathy is the antithesis of action, Bas. Coming up with great ideas still requires them to be implemented, otherwise they remain nothing but ideas," Espen said.

"Some of the greatest thinkers have been known to use marijuana, like my hero, Einstein, who said that was when his best ideas came to him. You have a deep-rooted bias, and you're using my women and their recreational habits as your scapegoat," Stijn said.

"How do you know that I don't hang out in pot houses? I don't tell you everything. And if I did, would you judge me for it?" Luka asked Espen with a challenging look.

He looked at her with a frown. "Well, if you did, I wouldn't like it."

Bas said dryly, "There's a shocker."

She gave a loud sniff. "Rest assured, I wouldn't put you or myself through the pain of telling you."

"I was only trying to illustrate a point about the women Stijn chooses."

"Espen, that rhetoric is stereotypical. Surely not all people who go to pothouses do so to talk about things in the way you've described them. Sometimes, believe it or not, people just hang out for the sheer enjoyment of their own or other people's company, and God forbid, they smoke a little pot too. You should try that, it might relax those uptight muscles in your head and in your rear," she said.

Espen didn't comment and Stijn and Bas chuckled.

Bas said, "Good point, Lukie. In Fraja's defence, she does work at Flick a Bean, so it's not as if she just hangs out there, getting stoned."

"Are you defending Fraja now?" Espen asked.

Bas shrugged.

"Are you going to pick a fight with everyone tonight?" Luka asked Espen, with raised eyebrows.

He didn't answer.

"Wanting to make the world a better place is a noble goal. We do need a better world," said Stijn, taking a sip of his coffee.

Espen changed the topic and asked Stijn, "Beside physical pleasure, what did you have in common with Fraja anyway?"

"Lots. For one, she thinks I'm funny."

"Yes, that's true, and you think you're funny too. And she likes to get stoned, which you like also. That's *two* things," Espen said.

"And his voice drips with sarcasm. What a surprise," Stijn said.

Luka said sympathetically, "It wasn't meant to be, Stijn. Don't give up, you're going to meet someone amazing who will appreciate you for all that you are."

"Based on his choices in women, that's a statistical hurdle, and for someone who's a skilled statistician, you have to appreciate the irony," said Bas and he chuckled.

Luka gave Bas a look.

"If only there were more beautiful women in mathematics," Stijn said in contemplation.

"How do you know there aren't any? Have you bothered to look at all? You need to broaden your scope so that you can meet women who'd be more compatible with you. You need to start going to other places," Espen said.

"What other places?" asked Stijn.

"I don't know, like bookshops for instance. Museums … I'm just thinking randomly here," Espen replied.

"Hmm, maybe I should give it a try." Stijn thought about the idea with his hands behind his head.

"Miracles may happen yet," said Bas. Luka gave him another look.

Later that evening, as they lay in bed, Espen asked her, "Why'd you get so worked up earlier?"

"Because you sometimes say things without thinking how it could hurt someone's feelings."

"It wasn't directed toward you. Did I hurt your feelings?"

"Not mine, Stijn's. And I don't like it when you try to put me in one of your little boxes."

"I think you're better than someone who just fluffs around through life."

"You can't control everything I do, and you're trying to make your argument sound noble, but to me it sounds like a form of manipulation. I don't like that, Espen."

"Do I sound manipulative?" She gave him a look and he sighed. "I have high expectations, I suppose."

"Then manage your expectations. Nobody can be everything, to everyone. I'm going to disappoint you at times—it's inevitable."

"I'm sorry." He took her hand in his and kissed it.

They were silent for a while, then Luka said, I know what I should get Stijn for his twenty-fifth birthday next month."

"A normal girlfriend?" He laughed at his little joke.

"A membership at a bookstore."

"You know there would still be a high likelihood that he'd end up meeting someone way out of his league and the fool would fall madly in love with her. That would simply repeat the same behaviour patterns all over. He can't help it. His own statistics aren't in his favour."

"It's worth a try. We can go with him and keep an eye out."

"What will you get me for my twenty-fifth birthday?" he asked.

"A book on how to show more compassion to your friends, even when they make choices you don't agree with."

"More compassion? Stijn needs to hear the truth. He keeps walking into the same trap and then ends up in a ditch. You think I enjoy seeing him get burned every time?"

"I know he does, but his heart is so good. Just tone down the tough love a little. You're not the boss of us all."

He chuckled, "I don't think I could ever be the boss of you. God, I'm lucky to have you." He rolled onto his side and pulled her to him and kissed her on the lips. "There's something I need to tell you."

"What is it?" She pulled away and looked at him with a frown.

"Don't look so worried, it's nothing bad. I've been offered a scholarship to do my PhD at the University of Utrecht in oceans and climate, and I've accepted. It's the golden opportunity I've been looking for, Luke."

"That's wonderful news. I'm proud of you." She scooted closer again and they embraced.

"Yes, it still feels a little surreal. I'll be busy for the next couple of years, though. And I'll need to move to Utrecht."

She thought about it. "I know, but I'll be busy myself. We'll just have to work around it."

He kissed her and said, "Let's go to Friesland for a few days, after school's out. I feel like being up there for a change."

"Okay, that sounds like a great idea. When we're back, we need to visit my grandmother. She's been nagging me about meeting you and I simply can't put if off any longer. She may disown me if I don't do it soon."

6

Espen and Luka took the train to Holwerd in Friesland, and from there the ferry to the village Nes, in Ameland, one of the West Frisian Islands in the Wadden Sea.

The islands had a strange, enchanting beauty about them, pulling the visitor into the heart of something unique. On the North Sea's side there were dunes and sandy beaches, while toward the Wadden Sea it was mainly a low tidal coast. The area was abundant in flora and fauna, especially birdlife. Luka wasn't surprised that Espen wanted to spend time there, it was a place a soul could find rest.

They had brought their bikes to make use of the numerous bike routes throughout the island. There were four villages on Ameland: Hollum, Nes, Buren and Bellum—they stayed at a B&B in Buren, the smallest of the four. The island only spanned twenty-seven kilometres, and it was easy to visit all the other villages in a day.

Espen wanted to stay in Buren because it was quieter. He said he could see the stars better and listen to the ocean. Luka was certain those goals were attainable in the other villages too, but she liked the quaintness of Buren.

In the little town centre was a statue of the witch, *Rixt van het Oerd*—Rixt of Oerd. Espen and Luka stopped to read the plaque.

The legend tells of an old woman who had tied a lantern between the horns of her cow and took her to the highest dune to deceive passing ships into thinking there was a lighthouse. They'd come too close to shore and would end up on the sandbanks, causing their valuable cargo to fall into the water.

One evening, after Rixt had practised her conniving ways, a ship had been overturned on the sandbanks, just as she had hoped, and she'd rushed to claim the loot. Rixt found the body of a dead sailor washed on shore and, to her horror, discovered it was her son, Sjoerd. From then on, according to legend, when storms brew over the island of Ameland, the voice of the old witch can be heard howling her son's name in the wind.

"The poor old cow," Espen said with a chuckle and shake of his head.

"What about the poor old woman?" Luka asked with a slight frown more out of concern than annoyance.

"Who do you think I was talking about?"

Luka gave him a shove. "You're heartless."

"Let's ride out to the dunes, I feel like spending the day at the beach," he said.

There were some clouds above, but it was a mild summer's day, and they walked around on the shore holding hands and squatting to look at the little clams and crabs blowing airholes in the sand. They watched the wading birds running up and down the beach in search of food.

"These guys need our help or they too will end up on the endangered-species list," Espen said. As he lightly ran his hand over the wet sand a crab quickly disappeared into its tiny hole. "Ocean acidification is causing havoc on calcium carbonate organisms like these, because their shells can't develop properly. They don't stand a chance of surviving at the rate things are going. And there are many other sea creatures, land animals and birds directly and indirectly affected. Not to mention the effect on humans, who rely on the oceans for food and jobs.

"We can't stand by and do nothing, Luke. We need to protect these beautiful masses of water and all they hold in them, as much as we need to protect the trees that give oxygen and shelter to the creatures on land. Our oceans are getting sicker by the day because of what is going into them. It's symptomatic of what people are doing to themselves." He sighed and looked out over the North Sea.

He was one person, and he bore the weight of it all on his shoulders. It was completely self-imposed, she knew, but he did it because he felt driven by a larger aspiration than his own limitations. She loved him more in that moment.

"Do you feel like having a picnic in Nesserbos? We can grab something to eat in Nes," she suggested.

"Sure. I was beginning to feel a little thin around the waist."

Nes was just over two kilometres from Buren. They stopped at a bakery, bought sandwiches, sweet treats, and water, but first had a cup of coffee while they talked with the owner.

Nesserbos—or Wood of Nes—wasn't a dense forest, but it was scenic and quaint. They rested their bikes against trees and found a comfortable spot where they could sit and have their lunch.

Luka looked up at the trees as she took bites from her sandwich. "They are so pretty."

"Yup," Espen said, spreading his beach towel out on the ground and lying down with his head resting on his backpack.

"Why don't you do the same? It's more tranquil to watch them from this angle."

Luka lay down next to him and watched the long, grey arms and legs of the trees above them. "You're right, they look like they are shielding us."

He turned his head and lay looking at her for a while. "I don't want you to worry about me going to Utrecht. It's only a quick train ride away, anyway. This next phase is just part of a bigger goal, we won't be apart forever. And I'm not going to get so wrapped up in my stuff that I'll forget about you. You're the most important person in my life, Luke."

She rolled onto her side and put her arm around his waist. "When I was a little girl, my dad used to tell me stories about the sun and its legends. I've always felt a kind of sympathy toward the sun, almost like people took it for granted. To me, it seemed that in those legends and myths about suncatchers, the poor old sun was always made out to be the villain, but I've never believed it to be true."

"People fear what they cannot comprehend," Espen said.

"Yes, that's true. My dad bought me a crystal suncatcher to hang in my bedroom window when I was six years old. I still have it, and it always makes me think of those stories," Luka said. Then added, "The sun is amazing. It shares its energy with us. We are totally dependent upon it for light and warmth. It's fierce, yet it can make things that are wrong feel so much better, like a dark mood or aching muscles. What a big, beautiful blazing ball."

He smiled. "You mean a ball of a nearly seven-hundred-thousand-kilometre radius of hot, nuclear plasma? It is fantastic, though. Tell me one of your stories," he said, running his hand over her arm across his waist.

She lay thinking.

"Many of the legends tell of how the sun had been captured or ensnared by some heroic god-figure in the ancient cultures," she began. "The First Nations people of Lake Winnipeg in Canada—the Bungee—have a beautiful tale. It goes like this: when the sun was deliberately ensnared by the god, Weese-ke-jak, he realized his dilemma, namely that everything was in danger of being burned to ashes. So, he made a deal with the sun before he released it. The sun was only allowed near the outer edges of the Earth, during the mornings and evenings. And it had to be far away enough so it wouldn't scorch the Earth, but close enough so it would still provide enough warmth. However, there was a snag—no one could get close enough to free the sun.

"Then something unexpected happened. The humble beaver, who at that time only had a few small teeth, a short stub of a tail and a bristly coat, offered to help Weese-ke-jak by gnawing off the cords that held the sun captive—thereby he placed himself in danger of being burned to death.

"Weese-ke-jak expressed his gratitude to the brave little beaver by giving him a lovely soft coat, fine, sharp teeth and that special paddle-shaped tail." Luka paused for a bit, then said, looking into Espen's eyes, "There's a moral to this story: the beaver illustrates to us that there is no one too insignificant to do great things—things that even the mighty themselves, could not accomplish."

Espen pressed his lips against her forehead and held them there for a while, then he said, "That's a fine story."

"I think so too, it's one of my favourites."

"And now it's one of my favourites too. The weather forecast for tomorrow is pleasant and sunny, let's walk the mudflats, let's do wadlopen."

"Great idea," she said.

* * *

They took the ferry back to Holwerd, where they met the other members of their group and their guide.

Luka and Espen came prepared. Their backpacks were stacked with snacks, water, an extra set of clothes, jackets, and a towel—all of which were wrapped in plastic bags to keep dry. They wore comfortable hiking sandals, which were easier than sneakers or hiking boots to wade through the mud with (in colder weather, warm, protective shoes were necessary, but not that day).

The hike was approximately ten kilometres, one way, and even though it wasn't the most difficult route, wadlopen was surprisingly challenging, especially the first time and for those who were not very fit.

Both Espen and Luka had done it a couple of times be-fore—although not together—and were familiar with the physical demands. After walking for about an hour the water reached the chests of most of the Dutch people in the group. Those who were shorter almost had to swim.

One of the foreign tourists asked, "Why on God's earth, would anyone want to do this more than once?"

The guide replied, "It's a Dutch tradition. We love walking out here where you can't hear cars or any other human activity. It's just you, sometimes the sun, often the wind, and always the sea. Just look at the changing sky. It's breathtaking to be an intimate part of nature for a little while. If you turn your gaze from your discomfort, you will see the wonders of the sea's life swimming around your feet. Here, you are a small part of a big picture."

Espen and Luka's eyes locked, and they smiled.

They hiked through deep water for another three hours and then an additional half-hour through lush green farmland. Luka thought the whole hike had been a gorgeous, deeply soulful experience. She was getting to know Espen better, and she loved his passionate heart.

The two of them abandoned the group, who continued to the ferry dock that would take some back to Holwerd, and others hiked back with the guide. Luka and Espen walked to the B&B in Buren, rinsed themselves off outside, took a warm shower, and then biked the short distance to Nes to get a proper meal with a mug of beer.

They fell asleep with their limbs still wrapped around each other, and Espen said, barely awake, "I love you, Sunna, my sun goddess."

Strange, she thought before drifting off, she just had a weird feeling: like she was looking back on the moment from the future; remembering it.

7

"My grandmother is one of the most courageous women I've ever met. She survived the Nazi invasion here in our country with conviction and strong resistance, and at eighty-seven, she's still going strong. She lives alone, and she insists that senior care is for old people. She manages excellently on her own, and she'll tell you to go somewhere if you dare suggest otherwise."

Luka was telling Espen about her maternal grandmother, Marit Feltes, as they were on their way to visit her.

"She's also still very active for her age and has a solid circle of friends. I suspect she's the leader of the pack. My mom and uncle keep an eye out for her, of course."

"How great that you still have a grandmother, and one who's so on the go. I hope you know how lucky you are. All our grandparents were gone by the time Bas and I were in our teens," Espen said.

Luka had told Espen about her uncle Arne, who was three years younger than her mother, an anesthesiologist and lived in Amsterdam with his wife, Betje, and their youngest daughter, Isa, who was doing her pre-med at UvA. Anouk, their eldest, lived in Paris with a rich lover only a few years younger than her father. Anouk had dropped out of university during her third year of art school, when the lure of a life of luxury in Paris (with a more sophisticated culture and higher art than in the Netherlands, apparently) had enticed her.

"Isa and I are the bland ones in the family, but Anouk's our heroine, even though she's causing my uncle and aunt sleepless nights," she said, laughing. "My grandmother prides herself on being a woman of the world, so she acts as if she's unaffected by Anouk's eccentricities."

"Sounds like a true Dutch woman's approach, I would say," Espen said.

"Indeed, my grandmother is the ultimate matron. But don't look so worried, you'll love her—she's a sweet old lady," Luka said as they took the elevator to the sixth floor.

"Meeting the matriarch of a family, is a little unnerving, and with you I've learned to expect the unexpected," replied Espen as he watched the light on the elevator panel move up and come to a stop at six.

"It'll be fine," she said reassuringly.

Luka knocked on the door and her grandmother opened. "Hoi, Luka dear. Here you are at last." They hugged and kissed each other on the cheek.

"Hallo, Omoe, I'm sorry we're a little late."

Marit had already turned to Espen before Luka could introduce him, and took both his hands in hers, turning her cheek for him to kiss, "And Espen, my boy, what a pleasure to finally meet you. Luka, I wish you hadn't taken so long to bring him over."

Luka ignored the accusation while Marit looked into Espen's eyes with a slight smile.

"It's a pleasure to meet you too, Ms. Feltes." Espen wondered what her scrutiny revealed.

Marit invited them in and asked Espen to have a seat, while Luka helped her make the coffee. He could hear them babbling in the kitchen as he looked around. It was neat and well-kept.

Luka came out holding a tray and Espen immediately got up to take it from her. Marit showed him where to put it. There was a plate with *gevulde koek*—filled cookies with a pie-like shape and texture, and filled with sweet, moist almond paste. It was a popular treat in the Netherlands.

"Oma, the cookies look and smell delicious." As she put one on a small plate, Luka said to Espen, "My grandmother makes the best gevulde koek."

"Please help yourself, dear," Marit said to Espen.

He took a bite and lifted his eyebrows. "Delicious. Thank you, Ms. Feltes."

Marit took a seat and sips of her coffee, while giving the young people a chance to eat their cookies before she engaged them in conversation. She had a lot of questions to ask.

"I always like to have something for the children and grandchildren when they come around," Marit said when she saw how much Espen was enjoying it. "What would a Dutch home be without sweet edibles to go with our coffee?" As soon as he put his plate down, she said, "So Espen, Luka tells me you come from a family of physicians."

"Yes, both my parents are doctors."

"How interesting. Do they live in Amsterdam?"

"No, ma'am, they're in Den Haag. That's where my brother and I grew up."

"Luka had mentioned you and your brother have a flat in Amsterdam. That's convenient."

"Yes, my parents bought it for when they needed to be in

Amsterdam for seminars and events, and I suppose also with the foresight that my brother and I would likely use it one day."

"You didn't want to stay in Den Haag then?"

Espen shrugged his shoulders and smiled. "Perhaps it's that need for independence. Your parents know you better than you think."

"That is so true, although it takes a man to acknowledge that," Marit said with a little laugh.

"My late husband and I lived in this flat for many years after our children left home. Luka may have told you her opa died eight years ago." Espen looked at Luka and nodded.

Marit continued, "Before then, we lived in Amsterdam. Rijk was a physician too. A wonderful, compassionate man and to the end, true to his Hippocratic Oath and, what I strongly believe, was his calling. It's strange how a single encounter with someone, can change your life forever." She paused, in thought.

Luka did too, as she looked at Espen for a moment.

There was a picture in a frame of a young Evi Gaal, standing with the famous Dutch conductor, Bernard Haitink. Espen looked at it closely and looked at Luka, "You really do look a lot like your mom. Is this—"

"The great Bernard Haitink, yes." Marit finished his sentence. "That photo was taken when she worked with him and the Royal Concertgebouw Orchestra in 1975. Evi was in her late twenties then. Oh, how her face beamed when she told us that she was going to work with one of the most famous conductors in the world, and our national treasure. They toured and recorded extensively during that time. He demanded a lot from Evi, but I think the high expectation that he set for her—and many other musicians may say the same—has carried through her musical career. I am truly proud of her accomplishments."

"Did you know that she would become so famous, when she was a little girl?" Espen asked with a smile as he put the picture back in its place.

"It was clear from an early age that Evi had a special gift. She understood the love relationship between the sheet music and her instrument, and she herself became like an instrument when she sat in front of the piano. Although she practised diligently, I don't think it was nearly as hard for her as it was, and is, for many students whose dreams are of becoming classical pianists. The competition to rise above the rest is fierce.

"After she finished at the Conservatorium van Amsterdam, she already had a string of invitations across the Netherlands and elsewhere. And so, it continues. She was given a gift, and she continues to pour her heart out, sharing that gift. But when you speak to Evi, she will tell you the two crowning achievements of her life were the day she married Ruben, and the day Luka was born." Grandmother and granddaughter looked at each other.

"Luka's told me you and your husband met during the Second World War," said Espen.

"Yes, the circumstances were grave when Rijk and I met. I was a nurse in my mid-twenties, and by then, he'd already made a name for himself, as a promising young doctor in Amsterdam. It was toward the end of German occupation here in the Netherlands, during Hongerwinter in 1944. It was a terrible time; people—little children—were dying because of malnutrition and the Nazi's hound dogs were everywhere, looking for trouble.

"Of course, doctors and nurses were forced to join the German doctor's guild, but not all of us were willing to comply. It was against everything human and decent to support an ideal that propagated the murder and torture of innocent people." Marit shook her head as she remembered.

"We were working underground for the National Organization for Helping People in Hiding, to help needy Dutch families and wounded soldiers of the Dutch Resistance, as well as Allied forces. Not to mention the Jews who were hiding from the Nazis. Our financial support came from the NSF: National Support Fund—they were our exiled government.

"Rijk had been instrumental in not only providing critical medical care, but also in dispersing medical supplies underground, and during one of those secret operations, I'd been assigned to work with the bright and brave Doctor Gaal. We'd gotten married right after the end of the war in 1945, and a year later, Evi was born. For all the terrible suffering and evil, some good has come out of that period ..." Marit was lost in thought again, then looked up and said, "Enough of that, let's lighten this conversation up, shall we? Who's ready for another cup of coffee and more gevulde koek?" Espen carried the tray with the empty cups back to the kitchen.

While Marit was busy making the coffee, Luka asked Espen, "Isn't she amazing?"

"She is. Her mind's so sharp. And the stories she's lived through to tell, boy. There's a lot of her in you, do you know that?"

"My grandmother can be willful and when she's made up her mind, that's it. Do you think I'm like that too?" she asked, surprised.

"Yes, I do. You both have strong characters, but you are also compassionate." He gave her a kiss, just as Marit came in with the coffee and more cookies.

Luka whispered, "Don't be too quick to hail her as empress. She's really going to interrogate you now."

"So, Espen, tell me about your studies. Luka says you'll be starting your PhD soon at the University of Utrecht." Espen took the tray from her and she sat down.

Luka recognized the glint in her grandmother's eyes, and she gave Espen a knowing look.

8

Luka was working through a mass of light detection and ranging (LiDAR) images collected from a hydrographic survey. Her task was to process the data using a specialized toolbox, and from there to construct her digital charts. It was painstaking work that required patience and visualization.

She had been working for an engineering firm since she'd finished her geography course—now already a year ago—while doing her honours in geographic information science part-time.

A large part of her firm's work was outsourced to the government. Known as the Venice of the North, Amsterdam lay on the Ijsselmeer and was connected to the North Sea. It was completely surrounded by water. The core of the city was built around canals. This necessitated upgrades to the constantly eroding structures and shorelines in and around the city.

Rubbing her tired eyes, she smiled, thinking how Espen would shake his head in a disapproving way, and say, uh-uh, as he held onto the four fingers of her hand.

She didn't mind her job per se. The work was challenging and to a degree, stimulating, but it was purely technical. At least the quality of her work was good, and it made her feel a sense of accomplishment knowing she was doing something worthwhile, well.

Espen had finished his PhD and was in his second year of a six-year tenure track at the University of Utrecht. The research they did was mostly numerical, and even though they occasionally had to do physical observations, the travels didn't impact their relationship more than the absences already between them. And sometimes she travelled with him.

With Espen in Utrecht, her studies gave her something constructive to occupy her time away from the office. When he'd moved to Utrecht, Luka had initially stayed over at his place—it was only half an hour's train ride from Amsterdam—but his schedule was busy. He worked until late at night and they didn't get to spend as much time together as they'd hoped.

So, alternatively, they've arranged to see each other over weekends, with an occasional visit during the week, and set one weekend out of the month aside to visit his parents in Den Haag. It was easy for them to incorporate her parents when he came to Amsterdam. She always stayed at the flat with him and Bas, and they popped over to Haarlem for dinner with her parents. Or when it was just her dad, they stayed over for the Friday or Saturday evening to keep him company—although Ruben insisted it wasn't necessary.

Luka checked her phone. She'd heard it vibrate earlier but didn't want to disrupt her focus. There were two messages.

The first message was from Espen. "Hallo. I miss you like crazy. Speaking of crazy, it's been wild over here. I'm really starting to feel like the stereotypical mad scientist, but we're making cool progress. Do you feel like going somewhere for the weekend, instead of hanging around here? I could do with a change in scenery. And by the way, I think there's trouble in paradise with Bas and Grete. He sounds off. Could you check in with him, perhaps? He tells you more than he tells me. Let me know about the weekend."

Bas had been dating a girl named Grete for the past six months. She had a master's in fine art and worked at the Rijksmuseum where she restored old paintings. Grete was more than a little Bohemian. Perhaps it was a default of her profession, maybe it was due to her equally strange friends, or it was a combination of her environment and her natural inclination.

Luka couldn't help but think that in overall tastes and appearances, Bas and Grete were a complete mismatch. She also had the sense Bas was simply cruising along in the relationship—neither pleased nor displeased.

Espen had said, "I doubt that the source of their love for each other springs from their hearts."

Judging by the sounds coming from Bas's bedroom, Luka had to agree, and she found herself wondering about Bas—the kind of lover he was.

But even though he tended to clam up, she and Bas had a close bond, and it was likely he would tell her what was going on.

The second message said: "Good day, Miss Bakker. My name is Frits Epperson, and I've been referred to you by a friend, Gustav Deremer. By his son Constantijn, to be exact. I own a yacht building company in Zaandam and have been making use of cartographers on a contract basis, but we've been expanding, and I feel it's time to find a dedicated onsite person.

"Stijn has mentioned you are currently employed but spoke

highly of you. I have taken the liberty of looking at your profile on your company's website. You still don't have a lot of practical experience, but your academic credentials are solid. The thing what struck me most, is your creative flare and attention to detail. Those are excellent qualities to possess in life, and for a person so young in your career, I congratulate you.

"If it is of any interest to you, I would like to set up a meeting, and perhaps we could discuss a potential employment opportunity for the near or distant future. I am not in a rush as such but as I've mentioned, we have seen tremendous growth and I wanted to reach out to you. You may call this number and if I'm not available, it will be redirected to my assistant, Val. I hope to hear from you soon, Miss Bakker. Have a good evening."

Luka sat holding her phone for a moment, then listened to the message again. Frits Epperson was the owner of Epperson Yacht Building, and one of the richest people in the Netherlands.

She was unsure about what to do, so she called Stijn. "Stijn!"

He gave a guilty little chuckle. "Hallo, Luka, by the sound of your voice, I guess Frits Epperson has gotten a hold of you."

"Stijn, why didn't you speak to me first?"

"I'm sorry, I didn't intend to go behind your back. Frits and my dad were talking, and he said that he was looking for a full-time cartographer, and I immediately thought of you. It was a reflex, I swear. Frits is a great guy. And he's known for his fair treatment of his employees. I thought you'd be a good fit for one another."

"I don't know what to tell him."

"You haven't spoken to him yet?"

"No, he left a message on my phone. I've just listened to it a few minutes ago."

"Luka, this is what you want to do, right?"

"I'm already doing that, Stijn."

"Uh-huh, but this would be exclusively nautical work. You'd have much more creative freedom as well."

She thought about it. "Yes, but I'm not sure about the timing of it—starting a new job while I'm halfway through my studies. Not to mention what Espen will have to say …"

"Speak to Espen first and tell him what a great opportunity this would be for you."

"You and I both know what his view on the topic is."

"Luka, you've said yourself that you would decide what's right for your career. Espen should support you in this, he damn well should."

She sighed. "I need to think about this. Just don't mention me to anyone else, okay."

"Okay. But promise me you'll think this through carefully, Luka. Don't let this chance slip through your fingers if it's something you'd really want for yourself."

"Thanks, Stijn. You're a good friend."

"I'll probably have to do some damage control with Espen, but don't worry, it'll work out."

"Before you do, let me speak to him first," she said.

* * *

Luka took a breath and called Espen. "Hallo, I got your message."

"Hallo, what's wrong?" he asked.

How did he always know?

"Nothing's wrong. I had a message on my phone earlier. I'm busy processing something, and I want to talk to you about it."

"A message from whom?"

"From Frits Epperson. He wants to talk about a job opportunity."

"Frits Epperson … the billionaire, who builds yachts for billionaires? Please tell me you're not seriously considering his offer. Wait a minute, does Stijn have anything to do with this—that rat."

"Don't blame your friend for being thoughtful, Espen. He was bona fide in mentioning my name. And why shouldn't I consider this? It would be valuable experience for me."

"Luka, this is nuts. These yacht companies are building monstrosities that are contributing to killing the oceans. How can you even give it a second thought? God, with all the shit our oceans must cope with, if there's something they don't need, it's a bunch of noisy rich mobiles speeding past each other just so that one guy can feel better about the fact that his is bigger than the next guy's. It's ridiculous."

The tone in his voice was rising and that wasn't a good sign. He was going to explain things to her that she already knew. This kind of conversation wasn't new, and she hated it, because there wasn't any getting through to Espen when he became like this. You had to go around him like a bird in a courting ritual: first this way, then the other way, walking on your tippy toes so you didn't crush the eggshells you walked on.

"Espen, bigger ships than yachts, are sailing the oceans using far less efficient fuel and they are the ones polluting the oceans and the air we breathe. Don't just blame rich people because it suits your argument." Espen made a gruff sound. "Besides," she continued, "I haven't even spoken to Frits yet. I wanted to speak to you first. This could be an exciting new path for me, and you're being overdramatic as usual."

She knew diplomacy was already out the door.

"I'm not being overdramatic. Billionaires contribute more to our climate problem, than average citizens do. They fly around in private jets; they own boats big enough to carry a cargo load of people. What on earth for? Besides the pollution which contributes to increased surface temperature in the oceans, the noise these vessels make is incredibly disruptive to sea life that depend on echolocation."

"C'mon Espen, people are savvier than you're giving them credit for. With all the pressure governments are now placing on not just companies but individuals, to comply with environmental requirements, you make it sound as if they just go around, doing what they please."

"That's exactly what happens. They do as they please, and when they get slapped on the wrist with a tax penalty that doesn't even make a dent in their pockets, they go on doing the same thing. Don't be so naïve, Luka."

"I'm not naïve. Why are you judging me?" Her blood was starting to boil.

"I'm not judging you. Don't you understand? What these people do, goes against everything I put my mind and energy into. Do you not care that they are contaminating our oceans? And what's wrong with where you are now, by the way?"

"Of course, I care about the oceans, and you *are* judging me. I'll tell you what's nuts, Espen, I get the feeling you want me to have a career that meets your terms of approval, no matter whether I'm satisfied or not."

He puffed. "You're exaggerating. Of course I want you to be happy, but I fail to see why you need to work for a luxury yachtmaker."

"You're making it sound as if I want to join a drug cartel. You know what, I called you, knowing this wouldn't be an easy discussion, but I was wrong. This isn't even a discussion. You're lecturing me, and you sound like a prig." Luka pressed the end button, then did it again with gritted teeth. Her hands were shaking. This call might just as well not have taken place. Why did she even bother?

She searched Epperson Yacht Building online and what she read, only infuriated her more. A large part of their research and development went into sustainable solutions. Their shipyard was state-of-the-art and eco-friendly, and they were designing fuel-efficient yachts. They were also partnered with a couple of global conservation institutions and made substantial financial contributions to marine research programmes.

She bet Espen didn't bother to read any of that. He said she was naïve and also implied she was ignorant, but what about him?

Her phone rang. It was Espen. She was too angry to speak with him and ignored the call. If he could be hard-headed, she could play him at his game. He tried four more times, then her phone stopped ringing.

She hated how acting tough didn't make her feel any better. What she wanted to do, was talk with him, not fight with him. Damn that stubborn ass!

* * *

Luka called Bas and left a message on his phone to tell him, as a courtesy, she was on her way to the flat, but she had a key to let herself in if he wasn't home. She was having coffee, going through her emails, when Bas walked in.

"Ah," he said.

"Hoi," she replied, watching him carefully. His eyes were red, and he smelled faintly of marijuana. "Are you okay?" she asked carefully.

"Sure, why wouldn't I be happy as can be?" He sat down on a chair with his hands behind his head, watching her with a grin.

"Would you like a cup of coffee?"

"That would be great, thanks, Lukie."

"I don't know, you seem a bit … you don't seem yourself. Has something happened between you and Grete?" she fished as she prepared his coffee.

"Has something happened between me and Grete?" Bas repeated the question to himself.

Luka realized he was more stoned than she'd thought.

"I guess a more suitable question would be, has there even been something between me and Grete? Besides wild sex, of course." He chuckled. "In truth, I don't think either of us ever understood what the other one talked about, and she certainly liked to tell me how my field of expertise was academically interesting, yet I was socially boring. Or was it the other way around?'" He sniggered. "Do you think I'm socially or academically boring, Luka?" he asked with raised eyebrows.

"Of course I don't. Grete doesn't know what she's talking about. You're wonderful and interesting at all times and on all levels." They both grinned.

Although this came as no surprise, her heart went out to him. Bas was one of her favourite people in the world, and she hated seeing him so down on himself. But Luka felt relieved that things had finally come to an end with Grete. He deserved much better.

"I'm sorry, Bas," she said after a while.

He looked at her for a moment and said, "You are something amazing, do you know that? You're the best person I know. If only there were more like you out there."

"You've just had a bad experience, that's all. Someone else will come along." She handed him his coffee.

"Perhaps. But we can't all have someone like you." He sat forward in his chair, elbows resting on his legs, holding the cup between his hands.

Luka was convinced it was the weed talking. She tried to change the subject, "Stijn is having a big party. You know what that means—there'll be tons of beautiful women. You're a free man now, and you'll have your pick."

"You're sweet. I'm useless company tonight, sorry." He looked at her more carefully, and said, with a frown, "But let's talk about you. What's the matter? You look miffed."

"I had a row with Espen. I'm really pissed off with him."

"Aha. What did my brother do?"

"Stijn had given my number to Frits Epperson—from Epperson Yacht Building—and Frits wants to speak to me about a job opportunity."

"That's great, Lukie. And let me guess, Captain Sunshine is not interested in joining the cruise." He tutted as he shook his head. "You know by now my brother's a purist. His life's mission is to make a clean sweep of the oceans and rid it of the dregs inside and out."

"Espen's unrealistic and he's being an ass about it. I just wanted to talk with him, and he gave me a big lecture. When he gets like that, I want to pull the hair out of my head, I swear."

"Luka, you must do what your gut tells you is right. Espen lives in a world of unbending absolutes. He's passionate about what he does, but he's not all-knowing. Just stick to your guns."

"Hmm …" She thought about it and said, with a smile, "Whatever will I do without you and Stijn?"

He had a skeptical look. "When Stijn and I are your best bets for support, something's amok. Why is it that you don't hang around with girlfriends more, by the way? I've always wondered about that. Not that I mind you hanging out with us. Please don't get me wrong. It's just that we're a couple of oddball loners."

"If you are oddball loners, then I fit right in. I don't know. Maybe it's because I've always spent more time with my dad. I'm used to male company. And women sometimes can be too much work, although Espen is making me question whether that's really true."

"Try having a relationship with a woman. And try being Espen's brother." He laughed. "But you're an all right girl, Lukie, don't go worrying your head."

She stood up to rinse out her cup. "I've got to get home. And then I need to think about this job-thing."

"There's nothing to think about. If it's a good match, you need to take a shot at it."

"If it doesn't cause a break-up between me and Espen first."

"Trust me, he'll never leave you out of his own free will."

"I might leave him for being such a knucklehead. Bye, I'll speak to you later." They kissed on the cheek and before he closed the door behind her, she added, "And I'm sorry about you and Grete."

He looked at her in his tender way, then shrugged and said, "*C'est la vie, mon chéri.*"

* * *

"How was your day, Lukie?" Ruben asked.

Evi was on tour in England.

"It was fine, thank you Papa. How was yours?" She tried not to let him see she was upset, but he most probably knew.

"It was all right. The students start getting a little restless toward the end of the school year, and they're hoping I'll drop more exam tips." He grinned but looked at her with searching eyes.

Luka was unsure whether to tell him about Frits' call, or about Espen's response. Her father would support her, but it would just make her angry with Espen all over again. She decided to wait a bit.

"Don't worry about cleaning up, Lukie. I've got it." Ruben said after they'd finished their meal.

"Thank you. I'm going to shower and work on my assignments." She kissed him on the cheek.

After finishing up her assignments and getting ready for bed, Luka lay, thinking about her decision. Why was it that she felt so torn about this? This was undeniably a dream opportunity. Frits Epperson sounded respectful and open-minded. His company certainly was a place she could visualize herself working at.

Both Bas and Stijn said she should go for it. Why couldn't Espen support her as well? Perspective wasn't a one-sided thing after all. One person's strong conviction didn't automatically disqualify the opposite side's equally strong conviction. You see and experience life in your own shoes, from your own platform. It's not always about one person being right and the other person wrong.

She was good at what she did, and Frits Epperson recognized that too. Perhaps she should quit mulling over it. Speaking to him in person was the only clear way of knowing. She decided to call him during her lunch break tomorrow.

Espen hadn't called again. That meant he was still angry. Well tough, so was she. She turned on her side and fell asleep.

9

"Mr. Epperson, this is Luka Bakker." She hadn't expected him to answer his phone, but he'd picked it up before the second ring.

"Miss Bakker, it's good to hear from you," Frits said.

Luka liked the pleasant tone of his voice.

"Please call me Luka. I have to be honest with you, sir, Stijn's initiative, although I have no doubt that he'd meant well, had taken me by surprise." Better to be forthcoming.

Frits laughed, "Yes, I suppose I hadn't thought of it that way, but he's a good boy and has a heck of a mind on him too."

"Yes, I'm extremely fond of him."

"Have you had a moment to process any of it yet?" Luka gave a little laugh, and he continued, "Fair enough, it's only been a day, and I'm sure you have your share of things to keep you busy. Tell me, is this something you would be interested in at all?"

"Most certainly. But I do have some things to consider," she said.

"I would have been surprised if you'd told me otherwise. I'm going to be in downtown tomorrow. Would it be possible for us to meet for a coffee after work, say at six?"

"Absolutely, thank you Mr. Epperson."

"Please call me Frits. I'll send you a text to confirm the time and place."

Frits texted Luka and they met for coffee. He was approximately her dad's age, and his demeanour was gentle and fatherly. She felt comfortable with him.

"Do you live here in Amsterdam?" he asked.

"No, I live in Haarlem with my parents, although my mother is away so often, it may as well be just my dad and me," she explained.

"Haarlem is a great place to live. What does your mother do that takes her away from home so much, if I may ask?"

"She's a musician, a pianist." Luka wasn't sure if she should tell Frits who her mother was, but then thought if she was going to work for him, he'd find out eventually. "You may have heard of her, Evi Gaal."

"Evi Gaal? My word, of course I know Evi Gaal." Frits was genuinely surprised by the news. "This is something Stijn didn't mention to me. The sublime Evi Gaal—my word," he repeated. "Come to think of it now, the resemblance is uncanny." He noticed Luka's discomfort and discreetly changed the subject, "I wouldn't have minded if my children had stayed a little longer in the house, but they couldn't wait to leave home. I have a son and a daughter—they are in their early thirties—and they both live here in Amsterdam. They tell me I should stop checking up on them but, as a parent, you can't help it. I've been a single parent for half of my children's lives, and I suppose I am a little overbearing." He added, "My wife passed away when the kids were still teenagers."

"I'm sorry to hear that," Luka said. She had no idea Frits was a widower.

"Thank you. As they say, life goes on—but not without

leaving you with a different perspective on how valuable the people in your life are. She was a wonderful woman and mother." He cleared his throat and said, "Anyway, Luka, let's talk about this job opportunity. I have the sense that you are indeed interested, and I think you'd be a good fit in our team at Epperson's. Tell me about the things that may be giving you pause right now and let's see how we can work around them."

* * *

Her phone rang. Espen. She let it ring a little before picking it up. "Hallo."

He hesitated before speaking, "Hallo. You didn't answer my calls earlier."

"I didn't feel like answering them."

"May we talk now?" he asked, but there was still a stubborn tone in his voice.

"If you are willing to hear me out."

He exhaled. "It is important to me that you are happy and satisfied in what you do, Luka—"

"But …"

"But I find it hard to reconcile myself with the notion that you'll work for a yachtmaker."

"Have you looked at their website at all?"

He ignored the question. "Have you already made your decision? It sounds like you have."

"And it sounds like you've only called me to try and persuade me not to take the job. Yes, Espen, I have made my decision. Frits Epperson has offered me a position, and I've accepted and will start in August. We still need to do the formal paperwork, but it's basically a done deal."

"So nothing I say, is going to change your mind?"

"No."

"I find that disappointing."

"I'm sorry that you do. I was hoping you'd support me."

"You know I'll support you in anything, Luke, but you can't ask this of me."

"And why not?" She sniffed. "You see it from one perspective, Espen—yours—and that influences your whole view on this issue. But it doesn't matter now. I've spoken to Frits. He's a great person and I feel as if I'll be able to learn a lot from him." When he didn't respond, she added, "Understand me Espen, I'm going to be who I am, and I won't conform to your idea of how that should be," she said firmly.

"Well Luke, you've certainly got this figured out, so there's no point in dwelling on it further."

Her insides twisted. This was the shittiest part of arguing with him. She was usually the one who gave in, for the sake of peace, but not now. Not this. Still, she tried to defuse the tension between them.

"Let's agree to disagree then," she said lightly, but he didn't bite, so she added, "Do you still want to do something over the weekend?"

"I'll get back to you on that."

That meant, no. Fantastic. The one who always had something to say, was going to give her the silent treatment—a tactic he favoured when he couldn't have it his way. She wondered how long his dark mood was going to last this time.

* * *

"Did you speak to Espen?" Stijn asked. He'd called her the day after her talk with Espen.

"Yes, I've spoken to him."

"And?"

"And I've also met with Frits Epperson—who's awesome—and he's offered me a position to start in August, and now Espen's giving me the cold shoulder—that stubborn, stubborn man."

"That's great news, Luka! About Frits offering you a job, I mean. Espen will come around. He can't stay angry with you forever."

"Well, we'll see how long this silent movie will go on."

"I'll speak to him. He has to see the logic in this."

"Fine, you can try, but be warned, he's feeling particularly sorry for himself."

Stijn chuckled. "Well, I'm proud of you for standing up to him and holding your ground, Luka."

"Thanks, Stijn. Now I'll have to play the waiting game."

Espen hadn't called her by Friday. His silence was deafening. What did this signal? Was he going to try to psychologically strong-arm her out of her decision?

She decided to pop by the flat after work and speak with Bas.

He gave her a big hug when she told him about the job offer. "Congratulations, Lukie. This is going to be great for you."

"Have you spoken to Espen?" she asked.

"About this? No, we haven't spoken all week. Is he still giving you a hard time?" he asked while making coffee.

Luka flicked her brow, leaning against the kitchen counter

with her arms folded across her chest.

"Tell me what he said." Bas handed her a cup of coffee.

"Thanks." She took a sip. "He said he's disappointed in my decision. He can't reconcile himself to the idea of me working for the loathed enemy. Do you know what the worst part is?" He shook his head as he took a sip of coffee. "Epperson Yacht Building is completely the opposite of what he's making them out to be. I mean, you should see their website, Bas. It's state-of-the-art technology. Everything is green focussed. These people are inspirational. Not to mention Frits Epperson himself. I'm proud that I'll be associated with them."

"And so you should be."

"But your brother has his one-dimensional glasses on. He sees only these evil rich people with black smoke rising into the atmosphere from their sinister boats contaminating the oceans."

Bas chuckled. "Of course he does."

"Did you know there's a trend for yacht owners to partner with scientists nowadays? Scientists go on research trips with yacht owners. It's totally collaborative," she said.

"I've read about it. I've also read that people can book trips on private yachts with scientists on board, for the same purpose. Must be awesome."

"Exactly. Surely Espen can't deny that this is a whole new ball game. These very people he's shunning, are the ones who are able to fund critical research for him."

"There's none as blind as he who will not see. When will you start at Epperson's?" he asked.

"The first of August. I'll stay where I am at the moment and finish my honours, and in June I'll hand in my month's notice. That would leave me enough time to learn the ropes in my new job before I start with my master's in September. I was worried about juggling all of that, but I think I'll be okay. And of course, I was also hoping it would give Espen and me time to spend together over the summer—if he decides to speak to me again."

"You've covered the important stuff. The rest will work itself out. I'm proud of you, Lukie. This is a major achievement."

"If only I had your brother's support."

"You will have it, don't worry. His sulk will wear off eventually. He can't do without you for long."

"Why can't your brother be more like you sometimes?"

"We can't all be cool," he said and grinned.

"I'm not giving in to him this time, Bas. I want this job."

10

"Lukie, you've been walking around with a frown for weeks now. It's going to become permanent if you keep that up, my love," Ruben said as he sat down opposite her at the breakfast nook with his Saturday paper and a cup of coffee. He took a scone from a plate of scones that Luka had baked earlier and smeared it with butter and thick blackberry jam, then added a dollop of cream on top.

She had already told her father that she'd been offered the job at Epperson Yacht Building and just as she'd expected, he'd been thrilled at the news. So had Evi, who'd called her from England, after she'd heard the news from Ruben.

Luka had also told Ruben about Espen's response, since she couldn't hide the fact that something was bugging her—he was far too intuitive. And it had taken Espen nearly two whole weeks to call her. She'd resisted the urge to call him, feeling that he was the one to apologize, not her.

However, when he'd come to Amsterdam last weekend to visit and had called and asked her to come over, Luka couldn't get to the flat fast enough to see him and the pent-up passion between them had been intense. But there was that scratchy little bug, crawling underneath her skin: Espen had still not let go of his prejudice of her accepting the job at Epperson's;

he just didn't say it out loud.

"It's this thing with Epperson's, Papa. Espen talks over it, as if it doesn't exist, but it's become the white elephant in the room. Everything's great on the surface, but it's there—all 12 tons of it.

"I was hoping by now he'd embrace the idea a little more, but even with all the evidence in my support, he won't budge. I don't remember him ever being so stubborn about something before. And I don't want to give in to him on this either—this opportunity's too important. But what should I do?" she asked.

"Sometimes people take longer to work through things in their minds. He's preoccupied with the research they're doing. Perhaps he's viewing this matter through his mental microscope because this is the way he can come to a resolution that would fit," he said.

Luka nodded and said, "That's what I feel he's doing. Only, it's like he wants to find a weakness in my argument, not a way of accepting it."

"Espen knows things are changing—there's a shift in people's minds from traditional ways of thinking and doing—both in the commercial world and in the field of science. Those two have long been at odds. It could be that he's merely acting out of reflex to the old ways." He paused for a brief second and added, "But I have another theory about this that may be worth exploring."

"Which is?"

"I wonder whether he sees this change for you, as a potential threat to your relationship, instead of a conflict in your careers."

"Why do you say that, Papa?"

"Maybe he has feelings of insecurity about you working in that industry."

"Why on earth would it make him feel insecure? Espen's one of the least insecure people I know."

"Well, I can only speculate, but perhaps the exposure you'll have to an environment of privilege and wealth makes him question his own worth. You're an attractive girl and it's easy to believe how other men would notice that too. Perhaps Espen feels he won't be able to compete with what a rich businessman, who owns a luxury yacht merely as a toy, could offer you."

Luka looked at Ruben. For a moment her frown intensified. She couldn't imagine how Espen would be threatened by someone merely because he had wealth. Espen—with *his* mind and soul—impossible! Money had never been worthy of a discussion between them. Yet.

Question was—was Espen truly frightened by such a perceived threat? Could that be the cause for his reluctance to accept her career decision? How should she approach this issue without him simply denying it?

* * *

Luka decided to wait until it was her turn to visit Espen in Utrecht before she confronted him. She still felt uncertain about whether it was the right thing to do, but as much as she disliked the idea, and more so his fervent denial, it would be better than not talking about something that could later become a major issue.

She liked visiting him in Utrecht. It was a beautiful city, and he had a great one-bedroom flat in the city centre, not far from the University of Utrecht's campus. It was an old building, but well maintained and his flat was in the corner, on the ground floor, facing east. It had trees outside, although they didn't block the light.

She'd helped him get set up three years ago, when he'd moved there to do his PhD. Espen was neat—a minimalist, and just like the flat in Amsterdam, everything was in its place and clean.

"It can't look too sterile, we need to make it liveable and cozy," she'd said, and had added some bright, feminine touches here and there.

He'd teased and said, "Why, thank you. Now all my other girlfriends will feel welcome too?"

She'd responded, "Sure, no problem. We wouldn't want them to think you're just a sex machine with no flair for style in your empty pretty head."

There was a three-seater sofa that was super comfortable but didn't have nearly as much character as Oude Oom in the flat in Amsterdam. They'd searched antique stores for a recliner chair and had finally found one—a gorgeous burgundy leather chair that kicked out a foot stool if you pushed it forward as you sat in it.

Luka'd given her suncatcher to Espen, as a housewarming gift and on a bright sunny morning—like this one—she loved sitting in the chair with her feet up, cup of coffee in hand, and staring at it as it reflected multi-shaped dots of colours on the sheer drapes. When she moved the drape lightly with her fingers, the suncatcher twirled like a ballerina, and she followed the colourful dancing dots with her gaze all the way across the room to the wall in the dining area.

Espen smiled at her fascination with it. "You should have

kept it."

"But what is the point of holding onto something so joyful and beautiful when it is meant to be shared with the person I love?" She smiled at him and looked up at it again, and the colours mingled with the green in her eyes.

"You're beautiful. I love you too," he said, hovering over her and looking deep into her eyes that shone like prisms, before kissing her on the mouth.

She hesitated, wondering if she should come right out and say what was on her mind, but before she could, he said, "Let's go grab something to eat at a bakery and bike out to Castle De Haar." She nodded, wondering if he suspected she wanted to speak to him.

They pushed their bikes to a café only a block away (Luka usually brought her bike for the weekend). They bought coffee and dripping warm chocolate croissants and extra snacks for later. Espen wiped a bit of sticky bittersweet chocolate from her lower lip with his finger after she'd finished and licked it off with a grin.

Castle De Haar was a 16.5km bike ride from where they were in the city centre. It was the oldest castle in the Netherlands; built between 1892 and 1907 and one of the most visited museums in the country. You had to purchase tickets to visit the museum inside, and to walk through the gardens.

The castle was built like a fortress with water surrounding it. Graceful swans swam around in loops, hiding for a brief moment in the shadows under the drawbridges, before reappearing. They occasionally swam closer to the water's edge where eager children stood around to feed them crumbs.

The rose garden—which had an impressive seventy-nine

species of roses—was still in the early spring bloom, but the flowers smelled wonderful, inviting buzzing beetles and fluttering butterflies to come and have a taste. Espen held Luka's hand as they strolled around. He'd brought a light blanket in his backpack to sit on and they found a spot under the trees in the park where they could have the snacks and drinks they'd brought.

After finishing her food, Luka lay down and watched Espen, who was in deep thought as he scanned the trees around them.

"Espen."

"Hm."

"May I ask you something?"

He looked down at her. "Sure."

She hesitated slightly, then asked, "Is the reason you don't want me to work at Epperson's, because you're scared?" She saw a flash of surprise in his eyes and when it turned into an annoyed frown, she added quickly, "Please don't become defensive. I want to clear this between us because I hate that it's there. We can't simply ignore it. What will happen once I start working at Epperson's? Will it become worse? I think it will."

"Luke, you've accepted the job. As you've said: let's agree to disagree."

"My dad thinks you don't want to accept this because you feel threatened," she pushed on.

He sniffed. "Threatened? And of course you believe everything he says, like you always do."

"What's that supposed to mean?"

"Oh come on, Luka. You'll never dare challenge anything your father says, you're much too worried about what your parents will have to say about anything you do or say."

"That is spectacularly unfair, and untrue." She sat upright again. "And why are you lashing out at my parents now?"

"I'm not lashing out at them but think about it Luka, you take the dutiful daughter to the extreme. When it's my turn to go to Amsterdam for the weekend, we always have to stay over at your parent's house for an evening. And how many times during the three years that we've been together, have we not gone away for a spontaneous weekend, because your mother was back from touring? It's okay for her to throw everyone else's schedule around, but there you are—dutifully at her side the minute she's home.

"Most people don't see their parents that often. I don't and that doesn't mean I love my parents any less. It's part of life as a grown-up and being independent, but you are stuck in your dutiful role as the perfect daughter."

Luka was taken aback by the accusation for a moment. "I don't even know how this has turned into me and my relationship with my parents, Espen. I've asked you a question about something that's really worrying me about my new job and how it will affect our relationship, but clearly you want to take no ownership of your role in this, so it's easier to blame my parents and my duty to them."

"You're the one who's been talking with your father about me; jumping to conclusions," he said.

"That's not …" She took a breath. "My father loves you; he doesn't have ulterior motives. He was merely trying to help me understand why you are so antagonistic about me working for Epperson Yacht Building. That is what's at the core of this, and you're avoiding it."

"He said I'm threatened by you working there. Threatened about what?" he asked in an agitated tone.

10

"About the environment I'll be working in. The wealthy people I will come into contact with." When he didn't respond, she asked, "Well, are you or aren't you? Because if that's not the case, I would like to know why you find it so hard to let go of this. And don't give me that 'I'm a wounded scientist and these monsters are killing my precious oceans' bull. I know you've seen Epperson's website. I know that you know they are above your high and mighty reproach here. So, what is really going on, Espen?"

He didn't answer but there was a storm behind his eyes. They sat looking at each other in silence.

Eventually she said, "Fine, have it your way. I want to go home now."

"Fine," he said in a restrained calm tone, as he folded the blanket and put it into his backpack.

They biked the long way back without speaking. At the flat, Luka started packing her things into her weekend bag.

"What's going on?" Espen asked, surprised as he watched her.

"I said I want to go home now, and that's where I'm going."

He watched her with a deep frown. She avoided looking at him.

Before she left, she turned to him and said, "I don't know why you're acting this way, and you don't want to tell me. So, if your decision is not to be honest with me and to silently continue resenting my decision to work at Epperson's, then perhaps I will choose not to be in this relationship any longer. This situation is making me feel tired and unhappy and I've had enough."

She closed the door behind her, leaving Espen stunned.

* * *

When she arrived with her bag slung over her shoulder around six in the evening Ruben was sitting on the sofa, doing crossword puzzles.

He took off his reading glasses, holding them in his hand and looked at her in surprise. "Hoi. And this?"

"Hoi, Papa. I'm going to take a shower. I'm sticky with sweat." She gave a weak smile.

As she walked to her room, Ruben's eyes followed her slowly.

When she came out of her bedroom in her pyjamas, he said carefully, "There's some leftover lasagne in the fridge if you'd like some."

"Thanks, I'm not feeling hungry." Ruben stood looking at her, not saying anything, and she added, "Something happened this afternoon. I don't quite know how to define it yet, but it could signal the end for me and Espen. We'll see."

* * *

Luka was already in bed, lights out, but she wasn't sleeping. She had a throbbing headache from crying, and every time she started drifting off, she had that strange sensation, like in a dream where it felt as if she was falling, but then suddenly jerked back to reality.

She'd told her father about what had happened but had left out the part about what Espen had said of her always wanting to please her parents. Ruben had listened patiently, but there wasn't much he could say. She'd asked him not to tell Evi yet; her mother didn't need the distraction while she had to keep her focus on her performances.

Luka lay thinking: something about her father's theory had felt true when she'd confronted Espen that afternoon—just the way he'd overreacted, something in his eyes. But she'd definitely decided that was something he'd need to admit to himself, and then to her, if they were to go further—as painful and unbearable as the prospect was.

The thing that had thrown her off completely, was what he'd said about her always wanting to please her parents. If that was something that had been bothering him, why had he never told her before?

Her thoughts were spinning, trying to find room to cope with the gravity of it. Was she overly dutiful? Did Bas and Stijn think so too?

Yes, she could be passive aggressive, but she wasn't like Espen who could always say what he felt, without overanalyzing. He was direct, but he wasn't malicious, although he certainly lacked diplomacy at times. That was just his way, and in many ways, she wished that she could also be like that. It was advantageous for people to know where they stood with you. She admired him for that. But why wasn't he telling her what was going on with him?

And how would she confront an issue that she'd never been aware of before? She couldn't possibly know how to be less dutiful—if that was the objective. What would her parents think if she suddenly started acting differently?

Ah, but therein lay the rub: according to Espen, she worried too much about what they thought. And it was clear he saw her sense of duty to her parents as a weakness; almost as if he resented it.

Her equilibrium had been disturbed. This was the greatest

of ironies: she felt confident standing up to Espen about her career, but now he'd thrown her a curve ball and she didn't know which of her seven arms to catch it with.

92

11

Two hours after Luka'd left, Espen called Bas. "Hoi."

"Hoi, brother. Geez, you sound low. What's up?"

"Did Luka call you?"

"No, why? I thought she was with you."

Espen blew out a long breath. "I've messed up, Bas."

"How much mess?"

"I think …" he swallowed hard, "I think she's broken up with me."

"What! What do you mean, you think she's broken up with you? When did this happen?"

"This afternoon. She took her bag and just left."

"No, no, Lukie wouldn't have just left. There's definitely more to this." Espen didn't comment, and Bas asked, "Is this about her job situation?" Again there was silence, and Bas said, "It is." He sniffed.

"Why should I act as if I'm okay with her working there, when I'm not?" Espen said defensively.

"Hey, you're free to not be okay with it as much as you like, and now you can have your way in peace. See how well that's working out for you already," Bas said sarcastically. Espen was silent again, and Bass asked, "So, you're going to let her go, because you're too dumb-ass stubborn, is that how it's

93

going to be?"

"No! I don't want to let her go. I can't lose her, I'll go crazy."

"You've already got the crazy part covered. How are you going to fix this?" When Espen didn't answer, Bas said, "You always have something to say when it's not called for, but when it is, you're suddenly mute—go figure. May I propose something?" Espen made a sound that could have been yes. "You need to sit down and think about why it is you've been acting like a jerk about this, brother. There's no justification for it and she doesn't deserve it. And you need to go down on your knees and beg her to forgive you—if it's not too late already." There was a long silence before Bas added, "God, she's the best thing that will ever happen to you, Espen. You won't find another Luka again. You won't," he said firmly.

"I don't want anyone else but her," Espen said helplessly.

"Then get off your high horse and tell her that, because I swear, I'll never forgive you if you cause her any more pain."

* * *

A month could feel like a lifetime, and every day for the past month, had sped by at the pace of light travelling billions of lightyears through empty space in the galaxy.

Every day, there was the same message from Espen on her phone: "Luke, I need to speak with you. Call me, please." Desperate, anxious.

She didn't call him, because she wanted to clear the cobwebs in her head; make sure they wouldn't simply be going back to square one if she gave in. But she missed him and listened to the message before she fell asleep at night; sometimes until her ear hurt, and it repeated over and over in her dreams.

She'd handed in her month's notice in June and completed her honours by the end of June. Now she had to bide the time until August when she'd start at Epperson's. They'd sent her an information package that she's been working through. A part of her felt excited, but the heaviness in her heart put a damper on her enthusiasm.

Bas and Stijn called regularly to hear how she was doing.

"He's in bad shape, Luka," Stijn had said a few days ago.

"Do you think this has been a picnic for me?" she'd snapped back and immediately apologized, "I'm sorry. Wrong audience."

"No worries, Luka. I'm just concerned. For both of you."

Of course he was.

Bas had called again yesterday. "Hoi."

"Hoi," she'd said.

"It's been a month," he'd said after a pause.

"I'm aware of the time."

"I'm not siding with him, but he has great remorse over his behaviour, Lukie. Won't you just hear him out?"

"Has he asked you to try and convince me?"

"He's desperate." When she didn't answer, Bas asked cautiously, "Do you think there's a chance that you won't take him back at all?"

The question shocked her. Her and Espen, not together again. "No … no," she said.

He paused again before speaking, "Then maybe it's time for the two of you to talk, Luka."

She thought about what Bas had said and knew he was right.

"Luke, I don't know what to do anymore, I'm going out of my mind. Seriously, my head's a stupid, crazy mess. I can't work; I can't sleep. Will you please call me? Please," Espen's last voice message said.

She sat on her bed, looking at her phone in her hand. She hit the call button.

"Hallo Luke," he answered immediately and with anticipation in his voice.

"Hallo Espen."

"Thanks for calling. How are you?"

He almost sounded out of breath. She wondered if he'd also been holding his breath, as she'd been doing.

"I'm okay. You?"

"It's been hell, Luke, but it's given me time to think. Boy, you certainly gave me time to think." He gave a nervous little laugh.

"Are you ready to be honest with me?" she asked.

"Yes."

"Okay, I'm listening."

She heard him swallow. "I've been thinking about everything you said. Epperson's do have an impeccable reputation; that's true and I can't deny that. And my resistance to you working there …" He cleared his throat, "Your dad was right; it was about my insecurity. I'm scared of losing you, Luke. It took me a while to really come to grips with it—damn, I can't believe how immaturely I've behaved—but you were right, and you called me out on it. My reaction was so severe, I know, and I'm really sorry."

"But are you truly afraid I'll succumb to influences from a world I know and care little about, Espen? Do you know me that poorly?"

He blew out a breath. "To repeat something I'd once told you, people fear what they don't understand. I guess I also fall into that category; talk about a grounding revelation. You're so amazing, someone's bound to discover you. How would I be able to hold on to you then?"

His honesty touched her deeply.

"Haven't I already been discovered at Albert Cuyp Market?" She could imagine him smiling, and said, "Espen, I just want this job. I'm excited about working for Frits Epperson. He's a gentleman and I respect his business practices. I want you to be happy for me, but I can't manage your feelings of insecurity; you will have to do that yourself."

"I know, and I'm going to keep that in check, I promise. I am proud of you, Luka, and I want to support you."

"Thank you." She hesitated and said, "But this conversation isn't over. You said some other things as well, and I'd like to talk about that too."

He sighed. "Yes, I did."

"Why haven't you spoken about it before?"

"Because I didn't want to hurt your feelings, so I waited until the worst possible time, when I'd already piled my other shit on you … I'm sorry, Luke, my passions got the better of me. I was a big-time prig and way out of line about all of this."

"Yes, you were. But you do think I'm overly dutiful. I feel as if this fatal flaw in my character had been exposed, but I don't know what to do with the information. And I also feel that you resent this flaw."

"It's not a fatal flaw and I don't resent it. I admire your love and devotion to your family."

"Yet you think it's over the top."

"I do think you try too hard," he said carefully.

She asked, "What must I do then; move out of my parents' house?"

"No, no, I'm not saying you should move out if that's not

what you want to do, although it is something we can explore. But maybe you need to loosen the cords a little; give it some slack. I think it would do a lot for your confidence in overall decision-making."

She sniffed. "My decision-making confidence has improved tremendously, thanks to your stubbornness."

"Well, you certainly stood your ground with me. You have tough stuff in you, lady. You'll be an asset to Frits Epperson; I have no doubt he's aware of that. And I'm sorry for being so stubborn."

"I'm sorry that you're so stubborn too."

He chuckled. "We both have things about ourselves we need to work on, it seems."

"It seems that way, yes."

"Are we going to be okay, Luke?" It sounded more like a plea than a question.

"If you are willing to respect my choices and support me."

"I am willing to do that. Am I forgiven?"

She took a moment before she answered him, "Yes, I forgive you."

But she thought about what he'd said about exploring the idea of moving out of her parents' house. Her poor father. He'd be by himself most of the time.

It wasn't so easy to loosen those cords.

* * *

Luka blossomed in her job at Epperson Yacht Building. The shipyard was located in Zaandam—on the Zaan River—a charming city north of Amsterdam and east of Haarlem. The city boasted many fun attractions and was famous for the

Zaanse Schans: an area where visitors could see a unique piece of life in seventeenth and eighteenth century Holland, with authentic wooden houses, windmills, a cheese factory, a bakery museum, and more. It was in stark contrast to the sleek, modern yachts and boats that were built in the shipyards along the Zaan River.

Frits Epperson had the respect of the yachting industry at large, and Luka was surprised and exceedingly pleased to discover how deep his commitment to the environment was, and how often he had meetings and workshops with environmental groups. And it wasn't merely a rumour that he took great care of the well-being of his employees—he listened with patience to input and concerns, and under his strong, focussed leadership, the business thrived.

Luka was learning the ropes in a high tech, fast-paced trade. The bar was set high and there was no time for being slack, but she loved her job. Frits allowed her the freedom she needed to explore her creativity and she didn't disappoint his confidence in her abilities.

Soon after she'd started working at Epperson's she and Frits had had an opportunity to talk about goals and expectations and had shared general views and interests. She'd mentioned to him that she was in a relationship with a marine biologist, and he'd been intrigued. There was a great comfort level between her and Frits, and she had felt at liberty in the moment, to tell him about Espen's initial skepticism toward the yachting industry. Frits had not seemed surprised at all, but what had followed, had surprised Luka.

Frits had contacted Espen—without Luka's knowledge—and had invited him to come and take a tour of the shipyard. It was a strategic move, and nobody had been more speechless (not to mention humbled) than Espen. Luka'd thought, check mate! What better way of silencing your critics, than winning them over to your side and befriending them. She was thrilled, and there developed a deep mutual respect between the two men.

Although she still lived mainly with her parents, Luka did attempt to work toward being more independent—she wanted to prove to Espen that she had it in her. Finding autonomy wasn't always easy. She felt sorry for her parents whose only crime seemed to be that they enjoyed having her around, as much as she enjoyed their company. Not that she didn't enjoy Espen's company, of course.

She'd suggested to Espen that she would stay with him in Utrecht on a more regular basis and when he came to Amsterdam, she made a point of sleeping over at the flat, instead of them going to her parents' house. He'd embraced the idea—and her—with enthusiasm.

And logistically it took the same time for Luka to get to work from either Utrecht or Haarlem—both were about a forty-five-minute train ride—but for Espen, who worked late hours, it was significant to live close to work, and he was liking this new arrangement.

It was a bit of a tug of war between her desire to please her parents, and to please Espen. But she had to acknowledge that he had been right, and she was overly dutiful compared to the norm. Espen bore her reluctance, sometimes with a clenched jaw, but sill, he bore it and she was grateful for that. Neither of them was perfect, but wasn't that the essence of love: to accept each other's imperfections?

She wasn't going to be able to please everyone—mostly Espen—all the time, but she was trying. Luka thought, touch wood, that she'd finally struck a happy accord on a sensitive topic.

12

In July the following year, right after she'd completed her master's in geographic information science, Luka accompanied Espen on a research trip to Scotland. The first part of the trip was in Oban at the University of the Highlands and Islands and orchestrated by the Scottish Association for Marine Science—SAMS.

Oban was a stunning little university town in the Argyll and Bute Council area and bordered the Highland Council in Western Scotland. It was known as the "Gateway to the Isles" and the "Seafood Capital of Scotland."

Espen's colleague was a big, burly Scot named Arran Haddow, who had flaming red hair, a thick, neatly trimmed red beard and mustache, and spoke in a deep voice. Luka thought she'd never seen such big hands on a person before. But his rugged appearance belied his nature—Arran was a gentle soul and as he spoke about the research they did and his passion for helping to conserve his beloved Scotland's coastal waters, his lovely cobalt-blue eyes had a tender look in them.

Espen and Luka didn't stay in the town itself, but rented a self-catering chalet in Cologin, a farming area surrounded by rolling green hills, and less than five kilometres from Oban. There was a short trail that led through a forest and up a hill to Loch Gleann a' Bhearraidh on the farm they were staying, and whenever Espen had a break from work, it was here they most enjoyed the serene surroundings as they sat staring at the lake.

Espen held her as she sat between his legs, and he explained to her some of the things they were busy with, as she listened attentively. She cherished these quiet moments of bonding between them.

There were plenty of other attractions around Oban, and Arran made sure they were never left wondering what to do next. He wanted to show Espen and Luka an area he felt would be of particular interest to them. It was at Loch Creran, a marine special area of conservation, north of Oban. They'd also brought their diving equipment to do scuba diving in the lake.

As they stood on Creagan Bridge, overlooking the lake and the mountains, he told them about the geological history of the area in his thick Scottish accent. "During the last ice age, Loch Creran and Glen Creran were carved out of the mountainous bedrock by glaciers. Loch Creran was occupied by a glacier twelve thousand years ago."

He took them down to the Dalradian bedrocks and explained as he pointed it out, "As you can see over here, there are scratch marks on these rocks that point west, in the direction of the ice movement. These marks are known as striations."

Luka took photographs and Espen was entranced as he studied it with a frown of concentration.

"This area is teeming with life," Arran continued, "You'll discover in a while when we go for our dive, there's a lot more going on than meets the eye. Loch Creran is a harsh place for animals and plants to survive. A mix of seawater and freshwater from Loch Linnhe brings in food for filter-feeding animals that attach to these bedrocks. When the tide comes in like a tempest, they stick out their wee arms and tentacles and hope for the best. Part of their challenge is to make sure they don't get swept away in the current, but other dangers lurk behind the rocks. Birds sit and watch for an opportunity to have a snack of starfish and mussels." He chuckled.

Luka smiled at Arran's sweet nature.

"These are horse mussels," Espen said to Luka.

"Aye. They are the most plentiful species here in the Loch and they provide a safe haven for many plants and animals," Arran agreed.

They walked around on the beach, looking at the intensely hued lichens. There was a lot of mainly brown seaweed, but here and there a patch of red and green also.

"The colours make the lake appear like a vase full of colourful wildflowers," Luka said, and the men smiled.

A colony of common seals lay between the rocks and curiously looked up as the three humans passed by.

"Do you notice those bright green patches on the grassy area over there?" Arran pointed toward it and Luka nodded, while Espen smiled—he recognized what it was. Arran explained to Luka, "That's caused by otter urine—a powerful fertilizer. The otters are entertaining to watch but look carefully: mink are often mistaken for otters.

"Mink aren't native to the area, but mink farms were the in thing during the 1950s, with the boom of the mink industry. Over time, many of the mink had escaped, but due to their destructive hunting habits—killing more than they need, common guls, common terns, and oystercatchers practically disappeared. There are efforts to bring the birds back. The roof of the marine resource centre is one of the safe havens for the gulls and oystercatchers to breed."

Espen said, with a shake of his head, "Just one more example of how damaging human interference can be to ecosystems."

To Luka, the underwater world looked like a type of outer space, inhabited by extraterrestrial beings: bright red sunstars with yellow armpits; spiny squat lobsters whose pinchers and legs looked like they had spikey gloves pulled over them; feathery sea pens; fireworks anemone with long, glowing tentacles; pink swimming crabs scurrying for shelter.

But most beautiful to watch, was Espen. She followed him closely, as he hovered over clusters of the worm, *Serpula vermicularis* (the only place in the world where they formed reefs that were so numerous), swaying their gorgeous crimson tentacles and suddenly snapping them back into tubes, sealed by scarlet plugs. His eyes looked like he couldn't get enough. They made eye contact and she saw another world alive inside him. It elevated her like nothing else—his passion was her addiction.

On their last evening, while having a hearty seafood dinner in Oban, Luka recalled some of the experiences they'd had, especially the scuba dive at Loch Creran. "The world under the sea perplexes me every time I scuba dive. It is such a dark place, yet it is filled with colours and shapes that knocks your breath away."

"Oh yes, that is true. We still have a lot to learn about what goes on in the depths but exploring it is half the fun," Arran said.

"The whole area around Loch Creran and Glen Creran is incredible, but I have to say those serpulid reefs were something special to see. Amazing that those worms grow so abundantly in Loch Creran," Espen said.

"Yes, it's amazing, but as you and I both know, even an educational activity such as scuba diving, can place a lot of pressure on delicate ecosystems when people don't know what they're doing. Novice divers inadvertently do more harm than good. Strict control is necessary to help preserve those unique reefs," Arran said.

The men talked more about research efforts to counter the effect of climate change on marine life, while Luka listened with interest.

Arran suddenly stopped speaking and looked at her with an embarrassed expression. "I've just realized something, Luka, I haven't asked you what it is you do. You must think me a self-absorbed bore, I apologize."

Before she could answer Espen gave a little chuckle and said in a joking tone, "Luka works for a luxury yachtmaker. Talk about damaging ecosystems."

Luka gave him a look, as if to say, are we really going to go through that now? But he shook his head almost unnoticeably. She said, "I don't think of you as boring in any way, Arran. Yes, I work for a luxury yachtmaker. No need to tell you how thrilled Espen was when I'd told him about the job but it's a great company. Epperson Yacht Building—have you heard of them?"

Espen nodded his agreement.

Arran said, "No, but I'm not a buff on that. I suppose people have to earn a living somehow, and not all boats are equal. What do you do at Epperson Yacht Building?"

"I'm a cartographer. I really love my job and the company I work for. Marine conservation is a top priority for the owner," she said.

"A map maker, how interesting. I've learned, Luka, that messengers bearing good news, sometimes come in the least expected forms. It always leaves me scratching my head though, when I think about all the scrap metal from used up boats—especially big cargo ships and cruise liners. Where does all of that rusty metal end up, if not somewhere where it causes damage." He shook his head.

"Luckily nowadays more shipyards are building yachts with sustainable materials. Not all of them do, but there's progress. Let's hope the time will come soon, when those big ships will also be more sustainable," Luka said.

Both men nodded.

"Do you guys live in Utrecht or in Amsterdam?" Arran asked both of them.

Espen answered, "We live partially together. I live in Utrecht. Luka and her parents are close, and she still lives with them—"

"Another controversial subject," Luka interrupted.

Espen said, with a smile, "But she also spends time with me in Utrecht and when I'm in Amsterdam, I stay over at a flat my parents own, and where my brother lives. She's sort of a nomad, moving between homes."

"There's nothing wrong with being close to your parents. When they're gone, you wish you could have back those times you were able to spend with them. My da had died a year ago, of a heart attack," Arran explained.

Luka instinctively reached out her hand and it disappeared in his huge hand. "I'm sorry about that."

Arran shrugged with a sad smile, and said, "Thank you, Luka." He patted her hand. "What a kind lass you are. You're a lucky man," he said to Espen.

Espen nodded and she wondered for a moment what he was thinking as he held her gaze.

Luka said, changing the subject, "You're fortunate to have grown up in this beautiful country. The mountains and the sea form a lovely partnership in nature."

"Aye, I feel fortunate. Oban's weather is milder compared to the rest of Scotland, but with an annual average of only 3.3 hours of sunshine per day, you often long to catch some rays. But I wouldn't want to live anywhere else," Arran said.

"Catching the sun is not an easy feat," she said with a smile, "Maui, was unsuccessful in capturing the sun, even after he'd beaten it mercilessly with his ancestral jawbone. But my father taught me you can trick the sun a little and capture it in a way it would never suspect that it could be caught," she said.

Arran smiled, "And how would I do that?"

"You should buy a suncatcher to hang in a window. It collects and distributes the sun's magical powers. I had one that my dad gave me as a little girl, and I gave it to Espen. That's why he's so sunny in nature," she said and gave Espen an ironic little smile. He raised a skeptical brow.

"Most fascinating. I shall have to look into that," Arran said, with a laugh.

They spoke about the second part of Espen and Lukas' trip in Wick—something Espen was eagerly looking forward to.

"You will love the Flow Country. The biodiversity is so rich, I will keep you up all night talking about it. But go experience it for yourselves, and fall in love with a special part of this beautiful planet of ours," Arran told them.

When they said goodbye outside the restaurant, Arran gave

Luka a big bear hug and said, "Goodbye, Little Light. It has been a pleasure to meet you. I will go in search of a suncatcher, as you suggested."

* * *

Wick was a four-and-a-half-hour drive from Oban. It was situated in the county of Caithness, to the far north of Scotland, and was bounded by sea to the east and shared a land boundary with Sutherland to the west. At its centre it was known as the Flow Country. This rolling expanse contained the largest area of blanket bog in Europe and provided a bastion for species that had undergone dangerous declines elsewhere. The area was mostly used for biological research and collection of scientific data.

The scenic drive took them through the heart of the Flow Country, and about halfway on their journey, they stopped at the Forsinard Flows Nature Reserve—a stunning conservation area, bustling with birdlife and mammals. They walked on a trail to the Flows lookout tower where they stood viewing the magnificent pool system, listening to birdcalls and water birds splashing in the water.

Luka said, "This area's so vast. My father taught me about the peat bog and its importance." She looked around in awe and when Espen gave her a curious look, she said, "This was when I was doing my geography course; not during one of his teaching sessions in his work shed."

"And what did you learn from your wise master?" he asked with a smile.

She knew he'd already know this but was indulging her for his entertainment.

"Quite a lot, actually. Blanket bog is a rare type of peatland, and it forms in areas with high rainfall and low average temperatures. The rainfall drenches the earth and covers it like a blanket, but the plants don't rot away completely. They build up deep layers of peat in the wet, acidic conditions.

"These bogs here in the Flow Country are more than ten thousand years old and, in some places, up to ten metres deep. It boggles my mind how amazing and intricate these systems are."

"It is remarkable," he said.

"And here's one you'll appreciate: bogs provide a defence against climate change because the dead plants in the peat store carbon. As long as they stay wet, it keeps the carbon dioxide locked in. Peatlands have an important place in the carbon cycle," she said and gave him a self-satisfied little smile.

"They absolutely do. Why didn't you mention to Arran that you knew so much on the topic when he was telling us about it last night?"

"I didn't want to curb his enthusiasm. He's so earnest about his love for his country."

"He has an earnest crush on you."

"He does not," she denied and added, "He's passionate about what he does but unlike you, he's sweet about it," she said, lifting her brow to emphasize.

"What do you mean? Last night you'd told Arran I have a sunny nature," he said in mock surprise.

"I was being ironic."

"It's a good thing he's not aware of your devious nature. That would end the crush," he said. She rolled her eyes.

"You haven't told me the story about Maui and his ancestral jawbone yet. When will you?"

"Perhaps later, after you've made up for being such a smart ass."

"Ooo, I accept the challenge."

As they were driving toward Wick and the breathtaking landscape switched between high mountains and flat peatlands, Luka stared through the window of the car, lost in thought.

Espen looked at her briefly and said with a grin, "Care to share what's causing that smile on your face?"

"I'll tell you about Maui now," she said, then proceeded to tell him the story as her father told it to her twenty years ago, in his work shed, while he was busy making his globes of the Earth. Espen listened with enjoyment.

* * *

"Tell me a story about the people from Polyhesia, who wanted to capture the sun," Luka said to her father. She loved the stories her father told of people who had lived long, long ago and of their fantastic legends about the sun.

"You mean, the people from Polynesia," he said, emphasizing the last part. "One of the legends tells of how the great demi-god, Maui, had returned home from many travels and conquests, and as he was sitting around with time on his hands, he noticed how the sun sped across the sky in a great big hurry, and he became annoyed. It always seemed as if daylight ended much too soon, and people could barely see what they were doing while they prepared their meals in the evenings.

"In those days, they didn't have lights to switch on at night, and they relied on the sun's light to perform their tasks."

Luka nodded and Ruben continued, "So, Maui spoke with his brothers and told them about this great plan he had, of capturing the sun—"

"But the sun is too far away from the Earth. How would they have been able to get all the way up there?" interrupted Luka.

"That's a good question," he answered, "but Maui was clever. The people in his village helped him, and they made long ropes out of flax, and then he and his brothers journeyed eastward, to the place where the sun slept. Maui told them to be careful and to hide, otherwise they would frighten the sun and it would run away."

Luka sat transfixed as her father continued, "When they came to the place where the sun slept—it was a deep, blackened pit—Maui instructed his brothers to build clay huts to protect them from the sun's heat when it woke up. They were terrified, but Maui encouraged them, 'Be brave and fight. I'll be fighting right here with you.'

"When the sun woke up and started rising from its blackened bed, Maui gave the signal, and they pulled on the ropes they had placed around the edges of the pit and tightened them around the sun. Maui used an enchanted jawbone of one of his ancestors to strike the sun with."

"And was the sun not angry, Papa?" Luka looked at her father in shock.

"Oh yes. The sun was roaring and thrashing, but Maui kept hitting it. Eventually the sun became tired and weak. Then Maui said to the sun, 'Now you listen to me. We can't get anything done in time. We will only release you if you promise there'll be no more flying across the sky in haste.'

"The sun was too exhausted to argue and agreed to Maui's

conditions. When they loosened the ropes, the sun slowly moved toward the sky. And from then on, the days were longer, and people were able to perform their tasks with more daylight at their disposal."

Luka thought about it for a moment, then said, "I don't think the sun liked to be captured in ropes and hit over the head like that. Perhaps it wants to share its light and warmth with us, but it feels tired from all the shining and moving around way up there in the sky. Is that why it gets cold in winter, so that the sun can take a break and sleep a little longer, Papa?"

"You know, my love, I think you might be on to something," Ruben said and winked at her.

* * *

Wick had an oceanic climate with low sunshine and high winds. Mountains on its western side created a rain shadow, causing it to have an annual rainfall below 800mm—a low average for its high location. Wick Bay formed a triangle with the river mouth at the apogee, and South Head and North Head at the base of the triangle. Beyond the heads, lay the North Sea.

The town offered a couple of interesting things to do. Espen and Luka visited the Wick Heritage Museum that showcased the history of the Herring Boom era. The herring trade relied on the export of herring, particularly to Szczecin in Poland and Saint Petersburg in Russia, but the trade had dwindled after the First World War.

Luka took a photograph of Espen, pretend-knocking on the only door on Ebenezer Place—recorded in the Guinness World Records as the shortest street in the world, only just over 2m. They also explored the areas north of Wick, and visited the town of Thurso, famous for its annual international surfing competitions. They strolled on the beach, but avoided the icy waters.

East of Thurso, they visited the Castle of Mey—previously known as Barrogill Castle—which was purchased by Queen Elizabeth the Queen Mother in 1952, and who had used it as a vacation home up until her death. The old castle had gorgeous gardens—almost inconceivable considering the exposed location—that were protected from the rough gales by the Great Wall of Mey and tall hedges on the one side, and a belt of trees on the other. On a clear day it was possible to see the Orkney Islands in the north.

Fascinating as it all was, the thing which sparked Espen's interest the most—and was not surprising to Luka—were East Caithness Cliffs on the eastern coastline between Helmsdale and Wick. It was a Nature Conservation Marine Protected Area, and more beautiful and intriguing than any man-made structure.

The coastline's weathered sandstone cliffs were a haven for breeding seabirds, rare mammals, and fish in and around Caithness waters. As they were exploring the rocky beach one afternoon, they counted a pod of twenty long-finned pilot whales out hunting close to the shore, possibly for their favourite meal of squid.

Luka was thrilled to get a couple of good shots in with her phone, and Espen told her about the usually highly social, matriarch-led whales, that were really a large species of oceanic dolphins. The long-finned pilot whales preferred colder water, which was why they frequented the waters around Caithness, whereas the short-finned pilot whales preferred warmer tropical and sub-tropical waters. They were a welcome sight any time, and both Luka and Espen gave long, but satisfied sighs when the whales finally swam off.

Later they were walking around the remains of the tall tower of the Castle of Old Wick dating to the fourteenth century. It was a hauntingly beautiful sight: the green landscape etched against the blue sky and sea below; the long finger-shaped coastline, relentlessly hammered by the angry, frothy waves at the feet of the high cliffs; and the ruins of the old castle covered by a shawl of moss. They sat staring at everything around them; almost hypnotized.

Luka then broke the silence, "My father bought me the suncatcher I gave you the day after he told me the story about Maui." Espen turned his head to look at her, and she continued, "I remember when he hung it up for me in the window of my bedroom, how the light bounced around in all the colours of the rainbow. On the walls, across my face, arms, legs, and hair—I couldn't stop giggling."

"I would have loved to have been a fly on that wall to see that happy face of yours." He paused for a second. "You do love your father, don't you?" he said and pulled her closer to him.

There was a hint of something in his voice—a little envy, perhaps?

She sat smiling and thinking for a moment. "Yes I do love him. When I was little, he taught me about the Earth and its solar system. And he also taught me about mapmaking. But the most precious gift he gave me, were the stories."

"You just can't resist a sun story," he said and kissed her on the side of her head.

They sat and looked at the views again, and she studied Espen's face at a side glance, thinking that her father was the first man in her life and in many ways, she still loved and adored him with the same childlike innocence. Luka knew he tried to understand, yet she wondered if Espen would ever be able to comprehend the bond between her and her father. Perhaps it wasn't realistic to expect that from him, just as she would not be able to fully understand the bond between his mother and her sons.

It wasn't meant to exclude him, but there were worse things in life, than loving one's parents. She should remind him of that, she thought, but not now. She didn't want to risk spoiling this moment.

13

Evi had been complaining about pain in her wrists for several years now, and Ruben finally convinced her to have it checked out. It wasn't good news: she had osteoarthritis—not surprising given her family history on her mother's side—and although she would be able to manage it with some natural remedies and occasional anti-inflammatory pain medication, the doctor told her it would become worse over time.

The inevitable hard truth Evi faced, was that she'd have to retire from concert performance. That meant no more touring, all she had known since she was a young woman in her twenties.

"For a pianist who's only in her sixties and is otherwise in good physical and mental health, this is like a death sentence," Evi bemoaned her fate. "Now I'll be nothing but a regular older person living at home, and I'll have to grow accustomed to being married twenty-four seven." She said the last part with a mischievous smile to Ruben.

"We'll just pretend we're dating again, sweetheart," Ruben said and grinned.

"What do you think we've been doing all these years, Rubie? But now we'll have to do marriage. Do you think we're finally grown-up enough for that?" she asked.

"I'm not sure we'll ever be grown-up enough." Ruben hugged her affectionately.

Luka had long suspected part of her parent's happiness, lay in the fact that they had never been under each other's feet for long periods of time. Come to think of it, that could also explain her own flawless relationship with her mother.

But she could also see the joy in her father's eyes. Although he had always been his wife's biggest fan, Ruben himself, had been retired for a couple of years. The idea of his darling wife here at home with him indefinitely, was understandably, an exciting prospect for a man who spent his days constructing paper mâché globes to sell to a niche market of young, inquisitive minds. Luka smiled at the thought of her youthful self, watching him hard at work.

After walking around in the house, coffee in hand, and speaking to herself, Evi told her husband and daughter, "I've come to a decision—I'll do five farewell performances here in Amsterdam, at the place that transported me into stardom: the Royal Concertgebouw. It will be a grand finale to the incredibly prosperous career I feel so privileged to have had." She touched her hand to her heart and her lower lip trembled.

Luka indulged her mother's slight melodrama and gave her a sympathy-hug. Ruben and Luka both told Evi the idea was grand.

Ruben reminded her, "You'll still be able to perform pieces for smaller audiences, but they won't be as taxing on your hands. Think of this as au revoir, rather than farewell."

And so began the months of preparation for the stately lady's exit. The dates were scheduled for early July when most people would already be taking time off for the summer and the weather would be conducive to having an evening out. The tickets sold out during the first week they became available.

Evi reserved seats for her family for the last evening's performance. Marit would attend with Ruben, Luka, Espen, as well as Bas, and they would all meet Arne and his family at the Royal Concertgebouw.

***

Ruben and Luka picked Marit up at her flat and they drove to the concert hall.

"Luka, my dear, you look like a picture," said Marit as she touched Luka's cheek.

Luka wore a long, sleeveless midnight-blue satin dress and her hair shone like pure gold underneath the ceiling lights.

"Thank you, Omoe, you look beautiful too." Luka hooked her arm in with the old lady's.

"You both look lovely," Ruben said as he caught sight of Espen and Bas and signalled to them.

"Congratulations on your daughter's wonderful achievements, Ms. Feltes. You must be bursting with pride," Bas said to Marit.

She patted his hand. "Thank you, Bas dear. Yes, we are all proud of Evi."

Bas then said to Ruben, "And thank you for letting me be a part of your special evening, Ruben."

"Yes, absolutely, Ruben, thank you," Espen added.

"It's great to have you with us, boys. This is a family occasion, and you both are part of our family."

Luka straightened Espen's tie and brushed a strand of hair away from his forehead.

"You've never looked more stunning," he said, putting his arm around her waist.

"Thank you." Luka turned to Bas, "You look quite handsome. I don't think I've ever seen you in a tux before. It's a good look for you."

Bas smiled and said, "Thanks. And you look incredible."

"What about me?" asked Espen.

"You look cute," Luka said, pouting her lips.

"Cute? What happened to very 007?" Espen asked in mock shock. He kissed her on the lips.

"We change with the times," Luka said, although she did think he looked impossibly handsome.

Bas gave his brother a triumphant look.

Arne, Betje, Anouk—who'd flown in from Paris with her silver-haired beau for this momentous occasion—and Isa joined them. The men shook hands and the women greeted each other with hugs, complementing one other on their dresses.

"Okay, lords and ladies, shall we take our seats?" Ruben suggested as he offered his arm for Marit to hold onto.

When Evi lifted her hands and played the first bars, Luka and Ruben looked at each. Luka turned to look at Marit, who's eyes were glistening as she watched her daughter perform. And Evi was sensational.

There weren't many dry faces during the encore as Evi bowed and blew kisses to the people who'd supported her for so many years—her own cheeks wet. It was the end of an era, and the air was thick with emotion as people stood and clapped, shouting, bravo!

Evi's backstage dressing room was filled with bouquets and notes from fans.

Marit took Evi's hands in hers and kissed her palms. "These hands have blessed many, many hearts and they have blessed my own heart. Well done, dearest daughter."

Mother and daughter hugged and cried together. Luka took a picture with her phone, choking up herself, and joined the two women she loved most in a group hug.

They had a celebratory dinner at a restaurant and lifted their champagne flutes to toast Evi's stellar career.

Evi squeezed Ruben's hand underneath the table and said softly, "I don't think I'd ever been so scared of anything in my life, as when I sat down in front of that piano tonight. My wrists were on fire, and I wasn't sure that I'd be able to pull it off, Rubie." She looked into his eyes as she shook her head in disbelief.

Luka had overheard and squeezed her mother's arm affectionately.

"Well, you did, my love. You most certainly did. And now these hands can rest from their hard work. I am so proud of the person you are," Ruben said, kissing her hand.

"Yes, Mama, me too," Luka added.

* * *

Luka didn't want to spend the night at Espen and Bas's flat but told Espen she'd go home with her parents. She felt it was appropriate to celebrate her mom's moment a little longer, as a family. Espen took it rather tight lipped.

"Why can't you sleep at the flat tonight? We've spent the whole evening with your family. Your mom's going to be around all the time now," he said.

"This is a once in a lifetime special occasion, Espen."

"Let me sleep here then. I want to be with you tonight," he said in a low voice as he ran his hands down her back. She knew that look in his eyes.

"We can be together tomorrow night," she almost whispered. His face told her it wasn't the answer he wanted to hear. "Don't take it so personally, Espen."

"How should I not take this personally? You always choose your family over us, Luke."

"That's not true, and don't make it into an issue now. Please. It's been such a wonderful evening. Try to understand; my parents and I can't make up for all the time we'd missed together as a family over the years, but I'd really like this time with them."

He shook his head and blew out a breath, "I can't win this battle. When will you ever free yourself from this … I'm going home now. I'll see you whenever tomorrow."

She knew what he wanted to say, but she didn't have an answer ready that would satisfy him.

"I'll come over to the flat right after breakfast," she said.

He kissed her on the cheek and said, "Whatever. Good-night."

"Goodnight." Luka watched him as he walked off with Bas, hands in his pockets and head drooping. The anticlimactic moment after a perfect evening.

They were having breakfast, and Ruben brought in *De Telegraaf*—the Dutch national newspaper—and opened it at the arts and entertainment section. There was a three-page article tribute to Evi's career, and a single, bold review of her last performance. Ruben read the review out loud for Evi and Luka.

"By Klaas van Leeuwen:

'*Last night at the Royal Concertgebouw, Evi Gaal gave a performance I can only describe as a sublime human experience. It was the final chapter of a career that had spanned over forty years. She performed Piano Concerto No. 2 in C Minor, Op 18, composition for piano and orchestra by Sergei Rachmaninoff.*

'*It was a daring move—Evi had been frank in media interviews in recent months about her struggle with osteoarthritis and the agonizing decision to retire. But if the lady experienced any discomfort during this challenging presentation, she made sure no one was aware of it. She was the ultimate professional and the truest of artists.*

'*The Moderato-Allegro opened, mimicking the dark mood of the soloist and her audience on this bittersweet occasion. The virtuoso led us into that lyrical world where sound guided the imagination.*

'*With the Adagio Sostenuto, her tender rendition of the melody, accompanied by the superb direction of the conductor and his orchestra, made us remember yet again the beauty of romance.*

'*Then came the Allegro Scherzando, and Evi demonstrated why she had been a darling of the classical world for decades: the magnificent force of her artistry and skill, exploded, as if it wanted to burst through the doors of the Grote Zaal, out through the foyer, and into the streets of Amsterdam in triumphant release.*

'*We had come, we had seen, and for one magical last time, she had conquered our hearts. What a grand finale. We salute you, Evi Gaal.*'"

Ruben and Evi looked at each other, and he nodded as he repeated, "We salute you, Evi Gaal."

Luka thought she had never respected another woman more. Besides her oma, of course.

Then she thought of Espen. Now she had to go and extinguish a wildfire caused by an innocent little spark.

14

It was a week before Luka turned thirty.

Evi told her, "You're going to love your thirties, sweetheart, they are the golden years of your life."

Luka had to admit, it was fun being at an age where you were considered mature enough, but still not too grown-up to dream.

Ruben and Evi had made reservations at a restaurant to celebrate her upcoming birthday. Her grandmother, Espen, and his parents—Anton, and Adelheid—would be there (they'd be staying over at the flat with their sons). Bas and Stijn had been invited too but both had commitments they couldn't get out of, and wouldn't be able to make it. They apologized and said they'd make it up to her.

Luka was fond of Espen's mother and father. Espen took after his mom. Bas was his father's personality clone.

Luka commented to Espen about this. "You take after your mom. You both have strong personalities."

"You mean, we're both stubborn. Admit it, that's what you wanted to say." He had that teasing look in his eye, the one that drove her crazy.

"I also think you have her sense of humour, which I'll admit, is an acquired taste, but I enjoy it," she said.

"Finally, after eight years, you're starting to get me. This is real progress."

"See, that's the acquired-taste part I was referring to."

He chuckled. "What's so wrong with having a strong personality?"

"Nothing. Must there be something wrong? You know what you do when someone makes a comment you don't know what to do with?"

"No, what do I do?"

"You dive off a cliff into deep water in the hope of making a comeback with substantial treasure, and then—"

"What then?" he had a pretend-anticipating look.

"And then you discover it's nothing but sand. Stop being so patronizing. I'm trying to prove a point about your personality."

He was laughing at her and it drove her up the wall. "You know you're awfully cute when you come up with these points of yours. And they've gotten better over time, so it must be true—with age cometh wisdom."

"You're so full of it."

"I'm sorry, it must be my strong personality that's the force behind it all."

"I can think of another force behind it all."

Espen pulled her to him. "You're so irresistibly passive aggressive. Let me brighten your mood. I have something in mind; think of it as an extension of your birthday and I'm pretty sure you're going to like it."

"What?" she gave him a curious-yet-skeptical look.

He kissed her nose. "I want us to go to Tromsø for a few days, in two weeks from now."

"Any particular reason why it must be Norway? Not that I

mind, I'm just asking."

"I have two words for you: aurora borealis."

"Yay, that will be fantastic!" She grabbed him around the neck and kissed him.

"So am I back in your good books now?"

"Perhaps, I'll need to think about it."

He chuckled.

* * *

It was Friday evening—the evening of Luka's birthday. Luka, her parents and Marit, met Espen and his parents at a popular restaurant in Haarlem.

Marit had given Luka an ultramarine velvet coat she had had restored and dry cleaned, as a birthday present. It was a gorgeous vintage coat with large matching velvet-covered buttons, and a wide collar. Luka had always admired it and was quite overwhelmed when her grandmother had given it to her. She didn't take it off when they arrived at the restaurant, and she received numerous compliments.

"I haven't worn that old thing in ages," Marit said. "It looks so beautiful on you, my child. Now, your mother might have a thing or two to say, but never mind her. She will have plenty when I'm gone. I want you to enjoy wearing it."

Evi winked at Luka with a smile.

It was a fun evening, although it soon become apparent to Luka that much of the conversation were stories their parents told of her and Espen, as little children. She poked him in the ribs and rolled her eyes in a knowing way. Perhaps parents did this to get back to their children for being rotten toddlers or teenagers.

Adelheid answered Luka's unspoken thoughts, "Indulge us, honey. It's more about reliving those days in our own minds, and they go by too quickly. And now you are grown-up people, making your own choices, living your own lives." She took Espen's hand in both her hands and smiled.

It made sense. Maybe there was a part of you, when you were a parent, that wanted to live vicariously through your children—or at least one of them. A sort of second chance at being a rebel. Luka decided that's what she was going to do when she had a daughter: let her be a hell-raiser. She looked at Espen. With his genes, there was a good chance of that.

He looked at her quizzically for a moment, then said, "I quite like the stories of you as a little girl with a gapped-tooth smile and braids." She leaned her head against his shoulder. He could be so sweet—for a rebel.

Ruben took the perfect photograph of Luka, Marit in the middle, and Evi. Three generations of women, having a private little moment. Evi was looking at Luka, and Luka was looking at Marit, who was looking at Evi. Three pairs of the exact same green eyes, captured in a joyful wink of time that would outlast the occasion. Luka printed it out on photo paper and put it in frames for her mother and grandmother. She also had one she kept at the office.

* * *

Bas and Stijn said they wanted to take Luka out as a belated celebration of her milestone birthday, since they'd missed out on her birthday dinner. They'd agreed on Wednesday evening. It was the middle of the week, and therefore Espen wouldn't join them, since he was in Utrecht.

Luka wasn't particularly disappointed that he wasn't there—she had such fun with Bas and Stijn when it was just the three of them sometimes. She'd never dare tell Espen that.

Of course, she had some idea of what they were up to but didn't tell Espen about her and the guys' plans, since he might just decide to show up. And sure enough, they took her to a marijuana coffee shop (not Flick a Bean, due to Stijn's still painful association with it). It didn't take much for Luka to feel the effects of the weed kicking in, whereas, her two male companions were more seasoned in recreational pot use and took long, slow drags.

"So, this is what people do when they want to philosophize about the meaning of existence," Luka said as she took a drag of her reefer and sat staring at it between her thumb and index finger as if it was about to cough up an answer. She hadn't smoked much before, perhaps once or twice. Espen didn't approve, but he wasn't here now, so it didn't matter what he thought about it. It wasn't his belated birthday celebration anyway.

"Our minds become too cluttered with popular ideas; it's good to weed them out and chill sometimes," Stijn said with a grin.

She contemplated what he'd said. "Hmm. Do you think I'm uptight? Do you think I need weed to chill?" Her eyes shifted from Stijn to Bas, and her mouth twisted to one corner.

"No. You're just well self-managed," Stijn replied.

"Well self-managed," she repeated. "Espen says I have everything well mapped out. That sounds suspiciously like the same thing."

Bas and Stijn both shook their heads and chuckled.

"You're overanalyzing. But tell me, Lukie, what do you think the meaning of existence is, since you've brought it up?" Bas asked, sitting back on the couch he and Stijn were sharing.

"I was just saying. I mean, it just seemed like exactly the kind of predictable question to ask in a place like this." She looked around.

"Maybe you're not high enough yet to answer that," said Stijn.

"Maybe," she said, taking another drag.

Luka didn't like inhaling smoke and didn't like the taste in her mouth either. Smoking weed was somewhat different. She still wasn't crazy about it. But it felt kind of cool sitting here with her two best friends, puffing away, and she did like the drifting-on-a-cloud effect.

She thought out loud, "It's a universal fact that you have much more fun with friends, than with relatives. Are friends just more fun, or are family just not as exciting? What's your verdict on that?"

Stijn said, "It's because our friends have no expectations of us, therefore we don't fear that they'll judge us. Family would be more exciting if they were less interested in pointing out our flaws. Friends point out the irony in our flaws, but they don't expect us not to have any." He took a long drag.

"True, we have no expectations of you or your flaws. What would be the point?" Bas said with a smirk.

"To answer your question, Bas, I don't think life has a meaning. I think we're just streaming along," Luka said matter-of-factly.

Boy, her mind felt like it was streaming along.

"I think you're stoned now," Stijn said.

"So, what you're saying is that there's no greater significance beyond what we see and do?" Bas probed.

"I thought we were philosophizing," she said.

"Philosophizing is stretching your mind beyond ideas that are safe and familiar," Bas said.

"Why waste your time asking questions there aren't any answers to? The meaning of existence isn't the same for everyone anyway. Everything is subjective. I like following a process and a routine because I like predictable outcomes. That at least gives direction to my life. Does that make my life any less meaningful than someone who's perpetually spontaneous?"

"You're definitely stoned now," Stijn said and laughed. "I think you're getting the hang of it. One can't sit in a coffee shop, smoking weed, without asking life's unanswerable questions, Luka. And by saying the meaning of existence is subjective, and that people have their own reality of it, you are opening your mind to philosophical ideas. That's good."

"So, you both agree with me then that the meaning of existence is an unanswerable question?" Luka asked and they laughed.

"Perhaps, but I believe it's based on something scientific as well as philosophical," Bas said. "Consider the law of con-servation of energy: energy can be converted or transferred, but not created or destroyed, right? So, we don't really create our own reality and destroy our own or someone else's life. That energy already exists as, let's say, kinetic, chemical, or potential energy, although it could be construed as another kind of energy too, and it moves and changes through our interactions.

"Consciously or subconsciously we are connecting with each other through invisible currents. We are feeding and starving one another, we are giving and taking at the same time. It's this exchange of energy between human beings, constantly moving through each other's holes, that gives life meaning. That's at least what I think it is." He took a long drag.

Stijn looked at Bas and gave him an affectionate hug around his shoulders. "That's beautiful, man. I love you."

Luka said, "If that is so, and it sounds as true and lovely as anything can be, then I'm glad you both are consciously and subconsciously passing through my holes. I love you both."

"Okay, I think everyone's high enough now, time to go watch a movie," Bas said.

Stijn had assured Luka watching a movie in a theatre while stoned, was a surreal experience and not to be missed.

"I get to choose which movie we see, since it's my belated birthday celebration," Luka told them. She decided on a romantic tear-jerker.

"No, no. We need to watch something sci-fi for the effect," said Bas.

"It's my belated birthday celebration, I want to watch a chick flick," Luka insisted.

"I don't mind chick flicks. They usually have hot chicks and sex in them," Steyn said.

She nodded to reassure him. "This is an American movie. They always have hot chicks in them."

"Then what are we waiting for," said Bas.

All three of them laughed hysterically from beginning to end and were hushed a couple of times, which only led to more laughter. Luka's cheeks and tummy hurt by the end of the movie.

"What did I tell you about watching a movie stoned?" Stijn

asked her.

"It was the best." Luka walked between them and hooked her arms in with theirs.

"You know what, chick flicks aren't half bad, and they're crazy-arse funny," Bas said as they were walking home.

Back at the flat, Luka made coffee and Bas took a box out of the cabinet, while Stijn stood watching them.

"America has always had iconic female movie stars. Take Marilyn Monroe: arguably the biggest American icon," Stijn said.

"Are we still on that topic?" Luka asked.

"The man has women and sex on his brain," Bas said, before commenting, "but it's not just America that's had iconic female stars. France had Brigette Bardot." He lifted a cake from the box.

"And Italy had Sophia Loren—they still do," Luka said. "Is that a birthday cake for me?" Her face lit up.

"It is," Bas said with a smile, and put three candles on top. He lit the candles. "You need to make a wish first. But remember you're a big girl now, make it count."

Luka shut her eyes tight and mumbled something with her lips. Stijn took several photos of her concentrating on her wish. She blew out the candles.

"Happy belated birthday, Lukie," Bas said and gave her a hug.

"Happy belated birthday, Luka. Welcome to your thirties," Stijn said, and he too hugged her.

"This is perfect for the munchies," Luka said, taking a little scoop of icing with her finger and licking it off.

Bas cut the cake into three large triangles, and they took it with their coffee to the living room.

"It's a pity our country hasn't produced any archetypal stars. You would think so, Dutch women are some of the most beautiful women on the planet," Stijn reflected as he took big bites of cake.

Bas and Luka looked at each other in disbelief, then back at Stijn.

"Yes, it has," Bas said.

"Who?" asked Stijn, surprised and with a mouth full of cake.

Luka and Bas exclaimed simultaneously, "Audrey Hepburn!"

Stijn slapped his forehead. "Of course. Good one. The fairest lady of them all," he said, as he put another fork full of cake into his mouth.

"You know, sometimes I wonder if there isn't a smart little man tucked up your sleeve who feeds you information, because it's hard to believe you come up with brilliant mathematical solutions by yourself," Bas said.

Luka was giggling when her phone rang. "Uh-oh, Espen. He'll know I'm high. He knows everything."

Stijn immediately said, "Don't answer it."

"It will only make him suspicious," she said.

"Answer it. So what if he knows you're high?" Bas said.

"That's easy for you to say." She gave him a look and answered almost too casually, "Hallo."

Luka's phone wasn't on speaker, so Bas and Stijn couldn't hear what Espen was saying.

Espen said, "Hallo, how are you?"

"I'm fine, how are you?"

"I'm fine ... something feels odd, are you okay?"

Luka pulled a face and mouthed, *see what I mean?* Stijn and Bas chuckled.

"I'm okay. Just having some birthday cake and coffee."

"Where are you?"

"At the flat, with Bas and Stijn. They took me out for a belated birthday celebration, and we went to see a movie, and now we're here, having cake and coffee." The way she said cake didn't sound natural. The c was much too pronounced. "There's nothing positively wrong with me." Did that sound right?

Bas and Stijn were in stitches now.

"Oh my God. Are you high?" Espen asked.

"Why do you want to know? So you can put your stamp of disapproval on me, Mr. Perfect Purist?"

Stijn gave her a wink and a thumbs up.

Espen said, "I don't approve of you using marijuana, Luka. You know that."

She could almost see him frowning like he usually did when he was annoyed.

"But that's your personal preference, Espen. My preference is to occasionally smoke a little marijuana with my friends, like to celebrate my thirtieth birthday, for instance. It's not a crime, you know."

"Your birthday was five days ago."

"So what? I'm still celebrating. It was a big birthday."

"Put my brother on the line," he said.

"I don't like it when you're bossy with me." She didn't hand the phone to Bas.

"You go girl," Stijn said.

After a pause, Espen said, "Luka, please let me speak to Bas."

"That's better. I'll put you on speaker, then you can speak to both him and Stijn."

"What are you two thinking, taking her to a pot house, getting her stoned?" Espen asked, clearly agitated.

"Stop being so bossy, or I'll hang up," Luka said, holding the phone close to her mouth.

"Hallo brother, don't you have better things to do than check up on your girlfriend? We just had a little fun, don't stress it," Bas said.

"Hey mate," Stijn said from the side.

"Hey. And how's she supposed to get home in her condition?" Espen asked.

"I'm sleeping over at the flat," Luka said.

"In your condition? I think not."

"I told you I'm going to hang up if you don't stop being so bossy."

"So, you don't want her to go home in her condition, but you don't want her to sleep at the flat in her condition either. What do you propose then?" Bas asked and Stijn and Luka started giggling.

Espen was silent for a little bit and Luka whispered, "He's thinking about it."

"I can hear you," Espen said.

"Don't worry, mate. I'm sleeping with Bas. Neither of us will come near Luka," Stijn reassured him.

"You're sleeping in the same bed? And the plot thickens," Espen said dryly.

"Trust me, brother, neither of us has anything the other one wants. And stop worrying, we won't smoke more tonight. We took Lukie out, we're having some birthday cake, and then we'll go to bed and go to work tomorrow."

"Luke, please take me off speaker now, I want to talk to you," Espen said.

"Okay, I'll talk to you in the bedroom, but stop being so bossy to me," she warned.

She closed the door. "What's the matter with you? I'm just having a good time. Is it such a terrible thing if I smoke a joint once in a blue moon?" she asked.

Espen sounded as if he wanted to say something, then paused. "No, you're entitled to do as you please. I just don't like—"

"Stop right there. I already know that, but this isn't about what you like or don't like. Bas and Stijn took me out and it's been an enjoyable and relaxing evening so far, but you're spoiling it."

"I don't mean to."

"Espen, sometimes I want to forget that I'm in control of my life and operate full of logic, and just let my hair down a little. I don't do it often."

"Do you feel you don't allow yourself that or that I don't allow you that?"

"Both. You and I have amazing times together, but you're rigid sometimes, when you can allow for a little leniency. You're not here and Bas and Stijn did something sweet for me. And yes, it was out of the ordinary, but I like that it was something unusual. I'm having a fun evening with my friends; couldn't you grant me that?"

He was silent for a bit. "You're right." Espen blew out his breath and repeated, "Yes, you're right. I guess I'm also a little envious that they get to spend time with you, and I don't."

"I know, but we're going to Norway soon, and it will be amazing. Just don't call me and treat me like a child, please. I'm a big girl now, after all," she said the last words in a devious way.

"Yes, you certainly are. I'm sorry. You know I love you completely."

"Yes, I do know that. And I love you completely also, except for the bossy part."

"Okay, go have your cake and eat it. I'll speak to you tomorrow."

"Stop being so bossy. And thank you, I will. Bye."

15

March was a prime time to see the northern lights because there were more clear nights, and Luka had never been to Tromsø—supposedly the best place to see them, at least in Europe, she would suppose. She'd loved the idea when Espen had suggested it. It wasn't usual for him to take time off work this time of the year, but he'd made special arrangements for someone to fill in for him.

Espen had earned his tenure at the University of Utrecht the previous year. However, between his and Luka's work at Epperson Yacht Building, time for quick getaways amid the academic year were few. He had some time off during summer break, so Luka planned her vacation time whenever Espen was able to get away. But as a research professor vacation was often combined with work. Luka didn't mind that at all. They've had incredible experiences as part of Espen's research. Seeing the world through his eyes was an experience in itself.

Last summer she'd accompanied him to the Magallanes Region in Chilean Patagonia—a strategic area for monitoring global climate change. However, July was the middle of winter in southern Chile, and they'd experienced rough weather while they'd been out on a boat with the research team. As they'd sat huddled, clutching their raincoats, Luka'd had a glimpse of what went on in Espen's intense, beautiful mind, as she sat watching him. He'd been looking at something bobbing on the surface of the choppy water a few metres away.

"Look." He'd pointed. "A grey-headed albatross." And he'd grinned with pleasure.

The grey-headed albatross was an endangered species, and the area was an important refuge for them.

Espen had stared at it in wonder and then he'd turned his head to look at her, "Do you see the trust, Luke? It allows itself to be carried by the sea, like an infant rocking in its mother's arms. There's no fear, absolutely none." He'd looked out over the ocean again in a reverent way, and her own calm sea had been shaken by the bare truth and sheer innocence of that moment.

This trip was a refreshing change of pace. And Norway was always wonderful to visit, winter or summer.

As their flight had descended toward Tromsø, and they'd looked out over the picturesque scene of the island of Tromsøya, surrounded by fjords, the captain had said, "Ladies and gentlemen, welcome to Tromsø, the northernmost city in the world. It is only 2,200km south of the North Pole, and approximately 350km north of the Arctic Circle. You are on top of the Earth now, so please don't fall off. At least not until you've done a couple of fun activities and seen the most beautiful northern lights in the world. Of course, I am from Tromsø, so you must please forgive my bias. Have a terrific stay in our charming city."

Luka and Espen now sat watching the aurora borealis as it danced across the Norwegian night sky. They had a blanket wrapped around them both and were sipping on grapefruit schnapps.

Luka breathed in Espen's warm scent, mixed with the cold, clean air and said, "They really are vivid here, aren't they? This is a great birthday present, thank you."

"Our natural world always leaves me breathless. Just like you do," he said, and smiled when he saw her pulling a face.

"Me? I leave you breathless, just as your first love? Wow, I don't know what to say, I feel so honoured."

"You are my first love, Luke, although only marginally."

"I'll take my marginal first place then."

"Are you happy?" His voice suddenly sounded serious.

"Yes, I am. Why do you ask that of all things now? Don't I look happy to you?"

"I'm wondering. I always wonder about you, Luke. You have a way of revealing yourself, and I think I have you figured out, then I realize I don't. After all these years you are still a mystery to me in many ways, but I like that you are. I suppose I want to know if you're happy with us still."

"I am happy with us still. Of course I am." She was silent for a moment, then said, "Do you know how much I admire you? Your whole being is purpose driven. Compared to you, my energy feels almost feeble. Sometimes I think you will swallow me up in your intensity."

On occasion, when she'd said something, Espen would look at her in a way, without speaking, as he was doing now. In such moments she wanted to ask him what it was he was thinking, but she didn't. Maybe because she liked the look on his face when he looked at her like that. He was breathtaking.

They sat quiet for a while, then he said, "I have a story I think you'll like. It's a myth reserved for special occasions."

"Oh? Like this occasion?" she asked with a grin.

"Yes, like this one," he said and kissed her head. "This story is about an isgudinne—ice goddess, here in the Arctic," he began. "Her name was Krystallinsk, and she lived in the heavens just above the line of the Arctic Circle." Espen pointed with his finger at the imaginary line in the sky. "She was beautiful and like her name, she was almost completely transparent. During the day, she appeared like unfiltered sunlight, and at night the stars shone through her and her eyes themselves, were like stars.

"But the thing most captivating about Krystallinsk was that you could see her golden heart—a luminous sun throbbing in her chest—and it had magical powers. When creatures from the Earth and sea became sick or were injured—those for whom there was still hope—they were placed on a sleigh driven by a snow-white spirit wolf named Gnist, meaning spark, and he took the suffering animals to where Krystallinsk lived.

"On winter nights, the wolf rode on the wings of the aurora borealis; in summer, he used the long, soft wavelengths of the midnight sun to sail through the sky. When a creature was brought to her, Krystallinsk would hold it to her heart, and its health would be restored completely." Espen looked down at Luka's face for a moment. She was transfixed.

He continued, "On an island, off one of the great fjords below, lived a jordforvalter—an earth steward, appointed by the gods. His name was Bjørn, meaning Bear, and he was the protector of the land and the water in his keep. Early in the morning, when the mist lay thick, he rose and rode through the forests and over the mountains with his sleigh that never touched the ground and was led by the bold spirit wolf, Gnist, who was his companion.

"When Bjørn was satisfied that the plants and the creatures on land were safe and well, he let Gnist run free. Then Bjørn himself, dived into the fjord, and as he swam through the cool green water, he called the creatures in the abyss to him—he was able to mimic their sounds. This was the place where his heart and soul felt freest. The gods had given him the ability to stay underwater for unusually long periods of time, and he could swim and dive to his heart's delight."

Espen stopped for a moment to think, and Luka said impatiently, "Go on."

He took a breath. "Then one day, as Bjørn was swimming in the fjord, he became entangled in a fishing boat's net, and was unable to set himself free from the thick ropes. The creatures around him feared Bjørn would be taken away from them, so they formed a weight that held him down, and the men in the boat were unable to pull him up. Eventually the fishermen gave up and cut the ropes loose, and they went on their way.

"But Bjørn was trapped inside the net. He became weak from the struggle and lay helpless on the bottom of the fjord, where the eelgrass formed a blanket around him, until the belugas came and lifted him up with their noses and fins. They swam underneath him and pushed him to shore.

"Bjørn was barely alive—he'd been underwater far too long. The belugas called out to Gnist for help. Gnist brought the sleigh to shore and used all his strength to roll Bjørn onto the sleigh. He then put his head through the harness and flew swiftly to the home of Krystallinsk. She loosened the ropes around Bjørn—he was cold and pale, and his heart was beating only faintly. Then she held him to her heart, and the life returned to his body. Yet something inside him felt different. When he looked down, he could see his new yellow heart beating in his chest and he realized he was now translucent, as Krystallinsk.

"Krystallinsk said to Bjørn, 'Your name is no longer Bjørn, for you have made the journey to the spirit world. Now, you are Åndebjørn—Spirit Bear; you are a man no longer, but a jordgud—an Earth god, and you will have more power to care for and save those who need your help.'

"So, Åndebjørn returned to the island that he loved. On foggy days, the bright light of his heart shone like a lantern, as he moved through the woods and over the snowy mountains where he watched and roamed with his trusted friend, Gnist.

"On warm summer days, Krystallinsk came down from above the Arctic Circle to play in the fjord with Åndebjørn, and the water turned a magnificent pastel blue when she entered it. And underneath the surface of the water, two glowing lights swam with the creatures in the deep."

Luka sighed. "That's a fine story."

Espen grinned as he said, "Yes, I think it's one of my favourites."

"Did you make that up just for me?" she asked.

"Yes, and I've written it down and saved it in an electronic file for you also. But I have something else that you can keep with you, something tangible." He reached in the pocket of his coat and took out a small box that closed with a hook in the front. Inside was a shiny brass compass. As Luka removed it from the box Espen said, "This is so you can steer your ship across the oceans and always find your way back to me, Luka, my golden heart." He held her tight.

She turned it around in her hand, examining it for a long time. The weight of it felt heavy in her palm, and it had a good balance to it. "This is beautiful. Is it an antique?" she asked.

Espen nodded. "I love you, Åndebjørn," she said, and reached up and pulled him to her, pressing her lips to his until they hurt.

144

16

"I have a proposition for you, Espen," said Frits Epperson. "One I think you might be interested in." Frits had called Espen on his cellphone.

"Mr. Epperson there's only one way to find out, and that's to tell me what it is," Espen said, with a little laugh.

"I'm having a fundraiser in July at the Felix Meritis. There'll be approximately two hundred guests: all businessmen, yacht owners, members of environmental clubs and foundations, and many of them will be showing up with their cheque books and credit cards. This is a great opportunity for you to bring your cause to the room. I would like for you to be a guest speaker. Nothing too lengthy, but something for them to take home and digest. It's all about education and awareness. What do you say?"

"Well, Frits, I feel flattered … I don't quite know what to say."

"Say you will accept."

"I will have to run this by the head of my department and check my schedule, but will gladly accept if there are no obstacles, thank you, Frits."

"Fantastic. My assistant will send you the details. You should have more than enough time to prepare."

Espen called Luka: "I've just spoken to Frits about the July fundraiser. Did you put him up to this?"

"I did not. Frits thinks the world of you, I didn't have to say anything. Are you going to do it?" she asked.

"Yes, on condition there are no conflicts, which I'm sure there won't be since, it would be to the benefit of our research programmes."

"That's great. It's going to be fancy—we're talking billion-aires galore. Don't feel intimidated. Just do what you do best."

He said in a sly voice, "You know, I'm also a billionaire of sort."

"Oh, how so?"

"I have the world's biggest diamond."

"Uh, that's borderline cheesy, but also kind of cute. Luckily you didn't say you *own* the world's biggest diamond, because that would have been it," she said in mock exasperation.

Espen chuckled. "Don't I know it. After eight years with you, I've learned to use my words wisely, Miss Bakker."

* * *

Located on the Keizergracht in Amsterdam, the iconic Felix Meritis was founded in 1777, as an intellectual society of entrepreneurs, scientists, artists, and philosophers. The society was dissolved in 1888, but a hundred years later, had been re-established as a centre for art, culture, and, science. It was a spectacular venue.

Luka held onto Espen's arm as they were escorted to the Zuilenzaal on the first floor.

"Geez, this is even more impressive than I imagined," Espen

whispered to her.

They both looked up and around at the fine architecture. The smell of food and expensive alcohol filled their nostrils, and people were mingling in an elegant and relaxed atmosphere.

"It smells delicious," Luka said softly.

"It smells like money."

"Think of the irony: plastic credit cards and paper money, for a greener Earth."

Espen looked at her and chuckled.

Frits walked up to greet them. "Ah, good evening young people. Luka, you look beautiful."

"Thanks, Frits. This is a gorgeous venue," she said as she looked around.

"It is one of Amsterdam's finest, isn't it? Espen my boy, are you ready to shine?" Frits asked.

"I have to be honest; I felt a lot more confident until I walked in here. But yes, I'm ready."

"Good, about fifteen minutes before we start. I'll make a quick announcement and introduce you. After the speeches, you'll have a chance to meet some of the people here," Frits said and patted Espen's arm.

"Sounds good," said Espen. He took a deep breath as Frits walked off to speak to someone else.

"Don't worry, you'll charm their pants off," Luka said, hooking her arm in with his.

"Now there's an image to hold on to during my speech," and he grinned. He looked her over. "I am lucky to have you by my side, elegant lady."

"It's not every day a lady gets to be a Bond-girl." She gave him a dazzling smile.

"I see. So I've been promoted to 007 status again." Luka shrugged.

Frits took a stand behind a microphone and said, "Ladies and gentlemen, if I may please have your attention." The general chatter ceased as all eyes turned to him. "I want to thank everyone for being here tonight. This is a special occasion, and I think you will all agree with me, in a truly magnificent place.

"Tonight, is about coming together as a local and international community to create awareness, talk about distribution of resources, and have a little fun while we're doing it. We will not occupy your time with long speeches, but I felt it would be appropriate to set the correct tone for the evening. With that, I want to introduce to you a bright young mind in the field of science at the University of Utrecht, Professor Espen De Cleene. He is part of a renowned research team in oceans and climate, a subdivision of marine biology. Without further ado, Professor De Cleene."

Espen stepped behind the microphone, "Good evening. This is an honour—thank you Frits, for this opportunity." Espen turned to Frits and acknowledged him with a smile. He turned again to his audience. "The hot topic in just about every conversation nowadays, is the environment and global warming. And with good reason; this is one of the biggest challenges we face as a species. Never have we been forced to look so deeply within ourselves, as in the times we are living in.

"Scientists have been wrestling with governments for decades, and although there has been tremendous progress in recognizing the importance of preserving the world's forests, there is still not nearly enough emphasis on the role the oceans play in the carbon cycle. To add to this, there has also been significant pushback from those who claim it's nothing more than scare tactics, and that it's simply the Earth going through its normal cycles." Espen paused, pursed his lips and ran his eyes over the audience. "So how do we know what is fact and what is speculation?

"One way to try and find the answers to the problems we face today, is for scientists to look to the past. Events, such as the Paleocene-Eocene mass extinction 56 million years ago, give us an idea of what the Earth went through, and what had caused such a massive destruction.

"There have been other mass extinction events, so why is this period of such importance to scientists, you may wonder. Because the current rates of ocean acidification—a direct consequence of carbon dioxide released into the atmosphere, and then absorbed by the oceans—have been compared with the same greenhouse event that has caused the ocean temperature to rise by nearly six degrees Celsius at the Paleocene-Eocene Thermal Maximum—"

All eyes were fixed on him; flickering as they were processing the information.

"From a scientific standpoint, we can derive this conclusion: The oceans' surface temperatures are rising—in fact, about ten times faster than during the Paleocene-Eocene mass extinction. The difference between now and then, is that ocean acidification today is caused predominantly by human activity and fossil fuels.

"We can't blame nature and say this is a natural cycle. The reality is, there are more than 7.5 billion people on the planet, and such high numbers have an enormous impact on the environment—"

Luka was looking around at the faces in the room. Some were watching Espen intently; others were whispering something in an associate or a partner's ear. What was going through their minds? She wondered.

He continued, "So what is the big deal, some might ask. Well, the oceans cover more than two-thirds of the Earth's surface and they absorb nearly a third of the carbon dioxide in the atmosphere. They provide more than half of the oxygen we breathe. That's a big deal indeed.

"With the current rates of fossil acidification in our oceans, they simply can't keep up. That doesn't include the garbage that is dumped into them at a staggering pace. The ocean floor is covered in plastic—it's estimated at 14 million tons—which, besides the fact that it's consumed by some animals, also gives off chemicals, thereby contributing to the death-cycle—"

As waiters walked around with trays of drinks, people reached out and took long sips, but their eyes remained fixed on Espen. He was a clear communicator, yet Luka couldn't help feeling nervous for his sake. This audience was the hardest kind to speak to. They were educated and savvy. She briefly made eye contact with Frits on the other side of the room, who gave her an encouraging little wink and a smile.

"There are practical ways for ordinary citizens to help reverse this: they can pledge their support in reducing the buildup of carbon dioxide in the atmosphere by using renewable energy versus fossil fuels; eliminate the production of plastic that's not biodegradable, use sustainable fishing practices, encourage marine protected green areas so that the oceans will be able to lock away blue carbon and fish carbon; to name a just few. Nature is amazing, it will re-generate itself, but it needs time, and our help.

"Scientists are working non-stop to create solutions, but it takes long hours of research and resources. You no doubt have heard this message many times over, but without your voices to carry it forward, our efforts in the scientific community could be in vain. In fact, without your financial contributions, they may not even be possible."

He paused, gave them his big, irresistible smile and Luka could see by their responsive looks that he had the whole room in his pocket.

Espen looked at Luka, then back at his audience. "Someone who's especially dear to me, once told me I shouldn't put all my hope in people, yet nobody believes in me more, than she does. We have no choice, but to believe in people and believe that they will come through for humanity, and for our planet. I thank you for your time."

There was a big applause. Luka sighed with relief, and she gave Espen a big smile as he made his way to her.

Frits came forward and said, "Thank you, Professor De Cleene, for giving us much food for thought. We've come a long way since the days of the Dutch East Indies Company exploring the seven seas. The commercial shipping industry is still largely dependent on toxic bunker oil, and that must change, but economically, ships make sense. That is why we are here, so that we can put our efforts and resources into support for research to find cleaner and more affordable solutions."

As he stood listening to Frits, Espen's eyes sparkled. "I can feel the winds of change in the air, Luke," he whispered. "This is what people should be putting their minds to. Exactly this kind of reasoning."

"I'm so proud of you," she said.

After his speech, Frits joined them. "Espen, that was terrific, thank you. The better our understanding, the more successful we will be in communicating these important issues. Are you ready to talk to a few folks? Luka, why don't you join us? But let's get you two a drink first." Frits said, leading Espen by the elbow, and with Luka on his other side.

Luka watched Espen as he spoke with people. They liked him and listened with interest to what he had to say. He was comfortable in his own skin, and he stood proud of everything he believed in. She didn't believe in anything the way he did, and she loved him for that.

* * *

"Tell me about that look in your eyes when we were at the fundraiser—while I was talking to those businessmen and -women. What was going through your mind, Luke?"

They lay in bed. Luka ran her hand over Espen's chest and stopped at his navel and held it there.

"You could tell something was going through my mind while you were speaking to them?" She gave a little sniff.

"I know you," he said in a low voice, speaking against her temple and running the tips of his fingers down the side of her body. It made her lustful for him when he did it like that. He knew and she could feel his mouth curl into a smile.

She pressed her lips against his shoulder, then said, "Espen, you know exactly what drives you forward. Your life isn't just a routine, it's a mission. I like my work, and I'm happy, but I don't have the kind of burning passion you do. I wonder sometimes if it means there's something lacking in me."

"Do you think I see you in a lesser light because I'm different from you?"

"I think you love me, and you accept my flaws."

"Accept your flaws …" He chuckled. "Aside from that, I also see the incredible person you are. You underestimate your strength to pull people to you. Let me tell you something: the reason I was at that fundraiser tonight, was because of you." She gave him a puzzled look. "It's true, Luke. Remember how skeptical I was when you told me you were considering working for Frits Epperson?"

"Hard to forget."

"Exactly. But you opened a door of possibility for me I would otherwise have overlooked, because I was too stubborn to see it. I've told you before, you're a force to be reckoned with. Just because you express yourself differently, doesn't mean you are not passionate. The sun burns in a state of low entropy. You are like the sun, and you stabilize everything around you but on the inside, you are a powerhouse of potential energy."

"That's what you think of me?" She looked up into his eyes.

He nodded. "That's who you are to me, my love." He kissed her as he pulled her to him.

She wondered if she'd ever believe that about herself.

17

It was a cool December evening. Decorated trees, fences, and shop windows glowed with warm holiday lights, and the smell of sweet waffles and spicy cookies filled the air. As Luka walked past a shop, she stopped, went back, and bought her father a few treats.

Her mother had asked her not to spoil him too much. Evi said Ruben was starting to look like Santa Clause around his waist, and there were still four more weeks left before Christmas. Luka couldn't resist spoiling her poor papa who had such a sweet tooth.

Her phone rang as she was making her way to the train station, and she pulled her coat's collar with her free hand higher up to cover her neck, shielding herself against the chilly wind.

"Hallo, I'm on my way to the station, you'll have to speak up," she said

Espen didn't bother to greet her. She could hear he was super excited. "Luke, I have great news: we've been invited to ski in Zermatt, Switzerland next weekend. Bas is going too. They've had fabulous snow and my sources tell me the skiing is out of this world."

"Next weekend?" She stopped and looked for a place to

stand where she could hear him better. "Espen, have you forgotten it's my grandmother's ninety-fifth birthday?" she asked.

"Oh no, I've completely forgotten about that. Damn."

"I'm afraid, yes." She felt as disappointed as he sounded.

"Can't we take her out for a separate celebration some other time?"

"Espen, she's ninety-five; she's already on extremely borrowed time."

"Are you kidding me? That saucy old mink is going to outlive all of us. Luke, c'mon! We're talking Zermatt, the Matterhorn, the romantic snow-covered Alps. And we won't even have to pay for accommodation." He sounded desperate, and she couldn't blame him.

She sighed heavily. "I would love to go, trust me, but my grandmother would never let it be. I would hear about it until she's six feet under, and even then, she'll probably still haunt me. And Uncle Arne and my mom won't forgive me either. They've been planning this for months."

"Shit." There was a pause. "Okay, I'll tell Hugo we can't go."

The great thing about Espen, which was also a not-so-great thing sometimes, was that he walked with his heart on his sleeve. There wasn't much guessing what he felt, she knew. What would be the point in having him stay? And he'd feel miserable for missing out on the skiing. Bas would only come back and relay the amazing time, the incredible slopes, et cetera, and she'd have to endure that sorry face. She would certainly have gone if she wasn't so susceptible to emotional blackmail from her grandmother.

"You know what, why don't you go anyway?"

"No, I want to go with you. Really, I do."

"Espen, it's not often an invitation to Zermatt comes up, take it. I don't mind at all. And you can take my grandmother out for a meal later. I'll soften her up for you." He hesitated, so she said, "You and Bas will have a great time, and we can always plan a trip there by ourselves. That would be more romantic, don't you think?"

"Are you positive?"

He was practically packed and out the door, she could hear it in his voice. And any other answer would have crushed him.

"I'm positive. Go and enjoy yourself guilt free."

"Make sure you sleep over at the flat next Thursday; I'm coming through, and Bas and I will leave early on Friday."

"Okay."

* * *

Marit looked like a satisfied, pampered cat as she sat with a glass of champagne in her hand. There were twenty guests, including Arne and his family, and Evi, Ruben, and Luka. It was a small, intimate venue and Luka thought her mom and uncle did well to make it festive, without making Marit feel overwhelmed.

Arne gave a touching speech about Marit's long and meaningful life, and how she was such an inspiration to them all.

Espen and Bas had called Marit in the morning to wish her a happy birthday. She'd beamed when she'd told Luka. Of course, she'd forgiven them on the spot for not being there for her party. They got away with everything. Luka wished she might be that lucky.

But looking at her grandmother, it was plain to see she was

old now. Her eyes were still bright and full of laughter, but she didn't move around as easily, and she became tired much sooner.

Luka showed Marit some photos of Espen and Bas, skiing in Zermatt, and a video of Espen, that Bas had taken at mid-day. It was a beautiful, sunny day on the Swiss Alps, the perfect skiing conditions. She couldn't help but feel a stab of envy for not being there herself.

Espen was so excited, he was almost shouting in the video: "I wish you were here, it's incredible. Look at this place, look at this day, Luke. We're doing the Plateau Rosa. Everything is amazing. Only thing missing, is you." He mouthed with pouted lips; *I love you* and blew her a kiss. Bas turned the camera on himself and said, "Hi, Lukie," with a smile and a wave. Then they were gone.

"He's such a show-off," Luka said with a grin. But he was her gorgeous show-off.

Marit expressed Luka's thoughts, "Look how handsome Espen and Bas both are. It looks like they are having a wonderful time. I'm sorry you're missing out, Luka. I would have wanted you to be there with him," she said sweetly.

Yes, on any other day, but not today.

"Nonsense, Omoe. I wouldn't have missed your birthday for anything."

She checked her phone again for messages, before putting it away. They were probably still skiing, or exhausted and in bed, lights out.

When she went to bed, he'd still not texted or called. She sent a text: *Party was fun and Omoe was a real diva. I miss you. Goodnight.*

* * *

The house phone rang, and Ruben picked up. "Hallo, this is Ruben Bakker … no, I'm afraid she's stepped out, may I take a message? … Yes, she's my daughter … Yes, I'll convey the message … Oh, dear God …Were there any others? … I see … I see … Yes, thank you. Goodbye." Ruben sat down and closed his eyes, pressing his thumb and index finger into them.

Evi found him there and asked, "What on earth's the matter Rubie? You look like you've seen a ghost."

He looked up at her and said with a long sigh, "Evi, I need to tell our daughter the hardest news I've ever had to tell her. Espen was killed in an avalanche yesterday afternoon. They've tried to get a hold of Luka, but I don't think she has her cellphone with her."

Evi took a deep breath in shock and disbelief. "Oh, Espen. Oh, the poor child." She sat down next to him. "What about Bas?" Evi held her hand on her heart, eyes wide.

"He's fine, thank the heavens. That would have destroyed Anton and Adelheid, bad enough that their eldest is gone. There were four of them: two Frenchmen, an Italian and Espen."

"How horrible, Rubie. How absolutely horrible." Evi burst into tears.

* * *

There were a couple of missed calls on her phone last night—unknown numbers—but no messages. Luka shook off a feeling of alarm. She'd gone to the market early, before it got too busy so that she could go home and curl up with a book. It was that kind of Sunday. She hadn't taken her phone with her.

When she walked through the door, her parents were sitting close together on the sofa and her mother's eyes were red and swollen. Luka's nostrils flared as she took a breath, but it still felt too shallow. There wasn't enough air in her lungs, and it seemed as if everything was swaying in the room.

Suddenly she was standing in the botanical gardens in Oslo, Norway. It was a bright, sunny day. She was seven years old again. There was a beautiful ivy tunnel, with sunlight shining on the other side, and she ran through it, giggling. She felt ecstatic. When she stood at the opening, she looked around, and realized she didn't know where her parents were. She'd lost them. The panic choked her, and it was hard to breathe. But her father had told her many times before, if she ever got lost, she should stay exactly where she was, they would come find her. She waited.

Ruben got up. The way he looked at her, made her turn her gaze. She didn't want to see what his eyes were telling her. She stood still. Her father was speaking, but she heard only parts of it. "Espen … avalanche … killed." If she closed her eyes, maybe it would all go away.

Ruben and Evi both embraced her. See, they've found her. Everything was all right.

"I'm sorry, my love, so sorry," her father kept repeating.

When she opened her eyes, waves of pain hit her—sharp blades slowly entering and exiting her flesh. She stood there, her heart bleeding out like a slaughtered animal hung on a hook, until there was nothing left.

18

Luka wandered in a timeless vacuum. She'd heard her father speak over the phone to someone, and then she figured out it was Frits.

"Yes, it's a tragedy—such a young life that had lived full of purpose. It's just an awful loss … not too good … thank you, I'll let her know … we'll see you at the funeral then. Goodbye, Frits, take care."

Espen would be buried in Den Haag. That's where they all were now, at a green burial cemetery. Espen had wanted a green burial—characteristically Espen, to every last detail of his life. His unembalmed body was wrapped in a biodegradable shroud and placed in a biodegradable casket with orchids on top. They'd been his favourite flower. He had called her his orchid.

The casket was sitting in a hearse. He'd expressly said there should be no viewing. Luka was glad. She wanted to always remember him as he'd been: beautiful and full of life.

Ruben and Evi were talking with Anton and Adelheid. She shouldn't be so consumed by her own sorrow, Luka thought. Looking at them from a distance, they'd lost more than she had. They'd lost their eldest son. She could see a father's pain, a mother's unbearable grief.

Thirty-three years ago, Adelheid had carried him in her womb, she'd given birth to him. They had nurtured him as a little infant, played with him, taught him, and seen him grow up into a man. He had been a part of them both. He'd given them so much joy. Espen.

Frits had spoken to her earlier. He'd told her not to worry about going back to work next week, and if she needed more time, she should let him know. There were also two of Espen's colleagues from Utrecht, but she didn't want to speak to them now.

Luka searched for Bas's face. They hadn't spoken since he'd been back. There he was, moving around like a ghost. He walked over to speak with his father, and they embraced long. The older man's head was bent forward, his face pressed to his son's shoulder. Anton's shoulders shook as Bas held him.

Bas's eyes found hers, and it seemed as if he wanted to say something, but then he looked the other way. Why did he feel so far away—as if there was an ocean between them?

Stijn came over, took her hands in his and kissed them, before giving her a tearful hug. "Luka, what will we do without him?" His eyes pleaded with her.

Do without him? Her heart wasn't even ready to accept that Espen was gone. Dear Stijn. The suit he had on probably was expensive, but he wore it in a way that made it look like he'd bought it at a thrift store. That was so typical Stijn. She hugged him hard while he cried.

Access to the grave site was limited and they had to walk on a temporary path. Anton, Bas, Ruben, Stijn, Hugo, and Klaus carried the casket. It took six big men, to carry the body of a man who'd carried the oceans on his shoulders.

Someone was speaking, saying something about Espen, and

the life he'd lived, the people he'd touched. Luka looked up at the sky, and down at the forest that was the cemetery. Espen would have liked this. Then she looked at the plain casket sitting there next to the hole in the ground. He was inside it, and soon, they would be placing him in that cold brown hole and covering it with dirt.

Luka couldn't breathe. He must not go in there. They mustn't put her Espen in that hole. "No, no, you can't do it." It started as a whisper, but her voice grew louder, "No, you can't put him in there! You can't do it!" she yelled as she fell to her knees and clung to the casket like a survivor to the wreckage of a sunken ship. "You can't leave me. Please don't leave me. Please, my love." And she sobbed her soul out for the beautiful face she would never see again, and the warm body she would never again hold, and for the voice that would never say, I love you, Luke, ever again.

She had a strange dream: her father and Stijn were helping her up. Her mother was wiping something off her dress. They led her away to her father's car. She sat in the backseat. Her mother sat next to her and was speaking to her.

"You just need a moment, my darling. It's all right, don't worry," Evi handed her a bottle of water. "Here, have some water." She stroked Luka's hair.

Luka heard her father speaking to Anton. "She hadn't cried since she'd heard the news. She's been repressing all of it until now," Ruben said.

Anton said, "She's in shock. I have something in my car I can give her now, that will help, and I'll fill out a prescription for her once we're done here. It will ease the next couple of weeks and help her sleep."

Luka heard Anton's shoes on the gravel as he walked off

and then came back.

Evi got out and Anton bent down and looked inside. "I'm going to give you something to make you feel a little better, Luka. Don't worry, we won't go on without you. Just take a moment," he said.

He slid in the backseat and took something out of a case, pushed up her sleeve, cleaned a spot on her arm and inserted a needle.

She thought how Espen had looked just like his father. They had the same features, the same grey-blue eyes. Bas too, looked like his father, but he had his mother's mouth.

Anton's eyes had a tired and defeated look in them now. She touched his hand and he held onto her hand for a moment, looking into her eyes.

It could have been a few minutes, perhaps longer; she didn't know, but they were back at the grave, and she watched as they lowered the casket into the ground. The soil made a hollow thud as it fell on the wood, and it released the fragrance of the earth into the air.

Espen had said he wanted to give back to nature, what he'd taken. He wanted to be part of the circle of life. Luka imagined what the ground would smell like when he became a part of it—sweet.

Adelheid stood to Luka's right, with her arm hooked in with hers. Evi stood to her left and her arm was wrapped around Luka in the back, holding on to Adelheid's arm in Luka's.

Luka thought how brave Adelheid was for not breaking down.

When the casket was covered sufficiently, Bas gave first his father, then his mother a hug. He turned to Luka for the first time. They stared at each other, and she moved forward and hugged him with all her might.

He softly said, "I'm sorry, Lukie. I'm sorry, I'm sorry." He let go of her and walked off.

19

A week after Espen's burial, *De Telegraaf* featured a lengthy article about his life and promising career that had been cut short, and then mentioned the nearly nine-year love story between the dashing young professor and the beautiful daughter of Evi Gaal. A month later, *Quest*—a prominent Dutch science magazine—published an article called, 'Death of A Star', mourning the untimely passing of the brilliant and influential young Professor De Cleene, from the University of Utrecht.

The condolences kept pouring in from all over the country and abroad. Luka couldn't bear reading any of it, and she refused to turn on the television out of fear she'd see his face and name mentioned in the news.

Frits wanted her to take more time off from work—he was generous and sincere—but she couldn't sit there at home and do nothing. Work was her ally because it prevented her from thinking and feeling. She could immerse herself in a project and when it was completed, move on to the next.

But she didn't cry anymore. After her breakdown at the funeral, she'd stopped crying. She'd trained her mind into a new routine: she got up, ate, went to work, came home, ate, slept. And she didn't allow herself to sit and think about the face she longed to see and touch. The voice over the phone who said he missed her like crazy. She didn't think how her body and soul ached for him so much, it was like a raging inferno inside of her.

And she especially didn't express these non-existent thoughts out loud when she talked with her parents. Ruben and Evi were loving and supportive, but they couldn't change anything, and she didn't want to lay her own sorrow on them.

Ruben watched her going through her routines, noticed how hard she was trying.

"I'm proud of you, Lukie, I know this isn't easy," he said as they were having coffee in the kitchen one morning before Luka headed off to work." She stood looking at him with a faint smile and he kissed her on her forehead.

But dreams were a different matter. She both longed for them and feared them. Her dreams were the one thing she couldn't control. Even the sleeping pills Anton had prescribed, couldn't keep him out, and he was always waiting for her there. Espen ruled her dreams, controlled them like a dictator. When she closed her eyes, she was his mistress, helplessly under his spell. He loved her completely, and she him. For a brief time, her world made sense again. Then, in the morning, a new death was lying in wait.

* * *

Luka stood in front of a door with 501 written in black, on a silver plaque. She touched the signage lightly with her fingertips. Holding the key in her pocket, she realized she couldn't let herself in anymore. She no longer had the right to call this place a home.

The fear of what would never again be on the other side, made her insides churn. She hadn't been here since that last night they'd spent together; before he'd left for Zermatt. Was his room still the same? Would the pillows and bedsheets still smell of him, or had everything been removed?

Yes, of course they would have been changed. Anton and Adelheid had been here since Espen's death, probably several times. And Bas would surely use the room as a guest room in due course.

Soon after the funeral, Bas had mailed some of her personal items and clothes that she'd kept at the flat, to her parent's house. She'd called him a couple of times and left messages, but he had not returned any of her calls or texts. Finally realization had sunk in; he was deliberately avoiding her. His body was around—somewhere—but Bas was missing. Luka couldn't reach him, and it made her feel a deep void.

For herself, she longed to know what had happened that day on the ski slope. A sick part of her wanted to know what it had looked like when that avalanche had overtaken Espen and swallowed him up, even if hearing the truth about his death would be noxious to her.

Had he yelled out? Had Bas seen him and heard him before he'd disappeared underneath the mountain of snow? When they'd found him, had his long eyelashes been frozen shut? Had there been bruises on his beautiful face and body from the impact? How long had it taken for him to suffocate to death from his own carbon dioxide? Had he thought about her, and their love before life had left his body?

Perhaps Bas feared that she would ask those questions he didn't want to answer because he couldn't bear the thought of reliving any moment on the day his brother died. But all she had were the endless scenarios her mind created and then turned into dreams that tormented her. In a way, that was a worse hell than knowing.

Bas had told her at the funeral, I'm sorry. Why did he apologize? She didn't blame him for anything. She only wanted to see him and talk to him. To know that he was all right.

Luka took a breath and knocked. There was no gap underneath the door to tell if he was home. Maybe he was and just didn't want to answer the door. She waited a moment and knocked again, but when there was still no answer, she turned around and walked away.

Had she lost Bas too?

* * *

"Luka, why don't you go visit Omoe on Saturday, hm? You haven't been there in a while, and she's always asking how you're doing. This thing has not been easy for her to digest either, especially at her age. And she misses you so," Evi said.

This thing. Luka sighed. She knew her mom was right. She has completely lost track of time.

"Sure, Mama, I'll go see her."

"Good, I'll let her know to expect you." Evi paused for a moment, then said, "Isolating yourself won't help, my love. You've barely been out. You've barely seen anyone aside from me and Papa, and people at work. It's been four months now, Luka."

Four months? Had she honestly not seen her grandmother in four months? She felt a stab of remorse. Her poor granny.

"I'm sorry, I'll try harder, Mama."

"Oh, Luka, I love you, and I know you're in pain but you're going to get through this." Evi embraced her.

Luka nodded.

Marit had *stroopwafels* (a sweet treat of two spicy, crispy thin wafers, sandwiched between caramel-like syrup) and coffee ready when Luka walked through the door. They hugged each other long, but Luka was careful not to hug too hard—the old woman was small and frail in her arms.

Luka felt tremendous guilt for her inconsideration and neglect toward her grandmother. It was clear Marit was trying her best to make it as pleasant as she possibly could and that she was starved of Luka's company.

"Mmm, thank you, Omoe, this looks delicious." Luka smiled.

"Luka, my dear, I've missed you," Marit said as she sat down with her coffee. "Around here, there's not much action going on nowadays. I'm about as good as it gets, and this old ship doesn't sail as smooth as it used to." She straightened out her dress and gave a little laugh. Then she looked at Luka with those knowing eyes. "I missed your birthday last month. Time goes by so quickly …"

Not much said yet said so much.

"I'm sorry I haven't come to visit you, Omoe. I feel bad about that. It's been hard."

"There's no need to apologize. I know you need time to process your grief. That's a thing that doesn't go according to a recipe, and for each person it's different. But I've longed to tell you in person, how sorry I am for your great loss, my child. Espen was like my own grandson." Marit's lip trembled, and she cleared her throat and shook her head to collect herself.

Her grandmother looked so fragile. When you were that old,

you just didn't have the capacity for carrying around stones anymore. Her own stone was weighing her down. Over the past couple of months, Luka had relived her choice—was it even a choice—of telling Espen, go! What would have happened if she'd said she didn't want him to go and that he should stay? It made her mad with frustration and anger, but she had no idea where to direct that.

"I know he was. He loved you too," Luka said.

There was a long pause. Luka ate her stroopwafel and drank her coffee as she watched her grandmother stare out the window.

Then Marit looked at her, and said, "Now it is still early in spring, and the frost lingers at daybreak, but hope is starting to bud and soon, summer will bloom in your heart again, my dearest. Although we will always remember, grief moves on when its season is over." She took Luka's hand in hers.

Luka nodded. "I love you, Omoe."

But she knew there was an unspoken thing between them. Something neither she nor her grandmother dared to bring up, but it lay there like a dead weight in the space between them—Espen had died on Marit's birthday.

* * *

The choice was either living or eating herself away from the inside like a lobster in a tank; a slow, agonizing death. Perhaps seeing the sadness in her grandmother's eyes had been the tipping point.

"Hoi, Professor Deremer," Luka said in the voice message she left on Stijn's phone, "I was hoping you'd have a spare evening to entertain me a bit. I know I've been scarce, but I miss you. Will you call me?"

He called back soon after she'd left the message, and they agreed to go out for dinner in Amsterdam. It was a deliberate choice to draw herself out further from home. When she walked in the restaurant and saw him sitting there, she swallowed down a sickening ball of anguish. He looked so forlorn, but when he noticed her, he smiled and stood up to greet her with a kiss and a long hug.

"Hallo, Luka. It's good to see you."

She exhaled as she sat down. "How's life for the University of Amsterdam's most beloved mathematics professor?"

"Going through the motions. You've heard it said before: it's that one passionate student out of the whole bunch who makes it worth getting up in the morning and putting on a brave face for. Sadly, no love life. Hanging out in coffee shops has been replaced with preparing lectures and grading papers," he said with a smile. "How are you doing, Luka? You've been on my mind."

"Not too bad. I've been coming out of hiding, so to speak. I went to see my grandmother for the first time in four months this week." She emphasized four months.

"How's she doing?"

"She's getting old, but she's a tough little nut."

The waiter asked them what they wanted to drink, and they both ordered a glass of wine. They toasted and Luka said after a long sigh, "Seeing my grandmother made me realize something: she's experienced a lot of hardship throughout her life, but she's ninety-five years old, because she's chosen to go on. I have my life ahead of me—I'm only thirty-one years old, that's young by any standard. As much as the idea of it is still swimming around in my stomach like a jagged object, I need to try."

He nodded and watched her carefully as she played with the stem of her glass.

Then she looked up at him and said, "Fact is, Stijn, I don't live in a little bubble with my own grief. My parents and grandmother experience it too. And they can't give me happiness as a substitute for my pain. I don't want to cause them sorrow by wasting myself away. So, my dear friend, I've decided to go through the motions more consciously." She smiled and took a sip of her wine.

"I admire you for your courage, Luka. It's encouraging to hear you say that. You are absolutely right, we don't live in little bubbles, we have people who care about us, and they experience our joy and our pain." He took her hand in his and smiled.

She squeezed his hand and said, "I've missed you. How is Bas? I wonder how he's doing. I can't get a hold of him; you see, he's disappeared off my radar."

"It's not because he doesn't want to talk to you, Luka, you know that don't you? And I know you wonder if we talk about what had happened. We don't. I know as much as you do. He doesn't talk about any of it. I think Bas is blaming himself for something that wasn't his fault."

Luka nodded. She too had that sense. "I miss him. I miss hanging out with the two of you."

"Yes, me too, Luka. Bas says he might be going to London to work there for a while," he said, changing the topic. "His company's headquarters are there. I think the new scenery will be good for him."

Bas worked for an independent research company that developed software tools for processing biological data.

"Oh, good for him. Change is as good as a holiday."

"Yup. Speaking of which, I'll be taking one in not too long from now. I'm going with my parents to Tossa de Mar, Spain, in July for two blessed weeks of not-giving-a-damn."

She smiled, "That should put a pep in your step. A soft, sandy beach, the warm sun, dark beauties in skimpy bikinis—what more can a man aspire to? Nothing like the sun's love to cure our ailments, is what I always say."

"Tell me about it. Why don't you come with us? My parents are renting a villa, and there's more than enough room. There'll be no expectations, other than you enjoy yourself. Come on, Luka, nothing like the sun's love; you said it yourself."

Luka and Stijn stared at each other. She thought about the image of the lobster in a tank, and then of her strong grandmother.

"Okay, I'll go."

20

The villa overlooked Platja Gran—Tossa Beach—and had its own outdoor swimming pool. Stijn took Luka's suitcase to a big bedroom with stunning views of the ocean. She objected, since it was obviously where he would have slept, but he shrugged it off with, "Just enjoy yourself."

Luka had known Stijn's parents for as long as she'd known him. And Stijn was right, there were no expectations. Gustav and Anitra did their own thing while Stijn took her sightseeing around the little town of Tossa de Mar. They visited the medieval castle on the hill, went to the beach and in the evenings, dined out with his parents, eating seafood and paella, and drinking cava—Spain's version of champagne—and rioja.

It was in a way strange how your friends' parents ended up filling the parental role as a default. It wasn't something they intended or perhaps even considered. Luka'd seen it with her parents: they weren't any different toward her friends than Gustav and Anitra were with her now. Careful not to mention anything obvious, but watchful and perceptive with a respectful distance.

They were having sangria with flatbread and hummus out by the pool, watching the sunset. Luka had to suppress a rush of melancholy. Espen would have held her hand if he were here now and said something academic, like: "There's a misconception that dust and pollutants make sunsets more vivid, but that's not true. They absorb a lot of the light and scatter it, thereby muting the effect of the sunset." She'd told him once he was a lot like her father—always teaching her things she already knew.

Gustav said sincerely, "Luka, we'd wanted Stijn to come on this trip with us, because we knew this break would do him good, but we are so happy that you've joined us."

"Thank you both for having me here. This is an amazing place," Luka said.

"Gustav and I have always had a soft spot for Spain and the Costa Brava," Anitra said.

Stijn said, "There is a place I want to take you to, Luka, maybe we can drive there tomorrow. It's about two hours from here, give or take a few."

Luka was curious. "Is it a secret?"

"No, it's the Cap de Creus Natural Park, and it's on the easternmost part of the Iberian Peninsula. Trust me, you'll love it," Stijn replied.

"Yes, Stijn love, that would be perfect. You will enjoy that, Luka," Anitra added.

* * *

They drove through Girona, and Stijn was full of facts about the city. "The Força Vella in the Old Town was founded more than two thousand years ago by the Romans, but its culture was also influenced by Moorish-era Arabs and Jews. I love the blended architecture in the Catedral de Girona. Its vaulted nave is the second largest in the world after Saint Peter's Basilica at the Vatican. Girona is an awesome city to explore." He paused for a moment to think. "I don't remember asking you, but have you been to Spain before?"

"Yes. It was the summer after I'd broken up with Espen. It was sort of our make-up trip."

"Of course, how could I have forgotten that!" he said, shaking his head as he thought about it.

"We wanted to go somewhere romantic, and my mother had it in her head that I had to see Barcelona. She had me when she was already forty, so she and my dad had done a lot of travelling together before I came along. To her, Barcelona represented laid-back elegance, art, culture, and I think to a large degree, fantasies about Julio Iglesias and his velvet voice and bedroom eyes. She and my dad went to his concert when they were in Barcelona one year, and she's never stopped talking about it since."

Stijn chuckled. "Many a husband has had to contend with the Spanish love god and my father was no exception."

Luka laughed, "Anyway, Espen and I went to Barcelona for six days. It was great. We stayed at this not too good, not too bad three-star hotel with surprisingly beautiful ocean views, and just as luck would have it, we were surrounded from both sides and above, by sex-crazed maniacs." Stijn was enjoying this.

"At one point, we left our room to go out, and the couple in the room to our right came out as well," she continued. "The guy looked like he could have been in the Russian mafia—or some other crime syndicate—and the woman with him was all hair and makeup and big cleavage and lips and long painted nails, you know, the whole deal." Luka demonstrated with her hands.

"And she wasn't in any way discreet about checking Espen out. I mean, really checking him out. I don't know if her man was oblivious or if that was just their thing—it most likely was. The worst of it was, I couldn't stop imagining the two of them diving into the sea of love. Isn't it strange how with some people, you can't help picturing them having sex? It's bizarre."

Stijn burst out laughing, "Yes, it's like you either can't believe they really do have sex with each other, or they make you visualize the amazing sex they are having together."

"Exactly. Well, they didn't disappoint us later that evening, although I think she screamed extra loud for Espen to hear." Luka smiled as she went back there in her mind.

* * *

"Aren't you just a little bit jealous that she was checking out my goods?" Espen had a sly smile.

"Your goods? You know I'm not the jealous type. Do you want me to be jealous?" Luka asked.

"No, but it would have been a huge turn on if you had moved closer and held onto my arm and had looked at her in a hands-off-chick-he's-mine kind of way."

"Aw, I'm sorry, I promise I'll be more possessive next time."

They were on their way for an evening out in the Gothic Quarter that was part of the Old Town. It was a fabulous summer night. Luka wore a red cotton dress with a little yellow flower print that buttoned down in the front and tan leather sandals. Her hair was down, and she'd put pins in the sides to keep it from falling in her face.

She seldom wore makeup, but Espen liked that she didn't. However, she did have bright red lip gloss on, which she reapplied when needed, and Espen kept gawking at her mouth throughout the evening.

They ate tapas plates of *picante* Chorizo, roasted sweet peppers, manchego cheese, olives and drank plenty of clara—beer mixed with lemon juice—to wash down the salty food. On the square, street musicians were playing nostalgic songs on classical guitars and Espen swayed with her. It was terribly romantic, and they were tipsy and full of I-want-you stares for one another.

Back in the hotel room, he pulled her to him, and said as he started unbuttoning her dress in the front, "Tonight, I want us to show all these animals around us what we Dutchies are made of."

"Show them?"

"Figuratively speaking," he said, running his hands all over her.

"Okay, but don't you think people who'd visited the island of Ibiza, for example, would have discovered the other side to the industrious Dutch by now?"

"Possibly, but let's not leave anything to chance," he said against her mouth.

When they lay on their backs, arms above their heads to cool off, Luka said, "If you ever leave me for another woman, I'm going to stalk you."

Espen chuckled, "I'll have you locked up."

"It won't work, I'll pick myself out of that cell. I'm good with picking my way out of things."

"Yes, you are quite the escape artist. But why were you thinking about me leaving you for someone else?"

"I wasn't really. I was thinking about how you wish I was jealous, so I imagined something a disturbed jealous person would do. I thought you'd be pleased by that level of possessiveness."

"Hmm, now that you put it that way, I am. Thank you, that's considerate of you. I don't think I'll have you thrown in jail after all."

"You can thank me later."

"Oh, such a devious mind, I think I'll thank you now and later." He turned on his side and took a hold of her waist, pulling her up against him.

Luka was positive the mafia guy and his vamp had heard her and Espen, because when they were in the elevator the next morning, the guy looked her over in a way that made her wish she had many more clothes on, and the woman looked like she was ready to bring down the house with Espen on top of her.

Espen said in English as he pressed the open button, "Our sex scheme worked, mission accomplished."

* * *

In Barcelona, Luka had fallen in love with the fast-spoken Spanish of the locals, the street cafés and restaurants on the squares, Spanish guitars, Picasso, the turquoise-blue water of the Mediterranean, and with Espen all over again, she thought, staring out the window of the car, at the blue ocean stretching far beyond.

They stopped in Cadaqués to buy something to eat and soft drinks for a picnic. In the park, they hiked along paths with views of the ocean and coastline. It took her breath away.

Stijn knew the area well. "This island is called, s'Encalladora, and it's a marine reserve."

They found a spot where they sat and gazed at the pristine landscape and crystal-clear ocean. The air was incredibly fresh.

"The Cap de Creus Natural Park was the first maritime-terrestrial park in Spain. We've been coming to Spain since I can remember. My parents love it. But my dad's been reluctant to buy a place here. He's pragmatic. He says it's better to pay for a rental and have the freedom to go wherever it pleases them, and they don't have the overhead of a house to worry about either," he said.

"That makes sense. Owning a property in another country creates all sorts of hidden complications," she said.

He looked out over the ocean. "I brought Espen here, one year, when we were still busy with our bachelor's degrees." Luka looked at him, surprised. "He was here a couple of times before he met you," he said. "We walked around, and he examined every little thing, like a kid who'd discovered a magical world. I wanted to show you this because it was a special place to him."

She smiled at his kindness and love for his friend, and for her.

"Thank you, Stijn. I can see him here and how he must have loved it."

Luka walked around, taking photographs, imagining the look on Espen's face as he'd explored. Then she turned, took a few photos of Stijn, and watched him doing the same with a serious expression, and she could almost see on his face how he was remembering his friend.

They had a picnic on the edge of a cliff and saw two eagles

flying overhead.

"Those are Bonelli's eagles. It looks like a breeding pair," Stijn pointed out.

"Did you know right away that you and Espen would be friends when you met him?" she asked, still looking up at the eagles.

Stijn exhaled slowly, "You know when you know, and I knew he'd be a mate I would be able to rely on. Espen had a stubborn streak in him; you know yourself," he said with a smile, "but once he committed to something, he was in it with his heart and soul."

She nodded. "You know, when you know," she repeated. "You're a friend, a friend can rely on, Stijn. Thank you."

"You're welcome, Luka." They ate their food in silence for a while, then he said, "Tomorrow we're going to spend the day on the beach, and I'm going to pick out a hottie who will help me brush up on my Spanish."

Luka said with a smile and a lifted brow, "*Pensé que tu español era fluido?*" Meaning, I thought your Spanish was fluent.

"Sí, señorita, but there's always something new to learn, and I'm a firm believer in remaining teachable."

He'd said it in an innocent, boyish way—the way Stijn usually spoke.

She loved her friend for bringing her here so they could both remember, in order to go on.

21

Luka was web browsing, just casually looking at vacation destinations. She didn't intend to go on vacation, but it was fun to imagine going somewhere—a sort of mental travel.

It was the name of the company that caught her eye first, before she noticed the advertisement underneath. It said: Byrne Luxury Yachts. They were in Vancouver, Canada. She noticed right away the ad was for a cartographer position—this wasn't something you saw often by randomly browsing the internet.

She scanned over the job requirements: a degree in earth science—she had one in geography. A postgrad in geographic information science—she had a masters. At least five years' industry experience in land surveying, mapping, photogrammetry, remote sensing—she had seven years' experience. High IT literacy, analytical problem-solving, eye for detail, high standards for accuracy, ability to work both in a team and individually, ability to work under pressure.

Luka fitted the criteria. She was also more than qualified. Vancouver.

She walked around for days with the idea playing in her head. What would her parents think of her living so far away? Her mom would probably be more open to the thought, her play-it-safe dad; hard to say. What about her grandmother?

After going back and forth in her mind, she sent an email with her curriculum vitae to the contact person and told herself this was just reaching out. Testing the waters. She didn't have to make a commitment.

A day later, there was a reply from Cianán Byrne, the owner and CEO, saying he'd like to have a video interview with her. Luka stared at the response in shock. She hadn't really expected a reply, and so soon—not to mention from the CEO—but she responded, and they scheduled a time for the interview: her afternoon, his morning due to the time difference.

"Good day to you, Ms. Bakker, I'm Cianán Byrne. How do you do?" He pronounced it, Keenan. "To be honest, I was surprised to see a response from the Netherlands." He smiled.

He looked young for a CEO, perhaps late thirties, early forties. She'd seen on the website that his father had started the company but had passed away about five years ago.

Luka liked his open face and direct, friendly manner. "Good day to you too, Mr. Byrne. It's a pleasure to meet you. Please call me Luka."

"And likewise, please call me Cianán. I have to ask, Luka; how did you find out about us?"

She gave a little laugh. "If I have to be absolutely frank, it wasn't a job search. I was web browsing and your company's name came up. Please don't ask me how. I immediately noticed the advertisement for the cartographer position."

"Then fortune smiles on us. I've had a look at your CV, although here in North America people like to call it a resume. I have to say I'm quite impressed. You have sturdy academic credentials, and Epperson Yacht Building—they are pretty major in Europe."

"Yes, they are. I've been extremely lucky to work for Frits Epperson. He's a gentleman and a phenomenal businessman."

"I haven't met him myself, but that is certainly what one hears about him. I am curious, though. Why would you want to leave a happy home, so to speak, in the first place? Why not remain in the Netherlands?"

It'd been a year since Espen had died, and she still couldn't shake him off, and doing something impulsive and out of character was perhaps what she needed to get herself out of this rut. She didn't tell him that.

"We all need change from time to time. I've been with Epperson Yacht Building for nearly six and a half years. I know the industry and have learned the ropes from the best mentor a rookie could ever hope to have. And now I can apply my combined skills and experience somewhere else."

"Pardon me playing devil's advocate here, Luka, but from what I can see on your CV, you could apply for work in a much bigger company who'd be able to offer more than I would. With your qualifications and exposure, you could have your pick," Cianán said.

"That's a fair observation. The first thing that has struck me about your company is that it's green driven. I have learned at Epperson's the positive impact of conscious business practices. It has an enormous ripple effect.

"I couldn't in good conscience associate myself with a company who doesn't have the physical well-being of its employees, as well as the protection of our natural world at the very core of its business. Money is a helpful resource but having more won't make me sleep better at night if it's earned in opposition to my values.

"Many yachting companies still have not adapted their

shipyards and other operations to meet these standards. I like that you do, even if it means you are smaller than your competitors. It shows integrity, and I respect that."

She may well have convinced Cianán Byrne, but was she ready to believe it herself? Years ago, she'd had to convince Espen about working in an industry he'd seen as the enemy, and she'd told him not to tell her what to do and she would be who she would be. She'd known then that she'd had it in her, but a part of her had also wanted to defy Espen's stubbornness at the time. And in the end, she'd won him over wholeheartedly.

This was different. Now she had to decide if she truly wanted to make this enormous change, and it would be entirely for herself. She knew she could do it if she wanted to.

"Luka, you speak my kind of language, and over time, I hope our ethics will become our biggest advantage. We need to set ourselves apart and stand for something meaningful. You've just revealed a lot about your core values but tell me a little about where you are at. Do you have a family?"

"No, I'm not married, nor am I in a relationship, so this would be solely my decision. I live with my parents in a pretty city just outside of Amsterdam, called Haarlem. It's the capital of the province of North Holland, and I've lived here all my life. We Dutch are not known for being boastful, so there's unfortunately nothing exciting I can tell you, other than I've had a good upbringing and education, and enjoy my line of work." They both smiled.

"I've been to Amsterdam a couple of times, and it's one of my favourite cities in Europe. The culture, the art, those gorgeous canals. I just love it. The Dutch are brilliant innovators. I admire your nation's gusto, albeit more subdued," said Cianán.

"Yes, I am proud of my heritage."

"Reading between the lines, this move would be a big change for you. You've been living in one place all your life. Do you think you'd be up for it? I mean, I won't have to sell you on the beauty of supernatural British Columbia, but culturally, it would be different."

"I realize that, but one of the biggest advantages of growing up in an open and embracing society such as we have in the Netherlands, is that different is good."

Cianán smiled and nodded. "That's a healthy approach. As far as your overall outlook and experience go, I'm impressed. But for the sake of due diligence, I have two more candidates to interview. I will get in touch by the end of the week, if you would kindly bear with me."

"I understand, that's no problem."

"Should I decide to go with you, we'd need to get your paperwork for a work visa in order. I'm mentioning this, since it will affect the hiring cycle and would give you an idea how much time you will need for planning on your end. We're talking about a couple of weeks, maybe a couple of months, but nothing excessive. The Canadian government is quite on the ball where it comes to this. But we'll cross that bridge when, or if, we get there."

"That sounds good, thank you."

"Luka, it has been my pleasure to speak with you. You enjoy your day and I'll be in contact soon."

"Thank you for your time, Cianán. Take care."

* * *

It was Luka's turn to make dinner. She grilled salmon in a pan and made steamed vegetables on the side with brown rice. Her dad liked the starch, but her mom wanted him to eat more whole grains.

Ruben shrugged and said, "Rice is rice. I don't care if it's brown or white, as long as I may have it."

Both Evi and Ruben sat at the breakfast nook to keep Luka company. It was also a favourite spot to sit and look out over the garden.

Evi was listening to a classical station while reading a gardening magazine. She was always full of ideas for improving her beloved garden and although spring was still a couple of months away, she liked to prepare for it in her mind.

She tapped with her fingers against the magazine's cover, humming softly. The arthritis was pronounced in her hands now, and she'd given up her small performances altogether. But she still played the piano at home.

Ruben was reading the newspaper he'd already read in part during breakfast. Occasionally, they looked up to engage with Luka as she was preparing the meal.

Luka has still not heard back from Cianán about the position in Vancouver. She didn't want to get excited, nor did she want to feel anxious, although she had a feeling in her gut there was a high likelihood of her getting the job. She wanted to speak to her parents to prepare them before she accepted the position. That was to say, if it were offered to her.

"I sort of accidently stumbled upon an advertisement for a cartographer the other day, and I have investigated it." She'd started with an awkward intro.

Both her parents looked at her. Her dad had a worried frown, her mom big, curious eyes.

"Oh, where is it?" Evi ventured.

"It's in Vancouver," Luka said, hoping to sound natural.

"Vancouver, Canada?" Ruben asked.

Should she jest and say, no, Vancouver, Washington State? Perhaps now wasn't the time for that.

"Yes, Papa, it's the one in British Columbia, Canada."

Both Evi and Ruben were silent for a moment.

Evi blinked as she thought about it. "I hadn't expected it to be so far, Luka. Western Canada … that's quite a distance from here."

Her mom had become soft with age, and from spending so much time with her dad, Luka thought. "Yes, Mama, it's far, but it's also beautiful there and it would be something new and exciting."

Her mom liked words such as, new, and exciting, but she was clearly experiencing inner conflict.

"When you say you've investigated it, how much investigation are we talking about?" Ruben asked.

Her father knew her tricks much better than her mom did. His questions were usually more probing. He knew her hiding places.

"I've sent my CV and had a video interview a few days ago with the CEO, Cianán Byrne. He's a terrific man."

"You've already had an interview?" Ruben couldn't keep the surprise out of his voice.

"Yes, Papa, and I think it went well," Luka said, trying to keep her voice light.

"Do you think they will make you an offer, Luka?" Evi put the magazine down that she'd been clutching rather forcefully since Luka broke the news.

"I can't say for sure, Mama, but there's a good chance I might get it."

"My word …" said Evi and sat back in the chair.

"Lukie, this would mean a big change, in every way. I'm sure you've thought about this a lot, and if it's something you feel strongly about, your mother and I can't, nor should we even attempt, to stop you. But I just want to make sure you want to do this for the right reasons," Ruben said.

"You're worried that I'd be running away."

Luka and Ruben looked at each other, and he nodded.

She exhaled slowly. "I don't think of it as running away. But I need to get out of this rut. It feels as if everywhere I go, I bump into Espen. Perhaps when I'm in a different place, a whole new environment, it will allow me to see beyond him, Papa."

"And what if you can't? You'd be all alone," Ruben said with concern.

"Papa is right, Luka. We'd be terribly worried about you," Evi said.

"I know this is unexpected news. There's still a chance I won't get the job after all. But please consider it as a real possibility. I need to do something to move myself forward. When Espen was alive, he was my pull. But he's not alive anymore. I need to find something else, and I'm hoping the distance will help me. I don't view this as a permanent change, but it would be a remedy for the time being."

Ruben got up and hugged Luka. "I know you want to move on Lukie, and I don't mean to be selfish. It's just that I've had you here all your life. The idea of you so far away is hard to bear."

Evi came and stood with them. "It's hard to bear for both Papa and me. But whatever happens, we'll support your decision."

"Thanks, I love you guys." She gave them both a kiss on the cheek. "The food's ready, shall we eat?"

Cianán called her the next day. "Luka, I hope you're still interested, I'd like to make you an offer."

* * *

"Tell me how you're doing, Luka?" Frits asked. He'd called her to his office to go over a few project deadlines.

She sat down in a chair opposite him. "I'm doing well, Frits. Everything's on track. I have a couple of finishing touches on one chart, but it shouldn't take more than an hour or two."

She knew what he'd meant but was trying to steer away from that.

Frits wasn't so easily deceived. "I want to know how it's going with you. How are you coping?"

"Some days are better than others, but I'm doing okay." She smiled and looked down at her hands.

Telling Frits she was leaving was something she'd been dreading for weeks. They liked to joke and say they'd adopted each other as backup father and daughter, but the truth was, he was a father figure to her. And he'd been so good to her over the years.

"I know exactly what you mean, Luka. Just when you think you're getting there, something trips you up. Our minds are full of memories that won't let go. At least you are still living with your parents. That should be a great comfort to you, and to them."

Luka nodded.

He studied her carefully, then asked, "Is there something else on your mind that you'd like to discuss with me?"

Just like a father who knows his daughter well.

Luka took a deep breath. "Yes Frits, there is. I've been offered a position in Vancouver, British Columbia, and I've accepted."

She could barely look him in the eye when she saw the flash of disappointment.

"I see. That would certainly be a loss for me, and everyone here. You have considered this carefully, I would assume."

She nodded. "I need to do this, Frits. I feel as if I'm clinging to a ghost."

"You won't be able to run away from that ghost, Luka, no matter how far you go. He lives in your heart, and that's where you need to release him."

"Everything here is a reminder. Perhaps I'm naïve, but I need to try. It's a good company too. They're smaller, but with the same motto and work ethics. That's important to me. I've learned so much here at Epperson's—from you. You've been good to me; I've been happy here. This wasn't an easy decision."

"You don't need to convince me of your sincerity, Luka. That there were more people like you in this world. I'll gladly provide you with a reference, or anything else you need, just let me know. My only wish is that you are happy with your decision. And should things not work out, you know where we are."

"Thank you, Frits. For everything."

"When will you go? Will we at least have time to give you a farewell?" he asked with a smile.

"A month and a half from now. I'll hand in my formal resignation before the day is over for admin purposes."

"Good, I'll tell Val to get started on the farewell right away. We will miss you." He walked around his desk to give her hand a fatherly pat and a squeeze. "And may good fortune go with you, Luka."

22

Luka and Adelheid walked quietly side-by-side, arms hooked in with one another. A thin layer of mist lingered in the upper branches of the trees, and the morning air was fresh. But Luka's mind was somewhere else. She was back in Ameland, and she and Espen were lying on their beach towels in Nesserbos.

He was looking up at the trees, and she was watching him intently; how beautiful and symmetrical the shape of him was. His legs were stretched out and crossed at the ankles, and his arms rested on his chest, fingers interlaced. He completely gave himself over to the moment. She wished she could dive in and swim around in his mind.

"Just a couple of weeks before the buds will start showing," Adelheid broke the silence as she looked out over the burial site.

They stopped at the base of a gorgeous old elm and stared at the name on the granite slab: Espen De Cleene. Age 33. It was a simple, unintrusive stone and blended in with the peaceful surroundings. The sunlight made long beams through the trees, illuminating spots on the ground like flashlights.

Luka thought of the story she'd told Espen there in Nesserbos, about the brave little beaver who had set the sun free. But

193

she realized now that Espen had not been the little beaver after all, he'd been the blazing sun itself. She couldn't contain his energy; it was too intense to hold onto. His indomitable spirit was free now, and he was a part of that which he loved with his whole being. But she ached for his scorching intensity.

"Remember how lovely the purple heather was in September, on Espen's birthday? And the daisies. Little drops of joy, he used to call them," Adelheid said, and they both smiled.

They've been going through this ritual once a month since Espen's death. Luka took the train to Den Haag and spent a day with Adelheid and Anton, and they came to the cemetery to visit Espen. Today Anton wasn't with them.

"Maybe he'd still be alive if I hadn't insisted that he go to Zermatt." Luka hadn't intended to say it out loud.

"Oh, Luka, we simply can't know," Adelheid said, and patted her hand. "Even if Espen had not gone, would we have lost Bas instead? We will make ourselves crazy with what-ifs." She sighed. "There is something unnatural about the young dying before the old. And it's a strange death you experience as a parent when your child dies. A part of you dies with him because he had been a biological part of you. And you miss his individuality, as well as the parts of yourself that you'd seen in him. But there's also a part in you that continues to live, because you know that is the way it must be.

"I need to continue because there are Anton and Bas. All of us live with our different pain because we loved Espen in different ways. You have lost your love, and you're still grieving over him, but it's my wish that you find love again, Luka. You are young, and you should."

"It feels so impossible," Luka said softly.

"Now it still does, but it won't feel like this forever, honey."

Adelheid gave her a hug, and said, "Come, let's go home and I'll make coffee to warm us up. Anton said he'd bring something to eat."

* * *

They had coffee with savoury as well as sweet crêpes that Anton had bought while he'd run errands. This was a goodbye visit, and the atmosphere was somewhat subdued. Luka'd already told them about Vancouver. Whatever their true feelings were about her going away, Anton and Adelheid didn't express them. Instead, they talked about the beauty of the Pacific Northwest and the endless outdoor adventures Luka would soon be able to explore.

Before she left, Luka went to Espen's room one last time. It still looked like he occasionally slept there. Adelheid hadn't changed the setup. She sat down at the desk in front of the window and ran her hand over the wood. There was stationary in the top drawer, and she took out a block of paper and a pen. She wrote:

Dearest Sebastian,

I'm sitting here in Espen's room—at his desk—in your parents' house. It's a strange melancholy: the sadness, but also the comfort that he once inhabited this space; sat here studying and making his grand plans for saving the oceans.

Your parents would have told you by now that I'm going to Vancouver, Canada to work and live there. For how long it will be, I don't know, but I'm hoping the new start will be a reset. I desperately need that.

It has already been over a year since I last saw you. Time goes by quickly, but it seems not everything always does.

I wanted to say goodbye, and tell you I miss you, Bas. My heart longs to sit and talk with you, the way we used to. Whatever your reasons are for keeping your distance, I hope you will be able to work through them, and that one day we shall stand opposite each other with a new light in our eyes and as friends—not again, but still.

Be kind to yourself. Take care of Stijn, he needs you.

With love,

Luka

She put the letter in an envelope and wrote, Bas on it. She asked Adelheid to please give it to him the next time she saw him. He was still in London but was coming home for a visit soon. Luka said goodbye to them, promising to keep in touch.

* * *

"Don't worry, Omoe, we'll do a video call once a week. We'll sit with our coffee and a cookie—mine will just not be your delicious homemade cookies, but I'm sure Canadians also have treats of their own—and we'll have a visit as if we were here together," Luka reassured her grandmother.

She'd come to say goodbye to Marit before her flight at eight o' clock in the evening. She was as prepared as she could be. Nervous, but ready to begin this new chapter. She was unfolding out of her chrysalis, ready to spread her wings. All butterflies had to take a moment before they took to the air, propelled by the need to survive. Every first was an uncertain step.

"Yes, my dear. And I don't want you to worry your head about me on that end either. I'll be fine. Your mother is around, and I do have two other granddaughters as well. Just think of what a wonderful new phase this will be for you, Luka. I'm proud of you for showing courage and determination. There would be no greater loss than to let your heart rust away because it's stuck in things that can't change. Now surely, the Canadians wouldn't mind you bringing a little treat across their border, would they?" Marit asked, producing a container of cookies. "This should provide a bit of home comfort for the first couple of weeks."

Her grandmother's strength blew her mind. Luka knew it wasn't easy for Marit to see her go. They'd always had a special bond. And knowing it could be the last time she saw her grandmother was a thought Luka didn't want to entertain.

She smiled and gave Marit a hug and a kiss. "Of course they won't mind these. Thank you, Omoe. I'll give Mama and Papa a call when I've landed, and they'll let you know, okay. I'm going to miss you. Goodbye, my dear, sweet oma."

The tears welled up in both their eyes, and Marit said quickly, "Let's not stand here and get mushy. Goodbye, my angel child. Have a safe journey. I'm looking forward to your news."

They kissed and hugged, and Marit stood watching by the door as Luka headed down the hall and turned around one last time to wave before she got into the elevator.

Ruben and Evi drove her to Schiphol Airport. Luka checked her luggage, and they had a cup of coffee before she went through security.

"Everything will be fine. I'll let you know as soon as I land in Toronto, as well as Vancouver," she said to her tearful mother.

"Of course it will. I'm just a little emotional, that's all." Evi agreed and dabbed her eyes with a tissue.

"It's good of Cianán to offer to pick you up at the airport.

You'll feel disoriented and the time difference will be an adjustment. Your night and day will basically be reversed now," said Ruben.

Luka knew he was reassuring himself, more than her.

"Yes, Papa, I have travelled before, it won't be completely new, but no doubt it will be an adjustment." She checked the time on her wristwatch. "Time to go."

Ruben and Evi walked with her to the side of the check-in counters. Luka embraced first her mother and then her father, giving a kiss. If she thought of this as going on vacation, instead of leaving indefinitely, it wouldn't feel so hard. She tried not to cry. Evi cried for all three of them.

"Bye, I love you," she said and periodically waved as she walked to the entry point, and they were finally out of view.

23

"How's life in Vancouver treating you, Luka? You've been here three months now, and you've had a chance to explore in and around the city. Are you still happy with your decision?" Cianán Byrne asked.

Luka liked Cianán. He was forty-two, with a slight build and was as tall as herself—tall for a woman, but average for a man. His black hair was turning grey here and there, and he had intelligent blue eyes. His attractive face made up for his less imposing physique, and he had a pleasant, easy way about him.

She didn't know of anyone she worked with, who didn't think Cianán a great boss and human being. He was a thoughtful listener and had a delightful sense of humour, and he felt like someone who could become a good friend.

"Yes, I'm still happy with my decision. It's been great so far, Cianán, thank you. There are so many options to choose from, it's hard to decide what to do when I make plans for the weekend," she said.

Luka told Cianán this, because it really was a place where she could immerse herself in the beauty of her surroundings. She told herself she was moving on with her life in big outward strides. She went out with co-workers for dinner regularly and had discovered the wonderful cosmopolitan culture and cuisine of Vancouver.

Her co-workers did things like plan ferry excursions to Vancouver Island, because it was a must-see, and the tulips in Victoria during summer were gorgeous. They joked and said they had their own mini-Netherlands in Canada. The reason they did all this for her, was because they were kind and sincere and wanted her to feel welcome.

And every time she saw the blue Pacific Ocean, she tried not to think what Espen would have said about this magnificent place.

Luka had told her cautious father and adventurous mother about hiking in the mountains with views that took her breath away. Ruben had not spoken much; she'd sensed he was listening for clues that would alert him that something was wrong, or at least not quite right.

Evi had been inquisitive, but there had also been concern in her voice. "Oh, that's wonderful, my darling. I am so envious. Are you making sure to stay safe, Luka? Do you have someone to hike with you, at least?"

"Yes, Mama, I'm watchful," she'd said, "I hike with bear spray and the trick is to make noise to alert the bears. Most of the time, they move out of the way when they hear humans approaching, although you almost never know when you've passed one. And I do hike with friends occasionally, but it is such a peaceful and emboldening experience to hike by myself. When I walk in a forest and see the big old trees covered in moss, I am reminded that these are becoming my own experiences. I am loosening the thoughts of wishing Espen was here, and I can feel myself moving forward."

"We are well pleased by that, and proud of you my love,"

Ruben had said.

Yes, she was happy with her decision to move to Vancouver.

Cianán said, "We are proud of our city and province. In fact, this whole country is worth seeing, but all in good time. How's your abode? Are you enjoying the proximity to everything? I know it's expensive, but there really aren't any cheap rentals in Vancouver."

Luka gave a little laugh, "No, there aren't, but then again, coming from a densely populated European city where it's nearly impossible to find affordable accommodation—and thus, I've lived with my parents—I'm familiar with rental woes. But I like my flat, and it's easy to get around with public transport. I'm enjoying biking to work, although it takes a bit of getting used to the flow of these traffic laws. In the Netherlands, cyclists probably have more rights than anyone else on the roads. Overall, I can't complain."

Luka lived in Killarney—a multi-cultural, family-friendly suburb in the southeast of Vancouver. Although not the hippest location, it was pleasant and affordable compared to many other areas in Vancouver, and it wasn't a complicated commute to work.

She was becoming familiar with her neighbourhood and knew where to go for coffee and a bagel with cream cheese—to have the true Canadian experience, she was told. And she liked the indie bookstore she now frequented on a Saturday or Sunday when she felt homesick and missed her mother and father, and needed to be with people, without necessarily engaging in conversation. She enjoyed calling her grandmother for their weekly video chat when she was having coffee with her feet up on the sofa, laptop resting on her legs—especially on a rainy day, and it reminded her of

Haarlem.

At night she lay in bed in her one-bedroom flat (or apartment as they called it here) and listened to the voice of the city that still sounded foreign, but she was gradually becoming used to. And while she lay there, staring at the silhouette of the suncatcher where it hung unmoving in the window—as if it could hear her thoughts—she imagined a certain window in a flat in Utrecht where it had hung for eight years. He was becoming dimmer in her dreams, and she realized he was no longer controlling them, she was the one holding on.

"That's the truth. There's no such a thing as affordable city living anymore," Cianán said. "On a professional note, I'm pleased to have you on board, Luka. You've already proven yourself an asset, and I can see you are committed. I'm excited for what lies ahead for us as a small but rapidly growing business."

"Thank you, Cianán. I'm excited about that too."

"Tomorrow, I want you to fly out with me and explore the Gulf Islands and the San Juan Islands on the US side. Sidney Russell will be here to steer us in the air. He's a pilot slash yacht captain, and a good friend. He knows his stuff and he's a great tour guide. We'll do a bit of surveying and I really want you to see why the yachting business is worth investing in for our clients here in the Pacific Northwest.

"The greater Vancouver area can't keep up with the growth. People from all over want to be here. Canada's also not as populated as our US neighbour, and people are settling on the mainland and the Gulf Islands and Vancouver Island," he said.

"That sounds great, Cianán. I can't wait to see it from the air."

23

"Good to hear. We'll drive to Delta Heritage Airpark at nine thirty. Sidney will meet us there. The weather for tomorrow looks perfect. Hang on to your hat, Luka, you're going to see views that will blow your mind."

* * *

He stood leaning against the side of his truck, reading emails or texting, when they arrived at Delta Heritage Airpark. Luka knew it must be him. He somehow looked like a Sidney. He wore khaki shorts and a light turquoise-green T-shirt, and had a cap on that said, Canucks (the name of the Vancouver hockey team). He was tall, lean, and tanned. An outdoorsman.

Cianán pulled into the parking space next to Sidney's and rolled down the window. "Ready to take us to high places, mate?"

Sidney smiled and peeped through the window at Luka sitting on the passenger side. She and Cianán got out of the car.

The two men slapped each other on the back with a brotherly hug, and Cianán said, "It's been a while, Sid. How the heck have you been? No, don't answer that, we'll catch up. First let me introduce you to the talented new addition to our team: Miss Luka Bakker from the Netherlands. Luka, this is Sidney Russell, our hands-on sky captain."

He took off his cap and they shook hands. "How do you do, Luka. Good to meet you."

"It's a pleasure, Sidney," Luka said.

He looked like he was in his mid to late thirties. His hair was medium brown, and there was something almost tragic in his milk chocolate eyes, until she looked at the corners of his mouth. They were curved into a permanent smile, making his eyes and mouth a contradiction.

Sidney looked at her for a moment, then turned to Cianán. "Plane's fuelled and ready, boss. Paperwork's in order. We can mount the scanner and then we're all set."

They secured the sensing equipment on top of the aircraft's fuselage. Cianán checked to make sure the system was working on his computer, and that the GPS was tracking.

"Sid, you'll calibrate your altitude to above mean sea level," Cianán ran over the checklist.

"Check." Sidney confirmed. He waited for clearance from air traffic control, and they were off.

"This is a neat plane," Luka said as she ran her gaze over the interior and watched Sidney at the controls. He seemed completely at ease.

"Yes, this Cessna model is a popular small plane, because it can seat four people, and it's easy to manoeuvre. The high wings make for great cruising views," Cianán said.

"Do you ever fly yourself?" she asked Cianán.

"Yes, I do, but mostly when I want to impress the fairer sex." He and Sidney both chuckled. "But sometimes I need to focus on something else, like what we'll be doing today with the surveying. It's much better to have this guy in the captain seat, and I trust him with my life," Cianán said, looking at Sidney.

"So he says now," Sidney said with a grin.

Luka looked down at the sea and islands below. "This is gorgeous."

"Those are our Gulf Islands." Sidney indicated. "The one closest to the mainland is Galiano, to the south are Mayne, Saturna, and Pender and right next to Vancouver Island is Salt Spring. They're all beautiful little islands with tons to offer. You've been to Vancouver Island by now, I assume?" he asked glancing back at her.

"Yes, a couple of times. I'm amazed how much there is to do and explore," Luka said.

"If you love Vancouver Island, you'll love the Gulf Islands," Cianán said. "They're quaint and full of charm and character."

"We'll cross the US airspace soon and you'll be able to see the San Juan Islands. They're America's version of our Gulf Islands," Sidney said to Luka.

"This is the reason why people buy yachts, Luka. There's an unparalleled freedom in sailing these seas," Cianán remarked.

They flew at a constant altitude to ensure the quality of the data that the light sensor captured. Luka knew they'd have to do this a couple of times from different angles. She looked down at the deep, seeming impenetrable water, and thought how surreal it was that she'd be able to create pathways with her charts to reveal what lay beneath the smooth blue surface. She'd always enjoyed the technical elements of the work she did but loved the imaginative and adventurous part of it.

They spent a couple of hours circling the islands and around Vancouver Island.

Back on the ground, Cianán said, "That was a fruitful effort. Now the hard work lies ahead for you, Luka. We're going to do plenty more exploring in the future. Creating personalized charts for customers is the thing they like to hear."

She smiled and said, "That's what I love doing: unravelling the data and creating paths to paradise."

"Indeed. Sidney will take care of matters here, while you and I head back to the office. Thanks, Sid. How about we all go out for a drink later?" Cianán suggested.

"Sounds good to me." Sidney looked at Luka for a second.

"I'll see you at the office."

* * *

On the way back, Luka asked Cianán, "How long have you and Sidney known each other?"

"For about seven, or is it eight years now?" He frowned thinking about it. "He started flying for us when my father was still alive. My dad died five years ago."

"I saw that on the website. I'm sorry," she said.

"What can you do when your folks start getting older and get sick? Anyway, Sid's a great guy. He's a hell of a pilot and a yachtsman too." He paused for a moment. "Sidney's one of those people who needs to stretch out his arms and touch nothing but freedom all around him."

"How old is he?"

"Thirty-seven."

"So I take it he's not the relationship type."

"Oh, he likes women a lot. But he doesn't like to hold on to them. I've seen a few hope they'd change him, but I've known him long enough to say he has a near-pathological fear of commitment, and it has to do with his need for freedom. He'll gladly admit to that."

"It sounds as if you're forewarning me," Luka said with a smile.

Cianán gave her a quick side glance, and said, "I'm not saying this for selfish reasons, I assure you. You seem curious about him, and I can tell he's definitely curious about you. Sidney's a good-looking guy, and he's charming. I wouldn't want you to be disappointed, that's all." He changed the topic. "Me, I don't mind a woman in my life. Problem is, once I've found someone I think is compatible, it's easy to start the relationship but staying in it is another matter." He chuckled.

"I suppose so," she said after some reflection. "It's not easy to let another person into your inner world and to trust them enough with who you are and vice versa. But when you do experience that, it's a wonderful thing." She looked out the window while she said it.

"You were in a long-term relationship, I take it?"

"Yes, for almost nine years."

"Why did it end? Did he leave you? I'm sorry that was bad style, you don't have to answer if you don't want to." He lifted his hand in apology.

"No … well, yes, in a way he did, but he didn't elect to do so. He died in an avalanche a year and a half ago."

It felt strange speaking to Cianán about it. This was the first time she was openly talking about Espen and his death to someone outside of her circle. She hadn't expected their conversation would end up going in this direction, but it also felt comforting in a way. Cianán wasn't pushy, he was genuine, and she liked that about him.

"God, I'm sorry to hear that, Luka. I sensed you'd been through a heartbreak, but didn't expect that," he said. She gave a wan smile. He said, "And this move to Vancouver was part of that, if I may venture a guess."

"Yes. I don't want to say it was because I needed to find myself again, because that wasn't it. I needed to untangle myself from him—we had a strong love. But the further away you are from something, the weaker the hold on it, or on you, becomes. That's the theory, anyway."

"That's still a lot to deal with on your own in a whole new environment. In a way, I wish you'd spoken to me sooner, but I know that's easier said than done. Personal matters aren't comfortable topics for most people. And from what I've learned about you so far, you don't walk around with your heart on your sleeve."

"No, I don't. I suppose opposites do attract because Espen was my exact opposite. I was the little pilot light, to his burning fire." She thought with a smile how Espen called her a geodynamo. Long ago, in Mittenwald.

"What was his field?"

"He was a research professor in marine biology—oceans and climate. And to say he was passionate about his work, is an understatement."

"Some people are extroverts and others have inverted energy. It sounds like you understood each other."

"I just wonder sometimes what the benefit of such inverted energy is. Espen's energy was explosive. It changed the world around him."

"Not everybody can save the world, but those who are capable of doing so need support."

"Funny, that's what I told him once."

"And how have you been coping, Luka? I know I asked you this at the office yesterday, but this conversation puts things in a new light for me."

"It's not always easy, but not every day is bad either. My family are supportive and I even video chat with my grandmother once a week, and she'll be ninety-seven this year."

"Ninety-seven, how about that?" He laughed.

"Yes, speak about burning energy. But she's old and I try not to think about the distance between us too much."

"That's probably the healthiest approach."

She was silent for a moment, then said, "I also have two male friends back home whom I miss dearly. I've always preferred friendships with males, they're easier," she looked at him and he turned his head and smiled, as she said, "One was Espen's best friend—and we still keep contact—and the other was his brother, but I'm not sure where our friendship is at, to be honest. I haven't seen him since the funeral.

"He was skiing with Espen on the day he died. I can't imagine how awful it must have been for him. He wouldn't ignore me out of spite, he's not like that. He's just carrying around a lot of pain." She looked out the window and recognized the shipyard.

"That's tough. Perhaps if you give it more time, he'll come around."

"I'm hoping for that. I really miss him."

Cianán parked the car and turned to look at her. "I consider the fact that you've confided in me a sign of friendship, Luka. Thank you. You're going to find your orientation again, just be patient with yourself."

She had to agree with him. This felt like a milestone, as well as a millstone off her neck. And the truth was, she had been curious about Sidney.

* * *

They went to a pub two blocks away from the shipyard, and Cianán ordered beer for the three of them. They lifted their glasses in cheers!

"How do you say cheers, in Dutch?" Sidney asked Luka.

"Proost," she replied and took a sip of her beer.

"That sounds like the German, prost. Do you speak

German?" he asked.

"Yes, I do, but most Dutch people speak German and French, and some also Spanish and Italian."

"Do you speak any of those?" he asked, looking at her from behind his tilted glass.

She nodded. "All, except Italian. It's rather ironic that Dutch people speak a couple of European languages, yet nobody else in Europe speaks Dutch, except for our Belgian neighbours."

"My only boast is that I also speak French," Cianán said. "I'm a first-generation Canadian." When Luka looked at him in surprise, he explained, "I was born and raised in Ireland and my parents moved here when I was twelve years old, but I've acquired the Canadian accent in school and university. However, when I speak to my kinsmen, I automatically switch over to an Irish accent. It's the darndest thing, and it doesn't seem as if my brain knows how to control it. And once I've had a couple of these." He lifted his glass. "It's like I've flown in from Dublin on the red eye." He rolled his eyes and took a sip.

Luka laughed. "I promise I won't look at you strangely when that happens, although I am curious to hear this phenomenon."

"It's bound to show its peculiar head at some point," he said.

"Do you miss home, Luka?" Sidney asked her. He'd been watching her carefully.

"Yes, but busy keeps you out of your own head."

He grinned and nodded.

"Luka's bought herself a bike and is braving Vancouver's traffic," Cianán said.

"Cool, but bikes are a Dutch thing, though. I haven't been to the Netherlands. Is it true that bikers there are crazy kamikazes?" Sidney asked her.

"Yes, every word of it is true. But you can just take a hands-on-wheels crash course on how to survive a day in Amsterdam when you get there."

Both men laughed.

"That's funny. You look like a wholesome Dutch girl. I'm a little surprised, I'd pictured you differently," Sidney said.

"I'm not sure what it means to be called a wholesome Dutch girl, but are you surprised by the fact that I look wholesome in general or does the part that I'm a wholesome Dutch girl, surprise you?" she asked, with an amused frown.

Sidney laughed. "Forgive me I don't know why it came out that way. I haven't anything against Dutch women. I think they're strong and smart, and beautiful."

Luka just looked at him.

"Sidney spends a little too much time alone at sea. His wires become slightly crossed sometimes," Cianán jested.

"I'm sorry Luka, I hope you won't hold that comment against me," Sidney said with a sheepish grin.

"All's forgiven," she said.

"Have you taken Luka out sailing yet?" Sidney asked Cianán.

"Not yet, but the weather's perfect now. We should do that. How about Saturday?" Cianán asked Luka.

"That sounds great, thanks."

"We can pack a picnic and refreshments, and Sidney can steer the boat while you and I sit back and enjoy the views, Luka."

"I'd be happy to take you around. It's incredible out on the ocean. You've seen it from a ferry, you've seen it from the air, but there's nothing like the freedom of a sailboat gliding through the water on a sunny day with the wind in your hair and the salt spray in your face," Sidney said, and his eyes lit up.

212

24

The ocean was sparkling blue, and there were only a few puffy white clouds in the sky as they sailed to Galiano Island. Sidney was steering while Luka and Cianán sat back and relaxed on the deck.

Cianán had changed his mind about having a picnic on the boat. They would have lunch on the island instead. It was a gorgeous sailboat with a large cabin, and a small, but sufficient bathroom with a shower and toilet. Luka wondered if Cianán allowed Sidney to take women out on it. Cianán was generous, he probably did.

Luka wore an above-the-knee jumpsuit and was aware of Sidney staring at her from where he was standing. She'd always considered her coltish legs too long and awkward, although she remembered with a throb in her chest how Espen had loved her legs and could never keep his hands off them. Right now, she wished she could tuck them in, without looking obviously self-conscious.

Her thick golden hair hung in a braid down the side of her neck and glistened in the sunlight. She reached for her hat and put it on, holding it down with one hand to prevent it from flying off.

"Do you have enough sunscreen on that fair skin of yours?"

asked Cianán. He was sitting back and was relishing every second, with deep sighs. "It's easy to misjudge the intensity of the sun when it feels nice and cool in the breeze," he said.

He too, had a wide-rimmed sun hat on and wore linen shirt and pants, with leather sandals. Luka thought he fitted the suave yachtsman to a T.

"My Irish skin doesn't become tanned. I just burn bright red and then it turns into freckles," Cianán said as he took a sip of icy-cold lemonade, that he'd made for them at home, and smacked his lips.

Luka sipped on her delicious drink. She was feeling mellow from the combined effects of the fresh air and sun.

"Yes, I've applied a broad-spectrum sunscreen," she said and looked back at Sidney, who looked cool and confident, and didn't seem affected by the sun's harmful rays.

"Enjoying yourself?" he asked.

She couldn't see his eyes behind his sunglasses, but the smile around the corners of his mouth suggested he was enjoying what he saw.

"I am. It's beautiful out here," she said.

Cianán confirmed with, "We couldn't have asked for better weather."

"We'll be mooring in a little while; island's just ahead," Sidney said.

It was close to lunchtime when they sailed into the marina. There weren't many open spots left.

"This is a paradise," Luka remarked.

"This is Montague Harbour Marina. It's great, isn't it? The little village is close. We'll hop onto a shuttle, grab something to eat and then we'll come back and walk out to the marine park. It's not too far from here, and worth seeing," Cianán said.

"This place is beyond tranquil," Luka said, as they walked to the marine park after their lunch. "The water's such an incredible turquoise blue; almost like the Caribbean. I didn't expect that. And the beach shimmers so." She stared at it in disbelief.

"Yes, there are several shell middens like this one. Native people lived, and harvested oysters and other shellfish, here more than three thousand years ago. Over time, the sea carved up the shells that had washed to shore to form this beach," Sidney said.

They spent the afternoon exploring. Luka felt completely relaxed and took photographs of the shelly beach and the driftwood that washed up in all shapes and sizes. She also photographed the men, sitting in laid-back conversation, enjoying the day and each other's company, while watching her explore like a curious little girl.

"Thank you for bringing me here. I grew up with water all around me, but this is so different," she said, as she took it all in.

"You're welcome, Luka. It gives us as much pleasure to be here, as it does for you. There's a lot more to explore but you can't do it in a day. It really needs a couple of days on each of the islands," Cianán said, as he stood up, stretched out his arms, and added, "We'll go back to Vancouver now and if you would like to join Sidney and me, we'll go out for dinner."

"That sounds lovely, thank you," she said.

The scent of the late afternoon sea breeze was intoxicating as they sailed back. Luka thought of Espen, and tried to suppress the image of his achingly handsome face and the exact expression he'd have had if he'd been there to experience this.

* * *

Cianán dropped Luka off at her place so she could take a shower. He picked her up again at eight and they met Sidney at the restaurant. They sat out on the patio and had seafood and white wine. The men told her about the history of the Gulf Islands and stories from their various travels in and around the Pacific Northwest.

Sidney was staring at Luka. Her hair was down and taken away with clips on the sides. She wore no makeup, and her cheeks were glowing, from the day in the sun and the wine. Her green eyes sparkled as she listened attentively to what was being said. She looked contented, and slightly tipsy. She wasn't aware of how pretty she was in that moment.

Cianán was by now, speaking in a delightful Irish accent, compliments of the wine—and Luka laughed at his colourful depictions. She became more certain of a genuine friendship between the two of them and felt she could trust him.

"Do you dance, Luka?" Cianán asked the out-of-the-blue question.

"Well, that depends on what you mean by dance? Casual or formal?" she asked with an amused frown.

"Formal, of course. Two-step, that sort of thing."

"Yes, I do. I took dance lessons as a child. My mother felt it was part of a well-rounded education, along with piano. She'd seen the two as inseparable. I first took ballet and later, I took dance classes to learn ballroom and more contemporary styles. I love Latin dances, like salsa, because it's free and fun, and dancing the tango with the right partner can be a thrilling experience," she said.

"Tell me about it. I also took dance lessons on the insistence of my paternal grandmother. She felt that no young man had a snowball's chance in hell—her words—of finding a respectable woman and had assured me of the endless possibilities that lay in wait for me, once I could take a woman in my arms and skillfully glide with her across the dance floor. After a rather reluctant start at a dance school, that taught the Fred Astaire essentials in Dublin as a teen, it soon become apparent what my dear granny had meant when she'd spoken of a world filled with endless possibilities," Cianán said.

"And has your granny's predication come true?" Luka asked with a smile.

"Sadly, no. But I remain hopeful, since thankfully, I'm only at the halfway mark," he said, with a chuckle.

"But I'm curious Cianán; why did you want to know if I could dance?" Luka asked.

"Oh, I was just testing you to see if you're a respectable woman. Now I know for certain you are." His eyes twinkled with mischief.

"You mean I'm a wholesome Dutch girl," Luka had a wicked smile as she looked at Sidney.

"Ouch!" Sidney replied.

They all burst out laughing.

"What about you, Sidney, do you dance?" Luka asked him.

"I'm no Fred Astaire, but I can shuffle my feet. I don't do a great foot loose on the dance floor, but I like dancing with a girl when the right song's playing in the background," he answered with a smile.

"There is something about dancing to the tune of Glen Miller and Count Basie and all those big band legends ..."

Luka thought about it. "That era's music will never go out of style for me. I find it both exhilarating and romantic.

"It reminds me of the stories my grandmother told me about the Second World War, and how people had found renewed hope when they socialized and danced under those stressful circumstances. Dance had been an act of defiance and rebellion against war itself, and it was also a reunion of souls. For many people today, dancing is still that," she said.

The men nodded their agreement. "I would love to meet your grandmother. To think a person has that kind of determination to live so long, and with such vigour. That's admirable," Cianán said.

"Perhaps you can chat to her when I video call her again and tell her yourself. She would love to share her stories with you," Luka said.

"She lived through the Second World War? How old is she?" asked Sidney.

"She'll be ninety-seven in December."

"And she video chats with you. That's impressive." He chuckled.

"That's nothing. She still lives by herself and refuses to get someone to help her out. I do love her and miss her," Luka said, as an afterthought and with a rueful smile.

"I bet she'll have killer dance moves and secrets of how I could enhance my skills. I shall have to give her a ring," Cianán said in contemplation.

"Secrets, yes. Lots." Luka raised her eyebrows to emphasize her point.

They watched the setting sun as they sipped on their wine.

Luka spoke her thoughts out loud, "Maui had thought he could capture and hold onto the sun, but the sun's force and beauty lies in its freedom. In the end, not even a powerful demi-god with a magical jawbone, could capture and hold onto it forever. It must take its course up and down the heavenly sphere." She made an arc with her finger in the air.

The men sat looking at her, intrigued, so she continued, "But it's really the sun that captures us—we are the objects of its amusement. We are like crystals that sunlight scatters off from to form a rainbow of colours. Electromagnetic energy, bouncing around, creating different moods. It's all caused by the playful sun. Isn't it absolutely marvellous?"

She took a sip of her wine as she looked at the unconquerable yellow orb that now hung low on the horizon, and she imagined that her sun didn't sleep in a blackened pit, but there was a special place, deep in the ocean, where he slept. He would be happy to rest there.

"The playful sun, playing with us. I like that." Cianán smiled broadly as he thought about what she'd said.

Sidney wanted to say something but stopped himself when he saw the far-off look in Luka's eyes. She was smiling—either imagining or remembering. She didn't notice him watching her.

25

Luka awoke from the ringing doorbell. She checked the time on her phone: five-thirty. Who'd be here so early on a Saturday morning? She walked to the front door and peeped through the hole.

"Hallo," she said as she opened the door for Sidney with a puzzled look on her face.

"Good morning to you," he said cheerfully, as he looked her over.

Her hair was messy, and she wore a large blue pyjama shirt that came to mid-thigh, with the constellations printed in white.

He chuckled, "I've wondered what you sleep in. May I come in?" He squeezed past her. "Where do you keep the coffee?"

"I'm sorry, you should have warned me you were on your way so that I could have brushed my hair and teeth and put on my negligee with matching fluffy heels to greet you in a kittenish voice. Coffee's in the door of the fridge."

He laughed. "I like your stary-sky look, it goes with the hair. Cups?"

"In the cupboard above the coffee machine. Is there any particular reason you are here this early or is it just one of the special, spontaneous things that makes you, you?" she asked.

220

"You have a great sense of humour, especially in the morning. I've come to get you. We're going hiking on Pender Island, and we need to take the ferry, so better hurry up. I've already booked the tickets." She stood looking at him and he said, "Go on and get ready. And dress in layers, it's cool outside." He turned to make the coffee.

"I like strong, black coffee, no sugar," she said, as she headed to her room.

"How Dutch of you." He sniggered, but she ignored the comment.

* * *

He drove to the north of Pender Island and parked his truck near the trailhead. They followed the trail in, and she was immediately struck by the beauty of the forest.

"These are Douglas fir trees," Sidney said when he saw Luka looking up at them.

"They're beautiful," she said, and took a close-up photo of the moss on the trunk of a tree. The ground between the trees was overgrown with sword ferns.

"I like the shades of green, and the forest smells so wonderful." She took a deep breath.

"Yes, this is a great trail. We're going to do a bit of climbing, but the views are going to knock your socks off," he said.

It was early September, but there were still plenty of wildflowers, and Luka took photographs of them too. They walked quietly. She liked that they didn't speak much, but it wasn't an uncomfortable silence. It was rather like two people who've known each other for a long time.

They didn't have to worry about bears (there typically

weren't any on the Gulf Islands), so noise wasn't required, and it made everything seem more mystical. Luka watched Sidney—he was lost in his own thoughts, but he looked happy in the moment. He turned his head to look at her briefly and smiled.

He was as unpredictable as the weather. He came and went without ceremony.

Luka had spoken to her friend, Carly, who was a co-worker and was already working at Byrne's when Sidney joined the company. Carly wasn't a gossip; she was happily married and a neutral female ear to borrow. Luka liked her a lot, and they occasionally went out for drinks, and she sometimes did activities with her and her husband on a weekend.

"What kind of work arrangement is there between Sidney and Cianán?" she'd asked Carly.

"Nobody knows, I doubt even Cianán does." Carly had laughed. "I guess it's on very short notice."

Luka had thought so too.

This morning he had shown up at her door out of the blue. They hadn't seen each other in nearly two months. When she'd gone out on the sailboat with him and Cianán, there had definitely been a physical vibe between her and Sidney.

She'd told Carly, "Sidney's interesting and well-read, I enjoy his company. But Cianán had warned me about him," Carly had lifted her brow and nodded in agreement, and Luka'd said, reflectively, "He does seem to be a contradiction to his own philosophy though. The feeling I'm getting, is that he yearns for a carefree existence, yet he's totally predictable in his hang-up about relationships."

"He's a commitment phobic, Luka. He likes honey but eats it with little spoons, so his hands won't become sticky," Carly had said.

Luka had smiled, "Yes, that's what Cianán had warned me about, but I like him. He has a visceral energy and it's very attractive."

"Hm, most women who don't know what's good for them, want some of it." Carly had not bothered to hide her skepticism.

Luka had thought about it. "He seems to be the type of man whom men with less confidence, admire, and most women swoon over—you're right. He's definitely used to female admiration."

Carly had lifted her brow again. "I'm sure you've noticed the way he looks at you."

Luka had noticed.

Still, it was a surprise to find him on her doorstep, but now that they were here, she had to admit she was enjoying this. They were both breathing hard when they reached the top, but the views left her breathless in other ways.

"This is George's Summit," Sidney said, and they sat down on a bench and drank their water.

"You can see forever," Luka said. She looked at him. "Why'd you bring me here?"

"It's good to be impromptu occasionally."

Impromptu was his middle name.

"And you don't think I'm spontaneous enough," she said and sniffed.

"You needed to see this." He ignored her comment. "Over there, to the west, are the Gulf Islands, and to the southeast, lie the San Juan Islands," he said, as he pointed with his finger.

They were quiet for a while, then he said, "It couldn't have been easy to pack up and move to the other side of the world."

"Are you talking about the islands or about me?"

He chuckled. "You."

"And you've made me climb up this mountain to come and sit down on this bench, so you could tell me this."

"I've been thinking about what it took for you to make the decision. I admire your courage. You're a strong woman, Luka."

"Many people do it; I'm not unique," she said, but thought of the fact that he'd been thinking about her.

"Do you miss it?" he asked.

"Of course, but life goes on."

Had he learned about Espen through Cianán, and was he indirectly asking her about him? It felt like that. They were close friends, it was possible Cianán would have told him.

Sidney looked at her for a moment, then looked out over the sea and islands as he spoke, "I'm curious about you, Luka. I can't decide if what you reveal is just enough or just too little. I'm drawn to you." He looked at her again and it looked as if he wanted to touch her hand, or her leg, but reconsidered.

"Are you drawn to the fact that I'm reserved with my emotions, and that makes it safe for you to be around me?" She knew it was probably the case but wanted to hear his response.

"I think you are interesting and you're funny, but you don't just blurt things out. Besides, emotions are overrated and too many people don't know how to control their emotions. I like being with you. It's sort of like the freedom I feel in solitude—there's breathing space."

They were quiet for a long time, just staring at the scenery. Luka thought about her and Espen and how they were able to be quiet together. Espen was never afraid of intimacy and expressing his feelings. He told her he loved her completely, and he also showed that love. She was able to move in and out of his energy field whenever and however she wanted to. It was a sensual thing, seeing him up close and from afar, as if she constantly zoomed in and out from him.

She sensed that Sidney craved physical contact, but he was afraid of the giving and taking intimacy required. He wanted her; it was clear by the way he looked at her. And he was drawn to something about her, but was it more than the safety of her emotional distance? After all, he'd brought her here to show her something beautiful because he'd thought she would appreciate it. But saying, I want you, wasn't the same as saying, I need you; you are valuable to me.

Luka didn't want to need this man who couldn't bear the thought of needing anyone. Yet she felt like giving in to something where she wouldn't have to give herself absolutely to someone else. Maybe it would fill part of the big hole where Espen had been.

26

"Now that I've gotten over the worst of the shock of my friends abandoning me to go and live in other countries, it's made me realize something, Luka," Stijn said, as he sat with his arms folded in front of his laptop.

At thirty-five, he still looked like a gangly boy with his unruly head of blond hair, shy light-blue eyes, and crooked smile. All of which made him irresistibly charming.

"What have you realized?" she asked.

"A couple of things, really, but the first thing is more a revelation about myself—I'm chicken shit. I never do anything daring."

"Aw, you're the cement that holds the academic foundation of Amsterdam together. What else have you realized?"

"Well, obviously with you living in Vancouver, it presents me with the opportunity to visit, but I've also realized another, not so much important as interesting thing—pot's legal in Canada too."

Luka giggled, "Yes, it is. You'd feel most welcome here. And you'd charm these Canadian girls no end. They wouldn't be able to keep their hands off you and your philosophizing ways."

"Think of the possibilities. Of course, the number one

reason for visiting the lovely city of Vancouver, would be to see my even lovelier friend. Here's an idea: we can go camping and smoke in our tent. How awesome would that be to experience the Canadian wilderness with an enlightened view?"

"Yes, and I'm hoping it would be a natural bear repellent too."

"Hm, you have the bears there. I'd forgotten about those fellows. But never mind, I'd have you to protect me," he said and grinned.

"You won't have to worry about a thing, I'll shield you from danger."

He looked at her for a moment and asked, "How are you doing, Luka?"

"It's going well with me. I work for a great company, and my boss and I have become good friends. You'd like him too. And there are endless things to keep me occupied."

"Have you met any people?"

She knew what he meant but didn't know how to answer. "I've made a couple of friends."

"Any of them guys, other than your boss?"

If they were just speaking over the phone, she could have dodged the question better, but he was looking straight at her. She had a flashback. "You are quite the escape artist" Espen had told her in Barcelona, when they joked about her stalking him.

"There is someone but it's not serious. He comes and goes as he pleases. I don't make any demands on him, and he doesn't expect anything from me. It's quite the little arrangement. Can you appreciate the irony of my organized and calculated nature suddenly becoming so spontaneous?" Luka smiled and looked away from his searching gaze for a second.

Stijn was watching her carefully, without saying anything. She knew he'd never judge her, but she recognized that concerned look.

"Bas is coming back to Amsterdam in a couple of weeks." He changed the subject.

"That's great. So he's done with London then?"

"Yes, it will be cool to see him. I mean, I've been to London to visit him, and that's just over the hill. Not like you there on the other end of the world."

"I'm happy that he's going home, and that you'll see each other more often. Is he doing well?"

"Yes, he looks and sounds okay. He's been busy, which is good. There was an English girl for a while, but it didn't last long. He's a cruiser."

"Yes, he is. Tell him I say hi when you see him."

"I will tell him that, Luka. I have to run, but it was great speaking to you. Will you take care of yourself?" he asked.

"Of course, I will. Now, you go look at your busy calendar and see when you can come visit me. Once you're here, you won't want to go back because it's so amazing."

"I'm definitely coming over to check things out."

She understood perfectly well what he implied, and said with a smile, "I'll be counting down the days. Goodbye, sweet friend," and she blew him a kiss.

"Goodbye Luka."

* * *

Luka stared into the illusional flames of the water vapour fireplace. The flames looked quite real and created a cozy atmosphere. She swivelled her glass of white wine lightly and took a sniff.

"Those are deep thoughts," Cianán said, putting a snack platter on the coffee table in front of her.

"Not so much deep as relaxing," she smiled and took a sip.

She was over at Cianán's place in Horseshoe Bay, a trendy area of Vancouver. He had a modern place with big windows that overlooked the Bay.

Tonight, he was cooking his signature lobster bisque, with, as he explained in detail, "… a freshly baked wholewheat loaf on the side, instead of croutons, as well as a crispy winter salad with toasted walnuts, shaved parmesan and green apple slices and a homemade vinaigrette." He was a competent cook and often entertained people with his culinary skills, except when he had bigger groups over. Then he used caterers or hired a venue.

Luka looked up at him as he stood eyeing her. Cianán knew about her and Sidney, although she wasn't the one who'd told him. He'd probably deduced it from Sidney staying over at her flat when he was in town, which for the past three weeks, he hadn't done.

Sidney was captaining a month-long superyacht excursion with billionaire clients and their friends, in the South Pacific. It was basically one long party on a yacht, and she imagined there'd be other perks involved for the enigmatic captain Russell who fiercely defended his freedom. No doubt, he may have those perks. Luka tried not to think how much she disliked the thought. She took a big sip of wine.

Cianán was more perceptive than most people she knew, and he could practically read her thoughts—an inconvenient ability from her perspective. But he wasn't most people. He had become a dear friend, and she had no doubt his motives were pure.

He said, as he topped up their wine, "Nothing like staring into the flames, thinking happy thoughts."

Luka smiled. He'd had a couple of glasses of wine while cooking and had already connected with his inner Irishman. She loved it when his accent suddenly switched. It was one of the most eccentric and likeable things about him.

"You are thinking happy thoughts, aren't you?" he asked with a lifted brow that said it all.

"This wine's delicious."

"Yes, it is. Why are you avoiding my question?"

"Because it sounds like a trick question."

"Not as tricky as you trying to avoid it." He sat down on a plush chair, put a snack into his mouth, closed his eyes momentarily, then he took a sip of wine and looked at her.

"My thoughts are floating in the wind. They are neither happy, nor sad."

"Is that so? Tell me, Luka, why are you doing this?"

She knew what *this* meant.

"I have to accept what comes with the territory, I suppose." She took a snack, tasted it and gave an approving, "mmm."

"That's rubbish. You don't have to accept anything."

"It gives me something to do with my hands. I don't knit." She avoided a straight answer.

Cianán didn't look convinced, however, he played along.

"Nonsense. There are plenty of knitting classes you can sign up for. Vancouver's renowned for their excellent training in the art of creating the most deplorable sweater for the holiday season. And I'm in dire need of one," he said with a mock-earnest expression. She sniggered and he said, more seriously,

"But come now, Luka, you can be with someone who'd give you a lot more than Sidney does. You know that. How much have you invested in this … whatever is going on between you two?"

"Nothing. That's the deal I've made with myself, to invest nothing."

He gave her an apprehensive look, "Your little charade isn't convincing me. Just make sure you stay honest with yourself on this deal of yours. I'd hate to see you get hurt."

"I don't plan on getting hurt, and there's nothing to be concerned about."

He changed the subject. "A group of us are going skiing in Whistler over Christmas, why don't you join us?"

She hadn't made plans yet, but she wasn't ready to face a ski slope. Not yet. She shook her head.

He registered what she meant and said, "Ah, right. That was thoughtless of me, I'm sorry."

"Don't apologize. You were being thoughtful. I appreciate the gesture. There's still time to come up with an idea, it's only the end of November. Otherwise, I'm open for one. If all else fails, I'll be knitting you a sweater."

He chuckled. "I'll think of some ideas. No good if you'll be all by yourself."

She knew Sidney would be spending time with his parents if he wasn't called away on a commission. But no expectations, was the name of their game.

"Food's ready. Let's eat, love," Cianán said.

Luka called her grandmother on Sunday, to wish her a happy birthday, since she'd be at work the next day. Her parents and her uncle and aunt were over at Marit's place, and they were having coffee and cake. She felt a pang of melancholy seeing them all together, but her grandmother was beaming from the attention, and more so because Luka had called.

"Luka dear, presents are a waste of money at my age. It will only end up going back to the giver or to someone else. This is what makes my heart feel joy: seeing your beautiful, smiling face and spending time with the ones I love. It's the greatest gift of all. But tell me, have you been doing well? I've heard from Bas that Stijn is thinking of visiting you. That would be wonderful. I don't suppose you'll be coming this way anytime soon?" Marit asked, with a hopeful gleam in her eyes.

Luka couldn't hide her surprise. "You've spoken to Bas, Omoe?"

"Yes, of course. We speak regularly. I'm so glad he's back in Amsterdam. I've missed our visits so. Bas is such a dear boy. He's taking me out for my birthday tomorrow." Marit was gloating.

Bas visited her grandmother? Luka wanted to ask more,

but Evi interrupted, "Sweetheart, you have a glow about you. How are things at work?"

It was probably the glow of shock from her grandmother and Bas's friendship she knew nothing about.

"Everything's going great, Mama. Business is growing, and there's never a quiet outdoor season over here. Summer activities just move to the side for winter activities. We'll have our holiday work party this coming Saturday. Just the usual stuff."

Luka wanted to speak to her grandmother about Bas but knew it was going to be useless to try now. Her dad had also stepped closer.

"Hallo, Lukie, are you well, my love?" asked Ruben.

"Hallo, Papa. Yes, I'm well thank you. Are you enjoying the birthday treats?" she asked, with a knowing smile.

"A man has to take his chance when he can get it." He cupped his hand to whisper in a conspiratorial voice, "Your mother's turned into some kind of lady hawk."

"It's for your own benefit, Rubie. We are not kids anymore. We can't just eat what we want." Evi said from the side.

"Well, Papa, at least you're allowed to eat Omoe's delicious coffee cake," Luka said.

"Thank goodness for that," he agreed.

They made small talk and Luka indulged her grandmother by staying online for a while longer, but she desperately wanted to know more about Bas and why he contacted her grandmother, but not her. Luka wasn't sure if Marit was aware that she and Bas had not spoken in two years, and she also didn't want to say anything in case it would raise questions. She felt frustrated with Bas.

When she hung up she sat and wondered if she should bring

it up with Stijn, but that seemed childish. Bas had a right to contact whomever he wanted. She sighed.

Tomorrow was the day, and he was going to take her grandmother out for her birthday. Was it his way of trying to forget, or was he simply doing something thoughtful? She didn't know what to think about their friendship anymore.

* * *

Luka was glad to be at work to keep her mind busy. And she was especially glad she'd called her grandmother the day before. It was easier to pretend there was no connection between her grandmother's birthday, and today.

She and Cianán went over a couple of objectives for the week. He had a lot on his plate, including the holiday party on Saturday evening.

He looked at her quizzically and asked, "Everything all right?"

"Yes, sure. I didn't sleep so well last night. I'll have more coffee." She put on a smile.

She set a priority list and started working through her processes; trying not to think of what this day meant. But her eyes wandered outside to the cold, grey of December, and it made her think of Amsterdam on the day she and Espen had gone on their third date, after their weekend in Mittenwald. He had told her he was in love with her.

* * *

They'd agreed to meet outside the entrance of the Rijksmuseum in Amsterdam on the Saturday—a week after they'd been to Mittenwald. It was cold and grey, and Espen stood waiting for her with hunched shoulders and hands in his coat pockets. Luka wondered how long he'd been waiting. She had butterflies in her stomach as she walked up to him. He planted a tentative kiss on her cheek, then kissed her on the mouth and gave her his great big smile.

After purchasing their tickets, they strolled around, admiring the works of Rembrandt, Vermeer, and countless other Dutch masters.

They carefully watched each other's body language in response to the paintings. She walked with her hands behind her back, and he touched them lightly with his fingers—a sensuous gesture—before interlacing his hand in hers. She couldn't stop staring at him. His handsomeness made her feel out of breath. When they'd walked the rounds, they had coffee at one of the espresso bars inside the museum.

"Which one is your favourite?" he asked with a curious smile as he leaned on his forearms, his face close to hers.

"That's an impossible question to answer." She took half a bite of the sweet cookie that was served with the coffee and put the other half into Espen's mouth. He'd already eaten his.

"You must have one that you find just that little bit more appealing than the others." He licked the crumbs off his lips, and held his thumb and index fingers close together, squinting his eyes.

"I don't know, I love them all. They draw you in. It's like being lifted off your feet and sucked into the canvas. Which is your favourite?"

"I don't have only one." He chuckled when she gave him a see-what-I-mean look. "But I gravitate toward the Vermeers. There's something breathtaking about the clarity and purpose of his colours, and the mystery behind the women in his paintings. They reveal a strength about themselves but it's subtle. I can see how you could have been a muse for Vermeer."

"Hm, I don't know if I would have been able to stand still for so long, fake inspecting my maps and charts."

He laughed. "Although it would have made for a killer painting."

"Hypothetically, I would have liked to have been immortalized as a Sunna figure from Norse mythology. A blazing symbol of strength, racing through the sky on her chariot."

"Is Sunna your alter ego?" he asked with an amused smile.

"I think so ... yes, I've just decided she is. I like sun stories, and Sunna is the embodiment of the sun's kindness, generosity, and healing power. She rides on a solar chariot, pulled by two golden horses. How would that not make a beautiful Vermeer? Just imagine what he would have done with all those bright colours."

"I'm not an expert on Norse mythology, but if I remember correctly, Sunna's chased by a wolf. Would he also be in this hypothetical alter-ego painting?" he asked and took a sip of his coffee.

"Yes, and the wolf's name is Sköll. According to the legend, he occasionally catches up with Sunna, and takes a bite out of her, thereby causing an eclipse."

"And despite having a couple of chunks missing from her lustrous form, the sun goddess survives her solar expeditions on her chariot pulled by luminescent horses," he ventured.

"Not quite. Sköll eventually catches Sunna and kills her, but before her death, she gives birth to a daughter, and thereby—with the aid of the sun—humanity survives in the coming of the new world, after Ragnarök, the great battle and death of the gods and destruction of the Earth. But Sunna had done her part for the survival of the human race," Luka said.

"Vermeer would have had a field day with that. It's a pity nobody told him this story, but he was more of an indoors painter anyway. Perhaps Van Gogh would have been a better candidate as your artist, since he liked painting in the outdoors," Espen said.

"You're right; he would have painted a marvellous scene. Yellow was Vincent's favourite colour because he said it reminded him of the sun. What evokes more happiness than the sunny sun?" She gave him a dazzling smile.

He looked at her with a grin and said, "Come, Sunna, let me show you where I live."

She took the hand he held out for her.

* * *

The day remained grey, and Luka passed through the hours, morphing between reality and dreams about a boy she'd once loved, and who'd loved her back. She went to bed early, not having an appetite for food or anything else. And she fell asleep holding onto her compass—how she longed for it to show her the way.

28

Cianán had booked a small, stylish venue for their holiday party. Luka wore a green dress with a wide oval neckline that accentuated her eyes and graceful features. She'd taken her hair up loosely in pins and had painted her nails bright red and wore matching red lipstick, and mascara. It had been a while since she'd paid this much attention to her appearance.

She greeted and talked to a couple of her colleagues when she walked through the door. Cianán acknowledged her with a wave, as he was talking with people. She scanned the room and saw Sidney, who was engaged in conversation with a woman called Amelia. Luka knew she was one of Sidney's options. Amelia's options were as wide open as Sidney's, and Luka thought it ironic that, in a sense, they were perfect for each other.

Sidney didn't seem to notice her arrival. He was back from his trip and had a deep tan. A month in the South Pacific would do that, she supposed. It had been unclear if he would attend the function, and he didn't call to let her know either, but that was just how he did things.

Cianán walked over and kissed her on the cheek. "Good evening. Wow-wee, you look stunning."

"Thanks. This is a cool place," she said as she gazed around.

"Yes, they've done a marvellous job with the décor. We're not going to fuss over anything tonight. It's all relaxation. There's room for dancing, as you can see, and tonight, my dear friend, we're going to show these people a couple of stylish moves. I've made certain there'll be some Glen Miller and Count Basie for you."

"Ooo, I can't wait," she said and smiled at his enthusiasm.

"But let's get you something to drink. The hors d'oeuvres are quite delicious if you're feeling peckish. Bubbly? You look like a girl who needs bubbly to go with that swanky look."

He signalled to a waiter, who brought over a tray with champagne.

Cianán took two glasses and handed her one. "Cheers!"

"Thank you. Proost!" She sat down on a square stool and crossed her legs.

"How are you? You didn't seem yourself this week," he asked, studying her face for clues.

"I didn't?" He gave her a look. She said, "I'm okay. I see Sidney's back." She turned her head in his direction and he was looking at her now. Luka gave him a half-smile, and Amelia gave her the same.

"Yes, the lucky devil. When I look at the life he has and the grind I put myself through, I wonder about the logic of it all. Here he comes," Cianán said.

"Good evening," Sidney said to Luka.

"Hallo." She took a sip of her champagne and looked up at him.

He bent down to give her a kiss on the cheek and lingered to smell her soft fragrance. "You're looking particularly lovely," he said with an admiring look.

"Thank you."

"Doesn't she just?" Cianán added. "Okay, Luka, you have your drink. Sid, you've got one too, I see. Let me go and mingle and we'll catch up later." He walked off.

"How was the trip?" Luka asked.

"It was good, but a month gets a little long when you're stuck with the same faces day in and day out." He sat down on a stool next to her and roamed her face with his gaze.

"There's just no way to win," she said dryly.

He laughed. "Glad to hear you've brought your sense of humour with that outfit. You really do look beautiful." When she didn't speak, he said, "I wish we could get out of here. I'd love to be alone with you."

"I'm afraid that's impossible. Cianán has brought Glen Miller and his Fred Astaire moves, and he intends to show off big band style, and I'm part of the show." She smiled as she searched for Cianán, who was laughing gaily at something someone had said. "Did you see and do a lot of interesting things in the South Pacific?" she asked Sidney.

"Yes, plenty. We swam with the dolphins and rays, and the reefs were gorgeous. Heart-stopping stuff. Have you been there?"

"Only as far as Central Pacific," she said.

"It's an incredible part of the world. The people, the ocean. I could easily live in a place like that. I was able to do a few scuba dives. Man, that was magic. Do you scuba?"

"I do." She thought about the exciting research trips she went on with Espen, and said, "I love scuba diving. There's a magical world inside the ocean."

"There sure is. Maybe we can do that in the summer. We won't need to go far, there are great spots to dive around the Gulf Islands."

Sidney liked using non-committal words, such as, maybe. Luka interpreted it as his way of feeling in control, so she played along.

"Sure, that would be fun. Are you going to be around over Christmas?" she asked.

Sidney's parents lived in Abbottsford, about seventy kilometres southeast of Vancouver, and on the Canadian-US border.

He chuckled. "My mom's been nagging me, so I think I might just have to." He scanned her face again and said, "It's good to see you, Luka." He put his hand on her leg.

She drank the last champagne in her glass and smiled with pursed lips.

* * *

Luka was checking emails and having coffee. Sidney had come home with her after the party and was going to stay over tonight as well but he had to go out to run a couple of errands and get fresh clothes.

He seemed genuinely happy to see her. Despite his barriers, he was a tender and affectionate lover. He liked to hold her after they'd made love, and they spoke about things that weren't important, but amusing. Things like:

"What do you prefer: rain or snow?" Sidney asked.

"Rain," she answered, "because I can smell it and it makes a sound. And I like thunderstorms too—both the rumbling and the loud crack."

"What makes you sleep?" he asked.

"The sound of the rain, and deep, rhythmic breathing," she answered.

"Do you listen to me when I sleep?" he asked with a curious

frown.

"Sometimes, but you're not around that often," she said, but it was too close to the untouchable subject, so he didn't ask her further questions about that.

And she didn't tell Sidney that nobody sounded as beautiful when they slept, as Espen had sounded. When she'd told Espen, not long after they'd met, he'd looked at her with a puzzled expression, and asked her why on earth she lay awake listening to him sleeping, when she should be sleeping herself. Luka smiled at the memory.

"What part of a woman's anatomy do you like best?" she asked. Sidney chuckled and showed her. She removed his hand and said, "Let me re-phrase: what visible feature catches your attention first?"

"I suppose, eyes do. You have beautiful eyes, Luka. There's a lot in them that you don't say in words," he said.

He was one to talk. But he didn't probe about those unspoken things behind her eyes, possibly because he was afraid of what he'd discover in there.

"Why do you like the sea so much?" she asked.

"Any person who doesn't like the sea is crazy," he said incredulously.

"C'mon, there are plenty of people who find such a massive body of water intimidating and frightening. When was the first moment you realized you're obsessed with the sea?"

He laughed, "So, now I've gone from liking it, to being obsessed with it. There was no clear moment. I grew up with it always there." He paused for a little and said, "It has always been a place to go when the need to escape took hold of me. To me, the sea's a refuge."

A refuge from what, she wondered.

Espen had loved the ocean because it breathed and lived and sustained. And he'd also loved it because of its vulnerability. He'd never sought protection from the ocean. All he'd ever wanted, was to shelter it. Sidney feared a loss of something inside himself, that was why he was constantly fleeing for safety. Espen's fears had been for a loss of something far larger outside himself.

* * *

There was a new email message. Her heart stopped for a moment before she opened it. It was from Bas:

Hallo Lukie,

As you already know, I've had lunch with your grandmother during the week, and you obviously know about our visits now. I owe you an explanation, I'm sorry. You're probably pissed off with me, but I've been meaning to contact you, I swear. I just didn't know how to approach this.

There hasn't been a moment when I haven't thought about you, and what you've been going through, Luka. When my mom gave me your letter from before you'd left for Vancouver—God, I wish I hadn't been such a coward, but I didn't know how to even begin to speak to you. The words were stuck in my throat. Please forgive me.

Anyway, I'm ready now, so, if you want to, it would be great if we could talk. I'd really like that. Let me know. I'll be waiting for your reply.

Bas

She stared at the screen for several minutes, then called him on his cellphone.

"Hallo?" he answered right away, but there was a slight

delay and static because of the distance.

"Hallo, Bas," she said, trembling from the shock of hearing his voice.

"Luka … you got my email."

"Yes, I did."

There was a pause and Luka collected herself.

"Thank you for calling," he said, but his voice had a hint of uncertainty.

"How are you, Bas?"

"I'm doing okay, Lukie. Better. How about yourself?"

"The same. It's good to hear your voice," she said, and she lost hers.

He blew out a breath and cleared his throat. "I've been such an ass about this, Luka. I'm sorry if I've put you through more than you needed. Truth is, I've only recently started talking about it, and it's still hard …"

"Bas, I understand. I meant what I said in that letter. I've missed you so much."

"And I you, Lukie."

They were both silent for a little bit.

He broke the silence, "Stijn is fired up about visiting you. That would be awesome."

"Yes, he wants to come check up on me. I'm sure he's told you that."

She wondered how much Stijn had told Bas.

"He's turned into some weird kind of parent figure. It seems that teaching has softened him," Bas said and chuckled.

"He's not quite as grown-up as you fear. He also wants to come to Canada because he sees the recreational benefits, if you know what I mean."

"Ah, that explains a lot." He hesitated and said, "I'd like

to see you too. I was thinking if you can spare a day or so sometime—whenever it would suit you."

"Can you come for Christmas? I mean, do you think you'd be able to get away on such short notice?" she asked on impulse and was surprised by her bold initiative.

The question had thrown him off too, and he said tentatively, "Well, sure, I can try. It's a bit late for airline tickets, but there might still be a flight with five stopovers available. Are you sure about this?"

"I'm positive. I could really do with the company over the holidays, but don't tell my grandmother that. She'll have them all in a tizzy.

"If you can find a flight for a few days before Christmas, and can stay at least until after the New Year, that would be fantastic. Longer would be better, because it's so far to travel, and there's simply too much to see over here in just a week. Don't worry about a hotel. I have a sleeper sofa that's super comfortable."

He thought about it. "This is unexpected but let me first see what I can do before we get our hopes up. If not now, we can always do it later."

"Absolutely." She paused for a moment, then asked, "Are you well otherwise?"

"Yes, I am. I've been in London, but you already know that. It's good to be back in Amsterdam. Much less smog and more friendly faces."

"And there's Stijn."

"Yes, I've missed the rascal. I'll talk to him about this, but he wouldn't mind. That's the thing about Stijn, he doesn't mind."

"No, he doesn't and that's why we love him." She checked her watch. Sidney would probably be back soon, and she didn't want Bas to know about him. Not yet anyway. "I have to go, but I hope you can get a flight. I'm going to keep my fingers and toes crossed."

"Yes, this is long overdue. I'll get on it right away. Take care, Lukie. I'll speak to you soon."

"Goodbye, Bas."

She hung up and sat staring at her laptop screen again, and her mouth slowly curved into a broad smile.

<h1 style="text-align:center">29</h1>

Luka took the airport Skytrain and stood waiting for Bas at arrivals. He had been able to get a single connection flight via Toronto—it must have been twice the price, she thought. At least he didn't have numerous stopovers.

It was three days before Christmas, and he was going to stay for a week after New Year as well. She'd put in for vacation time right after she'd spoken to Bas, and Cianán had been thrilled to hear she would have company over the holidays.

Sidnėy had asked her what she was doing for Christmas but had not offered for her to join him with his family. Perhaps taking her to his parents' house would send the message they were a couple. She'd said vaguely that a friend from home was coming for a visit. He hadn't pressed her for more, but she could see he was curious.

Arriving passengers started coming through the doors. Time stood still for a moment when Luka saw Espen, who then turned into a version of him, before changing into the form of her beloved Bas. He was walking toward her. They embraced for a long time.

Bas was the first to pull away. He looked at her with a shy, boyish smile, and said, "Hoi, Lukie."

"Hoi, Bas. Welcome to Vancouver. Come, we'll take the

Skytrain. It's only half an hour, then we can get you home and comfortable."

From downtown, they took a taxi to Luka's flat.

He commented on her bike in the entrance way. "Are bikes a big thing here?"

"Not as big as we're used to, but I think it's a growing trend. A lot of people bike to work but it rains a lot, so you need good rubber boots and a big raincoat," she said.

"This is a decent sized flat," he said as he looked around. "I see you have a little tree made up."

"In the spirit of Christmas," she said. "Yes, this is quite spacious for a single person. I like the area. There are a lot of great restaurants, and the public transport makes it easy to get around. We'll do some exploring tomorrow. Let's put your suitcase in the bedroom." They walked to her room, and she showed him where to put it as he scanned the setup. "You can take a shower. I've put out a towel on the cabinet and there's shampoo and soap and if you need anything just ask. I'll make us something to eat. Are you hungry?" She said everything in one breath and Bas stood looking at her with a smile. "I'm sorry, a little over excited," she apologized.

"I've eaten on the plane, so I'm not terribly hungry."

"Okay, I'll make something that's not too heavy, but the hunger might hit you later tonight. I'll leave you to enjoy your shower now."

"Thanks, I'm looking forward to that."

When he came out, he was clean-shaven, and his damp hair looked darker. She thought he was so handsome.

"I see you have an electric fireplace. That's a handy feature, do you ever use it?" he asked.

"Yes, it used to be gas, but the city has started to move

toward renewable energy, and my landlord made the switch a couple of years ago. Vancouver is going all green. You may switch it on if you'd like, it creates a cozy ambience."

He stood back to look at the panel that looked like real flames. "Cool," he grinned.

"Would you like something to drink? I have red and white wine, and beer. You would enjoy the Canadian micro-breweries," she offered.

"Sure, I'll try a beer."

She opened a bottle for each of them, and they both said, "Proost!"

"Thank you for coming," she said and gave him a hug with one arm around his waist.

He squeezed her shoulder and said, "Thanks for having me, Lukie. It's great to see you." He kissed the top of her head.

They had dinner and Bas brought her up to speed with news about his parents, and then he said, "I have something for you." He went to the bedroom and came back with a plastic container full of sweet and spiced Dutch Christmas biscuits. "I was specifically instructed to tell you, your grandmother sends these with all her love."

"Speculaas! Perfect for Christmas." Luka smiled broadly when she read the little note: *A sweet treat for Oma's sweet girl. You and Bas enjoy your time together, my love.*

"She's doing remarkably well, considering her age, but the old hands are getting a little shaky and the legs slower. Your mom wants to hire a caregiver, but she's resisting."

"She's stubborn, that's why. I don't even know how she manages to do all the baking and other stuff, with her arthritis. It's kind of you to visit her."

"I love her company. Trust me, it's no skin off my back."

"I'm going to clean up these dishes quickly, and then we can make your bed. I'm sure you can't wait to crawl into it," she said, when she saw him stifling a yawn.

"The thought of a bit of sleep does sound appealing."

He helped her clean up and they pulled out the sleeper sofa.

"Some of them can be hard to sleep on, but this is a comfortable one. I'm also adding a mattress pad for extra buffer. You'll sleep like a baby," she said.

"Don't worry. I can sleep anywhere. This is going to be heavenly, thanks, Lukie."

She thought how he was like his brother in that way.

"Tomorrow we'll do some exploring. You're going to love this city and everything else around it," she said.

Bas was already up by the time Luka woke up. He'd made coffee and was checking and sending emails—she'd given him her Wi-Fi password to use.

"Good morning, did you sleep well?" she asked

He smiled at her tussled hair and sleepy look. "Good morning. It's been a while since I've seen you in your early mode. Yes, I've slept great, thanks. But my internal clock woke me up at the crack of dawn. I've helped myself to coffee—that's a fresh pot. And I've had some of last night's leftovers."

"Perfect; first few days are weird in a different time zone. Just make yourself at home." she said as she poured herself a cup of coffee. "You'll feel the jet lag by late afternoon. I suggest we go and see a sight or two, perhaps grab something to eat somewhere, and then we can pop into the grocery store to get what we need for Christmas. By tomorrow the stores are going to be insane."

Cianán had given her a gift basket with a bottle of Veuve

Clicquot and fancy snacks, as well as a gift card for the grocery store.

* * *

The Christmas lights flickered on the tree. Luka sat with her legs up on a comfy chair, and Bas lay stretched out on the sleeper sofa with his head resting against the back. Each of them had a glass of red wine.

"I don't think I'll be able to look at food for the next couple of days," she said.

"I thought you were going to say, for the next couple of hours," he said and chuckled. "Give it a while, you'll feel hungry sooner than you think. I'm nearly ready for a little snack of turkey again."

Luka made a face and held her tummy.

It was Christmas Day. She'd cooked a young turkey, which was still a lot of food for the two of them. She'd sent a text with Merry Christmas wishes, and a photo Bas had taken of her, next to her golden roasted bird, to Cianán.

He'd replied with a photo of himself, wearing the bright green sweater she'd bought him for Christmas. It had a big (equally bright) red mistletoe on a circle of white across his torso. His text said: *Merry Christmas friend and traveller. Marvellous job on the bird. Thank you for the gift, it's fabulously hideous. I'm going to a la-di-da soirée soon and I'll be wearing it. Perhaps a lady will kiss me underneath the mistletoe. Hope you kids are having fun.*

Luka giggled as she read it to Bas. "Cianán is a sweetheart. I'm certain he's already a little tipsy. Beware, the Irish are coming!" She told Bas about Cianán's accent changing when he'd had a drink or two.

"Brilliant and helpful." He laughed and remarked, "Women can't resist a foreign accent, it doesn't matter where on the planet they are. It's a powerful pick-up weapon in a man's arsenal."

"Yes, and he's going to use his sweater as another pick-up weapon, mark my words."

Bas lay looking at her. She knew he had something on his mind. "Will you please just come out and tell me what that look's about?"

"Stijn said there's a guy."

Luka took a long sip of wine before she answered, "He's not my boyfriend. It's just … something."

"You don't have to explain it to me, Lukie. You are free to do whatever you want. Stijn had just mentioned it out of concern, he wasn't ratting on you."

"I know." She trilled through her lips. After a pause, she said, "Freedom's a strange concept, isn't it? I felt freer with Espen, than I do now, as a single person. Perhaps I will love a man again, but sometimes I wonder if it's possible."

The moment she'd said it, she looked at Bas and had a strange feeling as he held her gaze.

He said, "The two of you had something special, which is why I wonder if you feel contented with your current situation." She shook her head in a gesture of inconclusion, and he said, "I know what it's like to do the easy-way-out kind of relationship. There's nothing to it. You just take your bag and get the hell out, but it gets old after a while."

"I suppose I crave the contact. It's something tangible, at least."

"That's a normal human need, Luka. Are you happy here in

Vancouver, though?"

"Yes, I am. I miss home, but I guess I had to find space between me and my ghost."

"I know. But look at us, jochie." Meaning kiddo. "Here we are together; it's going slow, but we're making progress. Let's salute that."

He sat upright and they clinked their glasses.

"Yes, you're right, Sebastian. We are making progress, aren't we?" She sat back and said, "Before you go home, we must make a trip to Vancouver Island. It's a place full of magic."

* * *

They were dressed in layers, with long raincoats protecting them from the precipitation. A thick layer of fog hung low, like the forest's breath lingering there. Luka imagined it was filled with the whispers of souls who had walked those paths in ages past, making it appear even more esoteric. Apart from herself and Bas, there were only three other people. It seemed to her everyone was speaking softly out of reverence for the ancient giants.

They were in the Carmanah Walbran Provincial Park, on the southwest coast of Vancouver Island.

Bas stood looking up at the cedar trees. "How old are they, I wonder? Even a thousand years seem too young."

"Perhaps their souls are as old as time itself. They're marvellous. The map indicated a viewing platform up ahead. Let's go check it out," she said.

The plaque said Heaven Tree and they stood looking at it in awe. It was a 77m-high, 3.5m-wide Sitka spruce tree.

Luka said, "She is a grandmother tree. It feels as if she has something of my oma's stoutheartedness in her; or perhaps my oma has hers."

Bas smiled.

She kept looking up at the tree as she asked him carefully, "Do you and my grandmother ever talk about Espen?"

"Sometimes we do, yes."

Luka wanted to ask him what they talked about, but perhaps he considered it something private between him and her oma.

"She's always considered you and Espen the grandsons she's never had. Thank goodness she still has you."

"Yes, I suppose so, but it's a two-way street. And she has her own demon to battle with."

Luka turned her head to look at him, but she couldn't read the expression on his face, as it was turned upward. Again, he didn't elaborate, but Luka knew what he meant. It was the thing she and her grandmother couldn't talk about, and it was her own demon too.

But Marit had confided in Bas because it was something that obviously tormented her. Luka felt overwhelming sympathy for her dear grandmother.

"When I die, I want my soul to become part of the spirit of a tree," she said as she looked at the Heaven Tree again.

"A spirit tree," he said as he turned and looked directly at her with a smile.

His eyes were bluer than Espen's had been. She noticed for the first time more of Adelheid in his features too. He was even more handsome now at thirty-four, than he'd been when she'd met him.

"Does it have to be a specific tree?" he asked.

"If I die here in British Columbia, then perhaps one of the spruce or fir trees in this forest."

"And if you die in the Netherlands?"

"The elm by Espen's grave," she said without hesitation.

Bas took her hand in his and held it tight.

They spent two days in the area before driving to Ucluelet, nearly four hours north, where they stayed at a beach resort with ocean views. Storm watching on Vancouver Island's west coast was a novel winter activity.

They walked for a few kilometres on a partial beach trail, then sat on a cliff, watching the raging sea pushing the foamy surf toward the coastline. It was cold and damp, but the view was mesmerizing. They were quiet as they looked far out over the billowing waves. There was a patch of sunlight lightening up the colour of the water in the middle of the dark ocean, like a beacon of hope.

Bas started speaking slowly, "I saw it happen …"

Luka was numb. She looked at him, almost too afraid to breathe, and she could see how hard it was for him to relive it in his mind.

"Hugo and Klaus and I had gone down the run before him. We stood at the bottom, and first felt the tremor, then we heard that awful sound as the slab avalanche came crashing down. There were other people too, near the runout zone, but the rescuers were able to get to them quickly. Espen and the other three guys were higher up the slope. They'd borne the full brunt of it.

"I never felt so powerless in my life, knowing my brother was entombed underneath all that snow, and I couldn't do a thing to help him. Not a damn thing." He looked at his hands, then out over the sea again. "I thought you hated me for being the one who'd survived, and not him. If I could, I'd change that in an instant, Luka." He turned to look at her—eyes filled with anguish –and he squeezed her hand hard.

She shook her head as the tears rolled down her face. It took a moment for her to find her voice. "No … no, I've never hated you. How could I ever hate you? I wish Espen hadn't died; I really do. But I'm so happy you are alive, Bas."

They clung to each other and cried as the breeze sprayed them with saltwater.

When they finally pulled apart, Luka said, "I have longed to hear this, thank you." She took tissues out of her backpack and handed him one.

"I know you have, Lukie." He kissed the side of her head. "Thank you for bringing me here; this is an amazing place."

"This was one of the places Espen and I had on our wish list. He'd always said he wanted to come and watch the windy and rainy storms that come from Alaska's Aleutian Islands, here on Vancouver Island. He would have loved this scene," she said, gazing around.

"Yes, this had been his kind of drama, for sure." He thought about something. "You know we could still visit some of the places on your list, like we're doing now, in remembrance of Espen. Stijn can do it with us."

She smiled. "That's a cool idea. It can be in remembrance of Espen, but also for new memories for the three of us."

"I like that perspective."

They sat quiet again for a long while.

Luka squeezed his arm tight and pressed her face against his shoulder. "Bas, you are so important to me. Please let's always stay in touch. I can't bear not knowing that your heart is well," she said as they sat huddled together.

She realized suddenly that she dreaded the thought of him leaving.

30

"Do you think you'll come home for a visit this year at all, Luka? It's been a year now since we've seen you," Evi asked.

Has it been a year already? It hardly seemed possible when it felt as if she was standing still most of the time.

"I was hoping that you and Papa could come to Vancouver in the summer. The weather is so lovely and there's a lot we can do," Luka said.

"I would love to visit, my sweetheart, but Oma needs more care now. Your uncle and aunt can't keep a constant close eye on her from where they are in Amsterdam. I've finally convinced her that she needs a caregiver, but it's still not a live-in position, and I dare not suggest she come live with us—you know your oma.

"And I think Papa is getting old too, Luka. He's been so achy lately, and he's becoming fussier with his routine, like a grumpy old bear. Doing a trip by train through Europe is doable for him, but moving through airports, and time zone differences is another matter. I still feel up for adventure travelling, but there's simply too much at stake here at home. I'm sorry, my love."

Luka could hear Ruben mumbling something in the background. He was becoming a grumpy old bear, she thought with a smile.

"I understand, Mama. It just would have been so great for you to see this beautiful part of the world, that's all." Luka couldn't keep the disappointment out of her voice, but added, "Perhaps I can go home for two weeks over Christmas and New Year. I won't be able to make it for Omoe's birthday, but we can do a belated celebration. Let me first see how things work out before you mention anything to her. It's only March and a lot can still happen. I don't want to get Omoe's hopes up for nothing."

"That would be wonderful my darling, see what you can manage. We understand that you don't have that much vacation time. And I hope you'll have a wonderful rest of your day. Are you celebrating with anyone?" asked Evi.

Luka knew that innocent sounding voice was really asking a loaded question. And she could almost see her father's bat ears tuning in to hear what she was saying there in the background.

Evi and Ruben had called Luka for her birthday. Her grandmother had also called to wish her a happy thirty-third birthday. Luka wished there was a way to get all of them to Vancouver without the hassle. Her mom was right about her grandmother, though. Marit didn't have any health issues, but she definitely needed care and someone to keep a close eye on her.

The advantage of her going home, was that she'd also see Stijn and Bas. They had both emailed her, wishing her a happy birthday. She'd been thinking a lot about her reconnection with Bas. In fact, she hadn't been able to stop thinking about it. She missed him.

* * *

"We aren't there yet, not completely, but we're getting there," said Cianán, looking out the window of his office over the shipyard. "It's just a matter of time before we'll be able to produce bigger yachts that are fully electric. The electric sailboat sales are doing well, and we've seen great success with the hybrid systems, but the goal must remain a hundred percent self-sufficiency without compromising on standards.

"Customers are asking for eco-friendly solutions when they're shopping for yachts nowadays. They want vessels that leave no trace, and they want a more peaceful experience. It's a win-win for our environment as well as our customers. These are exciting times in the yachting industry." He turned around, smiled, and sat down behind his desk.

"That's good news. But there are still plenty of yachts out there running on fuel only, causing a lot of air and noise pollution. Our poor oceans," Luka said. She could almost see Espen smiling about her comment.

"That's true, but we're going to make sure we don't send any of our customers out on the seas in those. And I do believe the older-generation yachts will either be remodelled, or they'll be phased out over time. People who mingle in those circles, don't like to think of themselves as lagging behind the times. Word of mouth is a powerful advertisement," he said. He leaned back and looked at her for a moment. "Is something on your mind? You're not worried about getting older, are you?"

Cianán had given Luka a lovely lime green silk scarf for her birthday, and she was wearing it. He did no different for the other employees on their birthdays. He was one of the most conscientious people she knew, and by far one of the best gift givers. He always seemed to know exactly what to buy for each individual.

She shook her head and played with her scarf. "No, I'll just think how you'll always be ten years older than I am, and instantly feel young again."

He laughed and said, "As American financier, Bernard Baruch said, 'To me, old age is always ten years older than I am.'"

"That sounds like my grandmother's motto. Speaking of which, I spoke to my mom and will need to visit them. They can't come here because of my gran. My mom doesn't feel comfortable leaving her. I know it's early in the year and a lot can still come up but was thinking of going home for Christmas and New Year."

"But that's hardly something to worry about. Just put in your vacation request."

"Thank you, Cianán. It's a strange pull: the obligation toward one's family. I want to live an independent life, but I always feel as if a part of me remains there."

"Having that connectedness does something for the soul. For a lot of us, we can't stand too much of our family's company, yet at the same time we can't live without them either. You, on the other hand, have a great relationship with your parents, and you still have your grandmother. I love how you want to honour her by showing how important she is to you. Your heart's in the right place." He paused for a second. "But I'm getting another vibe. Are you sure there's not something else bothering you?"

"I'll let you know once I discover what it is."

"Uh-oh. Well, since Sidney's not around, why don't you let

me take you out for your birthday tonight? Has he called you yet?"

Their friendship was easy. Cianán could read her—a little too well—and he asked questions, but out of concern and never to the point of exhaustion. Luka enjoyed their professional relationship too. He gave her plenty of freedom and never imposed ideas on her, and she respected his leadership.

Her work environment wasn't giving her a reason for dissatisfaction, in fact, she was happy at work. And Sidney … she reminded herself it was what it was. But Luka was bored with her own complacency.

She and Sidney didn't do special treatment of each other—not for any occasion. The careful lines they walked never crossed boundaries between sensual pleasure and emotional intimacy. But were those lines still clear in her own mind? Sidney was supposed to have been a physical filler for Espen, but Luka wasn't so sure about her feelings for him anymore. Perhaps she was just imagining things.

"He hasn't called, no."

"I see."

The problem was, Cianán saw too much. "Can't I just live in a little pretend world without you snooping around in it?"

"I love snooping around in your make-believe world, it provides me with much needed entertainment, however, I don't always like everything I discover in there," he said, with a concerned frown.

"Need I even ask what you think?"

"You already know what I think, but what are your thoughts?"

"I think you're trying reverse psychology on me." He lifted

his brow and she said, "Perhaps I'm getting sick of my own agreeability. There, I've said it."

"Aha! We're finally getting somewhere." She smiled ruefully and he said, "It pleases me to hear you admit that to yourself. You know you need more Luka, and Sidney will always resist needing anyone. That's not to say I don't think he cares for you—God forbid, even loves you—but he doesn't want to change." He watched her for a moment and added, "My birthday wish for you, my sweet friend, is for you to nurture that extraordinary light inside yourself, and to embrace possibilities for love and happiness."

"You're a wonderful friend, Cianán." She smiled, looking out the window, as she thought of herself and Bas standing in front of the Heaven Tree.

* * *

Luka was just about ready to go out with Cianán for dinner when the doorbell rang. She was surprised to find Sidney standing there with a big grin and a bright bunch of flowers.

"I thought I'd surprise you for your birthday," he said.

"This is a surprise," she said as he handed her the flowers and kissed her on the mouth.

"You look good. Feel like being spoiled, birthday girl?"

"Thank you for the flowers, but I'm afraid I already have plans."

Why did it bother her that he'd shown up unannounced? This was nothing new.

"Change of plans. I've spoken to Cianán and the two of us are going out, instead of the two of you. He's kept the reservation. Isn't he great?"

"Yes, he is, but—"

"But?" He frowned slightly. "I thought you'd like the surprise."

"I do … The flowers are lovely, thank you." She put them in a vase and filled it with water, then turned to look at him.

"You don't look so happy about this," he said.

"Sidney, has it occurred to you that I may have wanted to go out with Cianán tonight, and he with me?"

He gave a little puff. "Well, if you want to go out with him instead of me, just say so. Is there something going on between you two?"

"Don't you think either one of us would have told you if there were?"

"I'm just asking." He shrugged.

"This isn't about whether I want to go out with Cianán and not you. It's you, showing up here and expecting me to change my plans to accommodate you, and being incredibly inconsiderate toward your friend as well."

"It was his idea."

"Sidney, I haven't seen you in over a month. You don't call me ahead of time to tell me anything. You just show up and I'm supposed to stand ready for you. Is that honestly how it works in your mind?"

That was how it worked in his mind, she knew that, but for some reason it was irritating her like a rash tonight.

"Why are you suddenly making a big deal out of this, Luka?"

"Because you never do." And she was tired of it not being a big deal.

"Do you want me to call Cianán to change back the plans?"

"No. That would be an inconvenience for him."

"Would you like me to leave?"

Luka shook her head. "No, I wouldn't." It was the truth. She didn't want him to leave. She wanted him to tell her he wanted to stay with her, and not come and go on a whim. It wasn't so much him, as the possibility of that existing.

Sidney put his arms around her. "I've craved you," he said and kissed her softly on the lips.

"Yes, you crave me as one craves sushi or Thai food."

"I have an exotic palate." He grinned and kissed her again.

Luka pulled away from him. It was time to go into the eye of the storm. But she knew this wasn't about getting out of it together.

She asked, "Amelia has also been on this trip, hasn't she?"

He looked at her and frowned. "I don't want it to matter to you."

"You don't want it to matter to me," she repeated and thought about it.

He wasn't denying it. He simply came from another woman to her, because now he craved her. Luka knew he came to her, more often than the others, but it was no consolation.

"Do I matter to you, Sidney?"

"Of course you do. That's why I'm here."

"Enough to have but not enough to keep."

"God, Luka ..." He ran his hands through his hair and exhaled deeply as he looked up at the ceiling. "I'm with you now, aren't I? And it's because I want to be with you. I like being with you."

"You want to be with me, but you don't want to need me. And you certainly don't want me to need you."

He didn't answer but his eyes told her, yes, and she could also see the conflict in them. Perhaps Cianán was right, and Sidney did love her. It felt as if he did, but he just couldn't say it.

Then he said, "You think you need me, but people don't really need one another, Luka. We need water and food and sleep. People confuse wanting and needing. It never fails to amaze me how they always do."

He leaned against the kitchen island with his arms folded across his chest. He wasn't going to let her inside—not ever. Luka realized that with clarity.

"Do you truly believe these things you tell yourself?" She sighed. "When your soul craves another person's soul, then you need that person. I think you're afraid of being new to the same person over and over. It's easier to make people believe you are mysterious, but once they start getting to know you, the mystery fades. That's why you go away, so that you can keep the illusion alive. You want to be like a mirage on the horizon, always out of reach.

"But that's what love is, Sidney. It's needing not only someone's body, but also their soul. And even when you know them inside out, they somehow become new to you again every time you connect. It's one of love's most wonderful mysteries."

Luka felt sadness for this man who wouldn't allow anyone to love him and who wouldn't give love. She didn't know what else to say to him, and they stood looking at each other in silence.

Finally, he took his car keys out of the pocket of his jacket, and before turning to leave, said, "Happy birthday, Luka."

He hesitated, then embraced her around the neck as he pressed his mouth hard against her forehead, holding it there for a moment.

When he let go of her, he looked into her eyes one last

time—his own eyes sad. He left, closing the door softly behind him. Walking away was easier than staying.

She sent Cianán a text:

I'm afraid there's been a change of plans again. Would you mind letting the restaurant know we won't be able to make it, please?

I'll let them know right away. Are you okay?

Not quite, but I will be. Rain check?

Rain check.

Luka thought about the times when she and Espen had disagreements, how she hated fighting with him, and how it drove her mad that he could be so stubborn. But he always came back to her and apologized when he knew he was wrong. Always. Espen was never too proud to need her.

* * *

Being the true friend he was, there were no, I told you so's, from Cianán. He simply continued as usual. But Luka didn't want Cianán to feel his loyalty was now split. He had no reason to feel guilty about his friendship with Sidney. After all, she didn't harbour ill wishes toward Sidney. She saw it for what it was, there was no point in wallowing in self-pity.

She went for coffee with Carly, who knew about what had happened between her and Sidney on her birthday.

Carly asked, "Have you spoken to him since he walked out?"

Luka shook her head. "No, he's been avoiding me. It's strange, though. I feel sad, but also not sad. He'd never been around that much for me to grow too attached I suppose."

"Well, you didn't have a conventional relationship. It was inevitable, Luka."

"I know. And he avoided talking about anything emotional,

and I was in self-denial, but that's not sustainable. Something would have had to give, and I feel relieved that I've finally spoken my mind. I'm sorry it's like that between us now—the awkwardness."

"Luka, we can't control how other people react. You had to be honest and ask yourself those questions. And now you know, and you can move on. I say, good for you."

Carly was right, of course, but nonetheless Luka missed Sidney's company and the physical closeness, even though it had only been occasional. It was a strange sense of loss—not a devastating grief, as with Espen. She wondered if Sidney felt it too.

Luka knew Cianán was right, and she needed more. She focussed on her work and on having a positive outlook about her growing independence. That was, after all, the reason she'd moved to Vancouver in the first place.

31

Luka had been home late December to visit her family for Christmas and New Year, and they'd held a belated birthday party for Marit. Bas had joined them, and Marit had beamed with joy at having both him and Luka there together.

Luka had noticed her father wasn't in high spirits, even by his usually subdued standards, and had seemed lacklustre. She'd also noticed his appetite was off.

She'd asked her mother about it. "Papa's lost quite a bit of weight, and he doesn't seem himself. Have you taken him to the doctor to have him checked out, Mama?"

Evi had replied, "Yes, of course we have. Everything's fine." She'd cleared her throat and had avoided eye contact when she'd said, "He says he's just tired. Between your oma and your father, I have my fair share of stubbornness, I'll tell you. Perhaps Papa's just getting old, Luka. He's not that far from eighty, you know. I have him on a strict regimen of high fibre, low sodium, minimum saturated fat, and no refined sugar." Evi looked over to where Ruben had stood, and said, with a sad smile, "He is allowed to indulge a little tonight, my poor sweetheart."

Luka watched her father holding a plate with a piece of cake on—moving it around with a fork. Was there something they weren't telling her?

It was true that Ruben was five years older than Evi, who herself was nearing her mid-seventies. But her mother's energy seemed to be a genetic advantage, Luka had thought as she'd stood watching her 98-year-old grandmother, laughing, and enjoying herself.

"Where on earth does that woman come from?" She'd shook her head in disbelief.

Bas, who'd been standing next to her, had said, "From a magical forest on Vancouver Island."

Luka'd smiled up at him, and said, "I've been thinking about you and the Heaven Tree."

"Me too." There'd been something in his eyes when he'd looked at her.

Stijn had a new love interest, whom Luka had met when they'd gone out for dinner in Amsterdam one evening. Bas had joined them. Her name was Beydaan, she was graceful, gorgeous, and smart as a whip. She was Somali and her family had been in the Netherlands for four generations: most were academics.

Stijn had met her at UvA, and she was also a mathematician. Stijn was head over heels in love.

Bas had told Luka, "I have a feeling Beydaan is the game changer."

Luka had to agree with him. Her darling Stijn's face was shining with happiness.

* * *

Cianán's business was growing, and they were busier than ever. He had bought an additional piece of land adjacent to the shipyard and they'd already started with the expansions. There was a list of new orders to fulfill before June and schedules were running tight. He was a nervous ball of energy, running around from one thing to the next.

Luka herself was busy with back-to-back projects and she was already longing for another break. She'd seen Sidney a couple of times during the past couple of months, since she came back from her visit to the Netherlands, but other than greeting her, he hadn't approached her to talk.

She'd caught him looking in her direction, but he obviously still felt awkward with the truth lain bare. It was his awkwardness to own, not hers. She would gladly speak to him, even be a friend to him, but the time for indulging his phobias was over.

Luka had confided in her grandmother about Sidney and his fear of intimacy when they'd sat together over a cup of coffee during her visit back home.

"I know it had been a deliberate choice to let him in, because I'd needed physical closeness, and at the time, my heart wasn't ready for more, so things were okay the way they were. But then I started needing more. I guess I just became confused. I imagined it was love."

Her grandmother had told her, "Luka, when you experience excruciating pain at the loss of someone, you know you've loved, and have been loved well. Pain and joy can never be separate, they are the two strings that make love's chord."

Sidney had not caused her excruciating pain or joy. He had been right about something though: she could have and nearly did, but she had never needed him. If nothing was what he'd wanted, he had gotten what he'd wanted after all.

When Cianán had asked her a while back how much she'd

invested in her and Sidney's relationship—or *thing*—she'd told him nothing, but then there'd been a shift in her, and now change was coming over her again, because it needed to be so.

Luka was looking through her office window at the construction outside and saw Cianán speaking to contractors. Seeing him immediately made her smile. He was an important constant in her life.

She had her work, her family, and her three male friends—one right here and the other two a mere phone call away. That was enough for now.

32

Bas's email had read: *Here's the itinerary, we'll meet up in Hanoi.*

Attached had been the flight details, the spot where they'd connect, as well as information about the resort where they would be staying on Cat Ba Island in northern Vietnam. This was one of the destinations Luka and Espen had had on their wish list.

She'd smiled when she'd seen Bas's email. He'd made all the travel plans and had booked the airline tickets so that he and Luka would arrive in Hanoi in close proximity, since they'd be flying from opposite directions. Stijn would not be joining them as they'd hoped. He and Beydaan both couldn't get away. It was September, and the new school year had already started. But he'd said he would be there in spirit.

The weather was warm and humid in Cat Ba, and although it was still busy, it wasn't too hectic. They stayed at the Monkey Island Resort, in a wooden bungalow with two double beds and splendid sea views. The resort also had its own beach. And monkeys everywhere. There was an abundance of things to explore on the island and they wasted no time.

"Did you know Ha Long Bay was named one of the new seven wonders a few years back?" Bas asked as they were kayaking through the Dark and Light, Doi and Sua Caves.

They feasted their eyes on the beauty of the limestone mountains and karsts; deep marine notches and caves caused by wave action that eroded the limestone islands.

Luka said, "Yes, I did. This place is like an amazing natural museum. Seeing this, I imagine myself in the underwater world. My eyes become light-detecting sensors, and my mind captures the images of these strange sea mazes that have been formed in the deep, and have been preserved out in the open over the past 300 million years. I am the chart maker, but I am also part of the geomorphology."

"That's a pretty cool thing to imagine," Bas said with a smile.

They spent quiet hours as they wove through and around the mythical dragons—some bald and some with grassy heads—gently dipping the oars and gliding over the surface of the salty emerald water.

The next day they rented a motorcycle and drove to Cat Ba National Park, where they hiked to the top of Hai Quan Hill, the highest point in the park.

"There are 1,600 floating islands in the Gulf of Tonkin," Luka said.

Bas nodded. "Incredible to think, isn't it?"

"The great philosopher and teacher, Anaximander, believed the world was shaped like a cylinder and that humans lived on the top part," she said as they sat looking out over the islands protruding from the sea.

"In those days, curious minds didn't have much to go on besides what they saw on their limited journeys. Yet it proves that even with finite facts and resources at our disposal, the human imagination is capable of being fantastically wild," he said.

"I've come to believe a wild imagination is actually a prerequisite for mapmaking. People look at maps and charts and they see order and direction. But it's really a mysterious fantasy world disguised as line and form," Luka said.

Bas replied, "That's what imagination is: it's just another version of reality. It's the part of reality that helps us make sense of the inexplicable."

"Perhaps that's my purpose in life," she said.

"I'm not following."

"My vivid imagination. If we're here in this life to give something back, perhaps I should see it as my way of helping people make sense of the inexplicable."

"Perhaps you should." He grinned as he thought about it.

They sat quiet for a while before she spoke again, "Espen had such a beautiful purpose. Everything he did was definitive. If I was the map, he was the compass. I wish I could always have that certainty of direction."

"His magnetic field had pulled on all of us. We were constantly influenced by the direction his needle pointed toward, whether we liked it or not."

She said, after a long pause, "Do you also feel as if he's becoming dimmer, Bas? I can't hear his voice so clearly anymore."

Bas nodded and stared far over the ocean. Luka wondered what was going through his mind. She reached out for his hand, and they sat in silence, looking at the shadows of a few clouds passing over the water below.

Inside the park was Viet Hai, the largest floating village in Vietnam. They were able to choose the shellfish they purchased, and it was cooked for them right there. The local fishermen and women travelled, sold, and lived on these floating vessels.

Luka was standing with her bowl of seafood, when an old woman approached her and started speaking to her in Vietnamese. Luka bent down to try and make out what the little figure was saying. Her face was wrinkled with age, and she had no teeth, but her eyes slanted in mirth. She was touching Luka's hair and eyes as she smiled.

A man standing by, said in English, "She says you have the sun in your hair, and the sea in your eyes. She wants to know how old you are. Please, Ms., don't be offended, it is common for Vietnamese people to ask someone's age," he explained.

Luka looked at the old woman, bowed her head and said, "Thank you for the compliment, wise Grandmother. I am thirty-four years old."

The man translated for the old woman.

"What is her name?" Luka asked the man.

"Her name is, Hung. It means brave. She is 101 years old and has lived in this village all her life. She understands deep matters of the soul and all in our village revere her."

Luka repeated the name and holding her hand on her own chest, said to the old woman, "My name is Luka. It means, bringer of light. I too have a grandmother who is almost 99 years old. When I speak to her again, I shall tell her about the honour of meeting you, esteemed Grandmother."

The man repeated what Luka'd said to the old woman. Hung gazed up at Bas, standing next to Luka. She looked deep into his eyes, then again at Luka and smiled for a while. She said something again, and the man translated, "Hung says, may your souls always journey joyfully together."

Luka and Bas thanked her and bowed their heads in respect. As they rode back to town, Luka thought about the old woman's words as she was holding on to Bas on the back of the motorcycle.

* * *

The moon was already in its first quarter, but the sky was dark enough and bejewelled with stars. Bas and Luka found their way into the resort by convincing a couple to tell the security guards they were vacationing together, since the beach was closed for public access after sunset. When they explained the reason for needing to be on the beach on this particular night, the couple happily agreed.

They found a spot on the cool sand. "Oh, it is even more spectacular than I could have imagined," Luka said with wide eyes.

"Yes, it is awesome," Bas agreed.

They were looking at the sparkling blue bioluminescent water caused by algae. "It's absolutely spellbinding. Don't you just want to dive in there and become a part of the magic? I couldn't wait to see this," she said, unable to hide the excitement in her voice.

"I know you couldn't." He watched her with a grin. Then he said, "I love the moonlight on the water also. The moon has such an interplay with everything in nature. Moonlight reveals things in a way that the sun doesn't. The line of the horizon, the movement of the water, human shapes—it's subtle. Feminine almost. Of course, I'm in favour of the moon being female." Bas smiled and leaned back, legs stretched out in front of him, and resting on his forearms.

Luka gave a little sniff. "I'm sure you are. But the moon's not female in all mythologies. I prefer the female sun and male moon of the Norse. And I have a soft spot for the sun. The sun gives us warmth and happiness. And what about the beauty of a sunrise or sunset? Moonlight does have its charm, I'll agree with you there, but it can't top the sun." She shook her head.

He looked at her and chuckled. "You're awfully defensive of the sun, where's that coming from?"

"Don't you know yet? I am a sun-defender. We are a rare kind, and we don't aim to prove we are great, just worthy. We have an armour around us that's sometimes hard to penetrate, but our energy comes from the sun, and although it's not always visible, it's sincere." She gave him a big smile.

"Your sunny face glows so pretty here in the moonlight," he said.

She shoved him. They stared at the shimmering blue surf in silence for a while. "The bloom of the algae on this beach is quite remarkable. This makes me think of when Espen and I were youngsters, and our parents took us on a trip to Toyama Bay in Japan one year, to see the firefly squid. Did he ever tell you about that?" Bas asked.

"Yes, he did. He said it was one of the most mind-blowing experiences of his life, and it convinced him he absolutely had to become a marine biologist."

"Yup. That was amazing to see. The firefly squid's biolu-minescence is nearly, if not exactly, the same colour blue as these phytoplankton."

Luka remembered something. "One year, Espen and I went to Hawaii for two weeks. It was in December and as part of collaborative research between the University of Utrecht and the University of Hawaii at Mānoa in Honolulu. Do you recall us going on that trip?"

"I do. I was super envious. December's a great time for whale watching in Hawaii."

"To your point, we went out on boats and saw the humpback whales right next to the boat. They were doing elaborate breaches and singing for us. We dived and swam with them underwater too. That was unforgettable."

Luka paused and sighed. "Espen told me about the amazing little bobtail squid with their glowing ink sacs. Only, he did it in his typical professor style, explaining how the bioluminescent *vibrio fischeri* live in symbiosis inside the squid and cause them to glow and mimic moonlight to distract predators." Bas chuckled and nodded his understanding as she continued, "Anyway, one night we went out on a shore dive, and saw a couple of those speedy swimmers. Espen was beside himself with excitement, you should have seen him.

"It's not easy to spot them—they're skittish—but a scant fellow of only about two inches, with big black eyes, swam right up to Espen's mask and hovered there, and the two of them properly stared at each other. I don't know who was more intrigued, the squid or your brother. I'll never forget the look of pure joy on Espen's face. By some stroke of luck, I was able to take a quick photo, but we're talking milliseconds."

"That's the one he kept in a frame on his desk?" Luka nodded, and Bas said, "That was a brilliant shot. Espen talked about that experience for months afterward." He reached inside his backpack, and took out two bottles of beer, opened them, and handed one to Luka.

"His passion for his work was unyielding, and his love for us was true. We were lucky to have had him in our lives."

Bas put his arm around her shoulders. "Yes, Lukie, we were lucky."

They raised their bottles and said simultaneously, "Happy birthday, Espen!"

Luka leaned her head against Bas's shoulder.

* * *

They spent the last day on the beach, swimming, and snorkelling. Luka sat on her towel with her toes in the sand, staring out over the water.

"The sun's really intense, we need to put more sunscreen on," Bas cautioned as he started smearing his torso and arms with lotion.

"Here, let me do your back," she offered. She smiled and slowly rubbed the lotion on Bas's broad, lean back. He already had a bronze glow from all the time out in the sun. His normally dark-blond hair now glittered with gold shots. He looked like something out of a myth—a beautiful Viking hero, returned from a long war, basking in the healing sunlight.

"We are passing through each other's holes, aren't we?" she asked.

He turned around and they looked into each other's eyes.

He said, "Of course we are," and she saw a flicker of something behind his eyes.

"I like that we are," she said.

"Me too. Now your turn, girl with the sun in her hair and the sea in her eyes. And four new freckles on her nose." He grinned as he put a dab of sunscreen on the tip of her nose, and she gave him an irresistibly cute little-girl smile.

She took her hair up with a band, and closed her eyes, enjoying the sensation of his big hands gliding over her back, moving over her shoulders and neck, then down again. He pressed his thumbs along her spine and the rest of his fingers were spread wide across her lower back, like he was feeling her form.

"Your hands feel wonderful," she opened her eyes when he stopped, but he held them there for a moment longer.

"Are you done with the rest of your body?" he asked. She nodded and he said, "Great, let's go for a swim to cool off a bit." He pulled her up, but she couldn't read on his face what he'd meant by the comment.

They swam a couple of metres apart. Luka kept watching him, but Bas was off in his own world, and he looked relaxed. It was good to see him like this.

After a while he turned his head in her direction, with a knowing smile and asked, "Do you have something to say?"

She hesitated slightly. "I'm not seeing that man anymore. You know, the thing … I'd had enough of not enough."

"I know."

"Do you know, because you assumed I wasn't, or did my oma tell you? She did, didn't she? So much for confiding in her," she said with an indignant frown.

He chuckled. "It was both. I'd assumed through the lines of our communications and then she'd confirmed my suspicions after your visit. I'm her sounding board, Lukie. And she loves you more than anyone, you know that." He swam up to her and said in a more serious tone, "I'm glad you're not seeing him anymore."

He pulled her to him and wrapped his arms around her. Their bodies felt good together in the water. She put her arms around his neck and her legs around his waist, straddling him so that he carried her buoyant body. Eyes locked, they didn't speak.

Luka woke up in the middle of the night and turned around to watch Bas sleep beside her. She lightly touched his face and, still asleep, he put his hand on her waist, saying, "I love you."

She fell asleep again, not sure if he'd really said it, or if it was merely a dream within a dream.

* * *

At Noi Bai International Airport in Hanoi, Bas waited with Luka at her terminal until she had to go through security. His flight to Europe departed later, and he still had plenty of time.

"Are you going to tell my oma about the old woman we'd met in Viet Hai village?" she asked.

"Of course."

"But it's my story to tell."

"You can tell her again. Don't worry, it will be a different version from mine," he said with a slight lift of his brow to emphasize his point.

"How will it be different? You were right there with me."

"We don't remember things the same way. Besides, my version will be much more interesting." He looked away, unable to keep a straight face.

"Is that's so?" she asked but thought about it. "We do remember things differently, it's true."

Luka stared at something in the distance, then back at Bas. She wanted to ask him what he thought about the old woman's words, but she didn't, because they weren't going to journey together, and she didn't feel joyful about that. Instead, she roamed his face for these last moments before they were going to part. Bas did the same with her. Neither of them spoke again until it was time for her to leave.

"Goodbye," she said, holding on to him.

He said softly, close to her ear, "Goodbye." He kissed her on both her eyelids, then on her mouth. A hard, yearning kiss.

When she'd settled in her seat, she took out her phone and saw there was a message from Bas. He'd sent a photo of her and the old woman he had not shown her previously. A beautiful human connection: her bending down, while Hung gently touched the side of her face as they looked into each other's eyes. His message said: *May our souls always journey joyfully together.*

33

When Anaximander created his map of the world in the sixth century BC, he believed the Earth was shaped like a cylinder, and humans lived on the top flat part. Perhaps he saw an advantage to sitting above it all. Sort of like the floating islands of Vietnam, only a big flat, floating Earth. That way, one could see far ahead and had a 360-degree view. Not like the real round Earth that swallowed everything up on the horizon.

Luka wanted to process what had happened between her and Bas in Vietnam. She wanted to remember what it had felt like when they'd sat on top of Hai Quan Hill, and she'd told him about Anaximander's comically shaped world.

Bas had told her that imagination helps us make sense of the inexplicable, and she'd claimed it as her purpose, but not even the keenest of imaginations could get her to escape the reality she faced up ahead.

She'd just finished getting ready for work when her phone rang. It was her mother's name on the screen. Luka felt a twitch of panic. Her mom never called during the week, especially at this hour. The first thought that came to her mind was her oma.

"Hallo Mama," she said cautiously.

Evi said, "Hallo Luka," then burst into tears, and Luka held her breath. "Luka—" She started crying again before she could finish her sentence.

"Is it Omoe?"

Evi tried to get a hold of herself. "No, it's Papa …"

Her father?

"What's wrong with Papa?" She could barely get the words out and felt nauseous. Her legs were numb, and she had to sit down on her bed.

"He's sick, Luka. He's going to the hospital on Friday. He has to have surgery."

Her mind was in a whirl. He was going to the hospital on Friday to have surgery. What for? And that was three days from now.

"Mama, why are you only telling me this now? What does he need surgery for?"

"Oh, Luka, I've wanted to tell you, but he made me promise not to. But I just couldn't bear keeping it from you any longer, it's been driving me mad. I am so scared. I can't lose him now."

Lose him? What was her mother talking about?

"What's wrong with Papa?" she asked again.

"It's colorectal cancer and it has spread to his peritoneum. That's the lining of the abdominal cavity."

"Yes, Mama, I know what the peritoneum is. I just can't believe you haven't told me this sooner." Luka took something between a breath and a gasp. Getting upset with her mother, who was clearly and understandably upset herself, wouldn't help anything. "Is he in a lot of pain? Will they able to remove everything?" The last was a desperate question she knew her mother couldn't answer.

"I know it was wrong, and I'm sorry for waiting so long to tell you, my sweetheart. Papa's in a lot of pain, yes. It's a complicated procedure. They will remove all visible tumours and administer some advanced kind of heated chemotherapy there in the operating room. I forget what it's called, my mind's a blur. But he may need more chemo after the operation."

Evi sighed heavily and added, "The doctor says the procedure has been successful for many patients and there's a good chance of survival, given there are no complications during or after surgery. That's all I can tell you for now …. Do you think there'd be a way for you to come home before he goes into theatre? I know this is asking a lot."

Luka could hear the fear and anxiety in her mother's voice, and she felt the tears welling up in her own eyes. A good chance of survival, but not a definite chance of survival. Her papa. Her dear, sweet papa. He couldn't die, he just couldn't!

She tried to pull herself together. She needed to think rationally, and she needed to put her mother's mind at ease. This wasn't the time for falling apart. She needed to be strong for her poor mother who'd been carrying this burden by herself, and for her father.

"Of course, Mama. I will speak to Cianán, but I know I can depend on him for his support. I'll see what I can do to get back home as soon as possible. Promise me you'll take deep breaths and try to calm down. Papa needs that right now, okay?"

"Okay, my love," Evi said and blew her nose.

"I'll let you know immediately when I'm able to fly out, and if anything happens, please let me know right away, even if it's in the middle of the night. And you must also try and get some rest yourself. You won't be of any use to him if you're too tired to function. We're going to take this one step at a time."

"One step at a time, yes. I feel so relieved for having told you, Luka." Evi started crying again.

"Don't worry, Mama, I'll see you soon. I love you."

"I love you too my sweetheart."

Luka sat with her elbows resting on her thighs and her palms pressed against her eyes, and she sobbed.

* * *

"Would you like me to help you with your flight arrangements?" Cianán asked as Luka sat in front of his desk. He walked around and put his hand on her shoulder.

Luka felt like she was having an out-of-body experience. Everything felt unreal.

"No, I'll manage, thank you. I don't know when I'll be able to get back, but I can finish the current projects on my laptop and just send them to you."

"You will do no such thing," he said firmly. "I don't want you to even think about anything over here. You need to be physically and emotionally present when you're home. Your mother's going to need all your support, Luka. Trust me, I speak from experience."

"Yes, of course you do. Thank you, Cianán." She squeezed his hand. "I wish I'd known sooner." She swallowed back the tears.

"What would that have changed? Don't blame your parents. Your father didn't want you to worry, and your mother's in the middle of it all. Go home and be there for them. And keep me up to speed with his progress."

"You're an amazing friend," she said.

Her mind was racing ahead. All she could think of was getting home in time.

34

Ruben was sleeping. Luka held his hand while she sat watching him. There were tubes stuck all over him and his face, hands and abdomen were swollen—a side-effect of the surgery—but the rest of his body looked gaunt.

Her mom had gone to the cafeteria for a coffee break. Evi too, had lost a lot of weight and there were dark circles under her eyes. They would have to work out a schedule to relieve one another to get some rest, Luka thought. She felt tired to the bone herself, and even though she longed for sleep, her mind couldn't shut down. No doubt her mother had the same problem.

She'd been able to get a flight the day after Evi had called her, to let her know about Ruben, and had arrived in Amsterdam on Thursday. Bas had been at the airport to pick her up. He'd hugged her hard, and had simply said, "I'm sorry about your dad." Then he'd taken her home, and had left again, saying he'd see her at the hospital on Saturday—which now was today. Ruben had been in theatre for almost ten hours on Friday and hadn't received visitors, except for herself and her mother.

Luka had thanked Bas but had no energy, mentally or physically, to begin to think about them now. Everything was her father.

The doctor had explained to them that even though the operation was a success, meaning there were no glaring issues, Ruben still wasn't out of danger, and would have to undergo further chemotherapy due to the risk of undetected cancer. He would remain in the hospital for another twelve days, and once he was home, a nurse would visit him frequently for the first few weeks. The nurse would assist him with his medications, dressings, and make sure he was doing his deep-breathing exercises and moving around enough.

Fatigue was common after such invasive surgery, and would last anywhere between two to three months, but it was equally important for Ruben to rest as well as move around. The nurse would be able to help Evi and Luka establish a routine for him and answer any questions and concerns they may have.

There'd be a follow-up visit with the doctor as well as the oncology dietitian a week after Ruben has been discharged. A high calorie diet consisting of especially dairy fat and protein was crucial for Ruben to regain his strength. There would also be follow-up lab work, and CT scans in a couple of months.

It was a lot of information to absorb, and the doctor reassured Evi and Luka that they needn't worry about any of it now, they'd receive a package explaining everything in detail before Ruben went home.

Luka looked around the white, sterile room, then back at her father. The heart monitor indicated a steady heartbeat, but watching him, it seemed as if he wasn't breathing at all. She noticed how shallow her own breathing was. She wasn't ready to let him go—this sweet man who'd given her far more than love and kindness.

"Remember how I used to sit and watch you in your work

shed, Papa?" she asked in a soft voice. "That was my favourite place in the world: sitting on the stool next to you as you made your globes from old newspapers while you taught me the most wonderful things." She stroked his hand lightly and smiled as she remembered.

* * *

"What do you see when you look at a map or a chart, Lukie?" Ruben asked as he held a globe close for his daughter to look at.

Six-year-old Luka studied it with a serious expression, then said, "I can see countries and the sea."

"What else do you see besides those things?" He turned the globe slowly.

"There are also lines."

"Good. And do you notice how there are lines that run from the top to the bottom, and lines that go all the way around?" She nodded and he asked again, "Do you remember what we call these lines?"

She thought for a moment. "The lines that go around are called horizontal lines, and the lines that go from top to bottom are vertical lines."

Ruben smiled. "Good girl. But when we talk about maps and charts, the horizontal and vertical lines are called latitude and longitude lines," he explained as he indicated with his finger. "These lines are very important, because they can tell a person the exact location of any place here on Earth, even in the ocean."

Paper mâché globes in various stages of completion, hung from the ceiling on thin wires, curved on the ends into hooks. The globes had small hooks screwed into their tops from which they hung on the wires. Others were sitting on old newspapers on the large worktable—dwarf Earths, growing bigger by the week, to become multiple football-sized Earths, painted with vibrant turquoise-blue oceans and ochre continents and islands, shiny with glaze.

Luka loved to sit and watch Ruben while he created his masterpieces. Her father's work shed, filled with objects and tools and paint, was her favourite place to be.

He continued his education as he mounted a globe on an apparatus, clamping the axis on both ends, so that it could turn but was stable.

"Maps give us information about landforms. We call that topographical information. Charts on the other hand, are used to navigate through bodies of water, and where maps are useful, charts are extremely important, because they give a detailed description about the navigational course, especially of any dangers underneath the surface, like big rocks or icebergs or dangerous currents. But both maps and charts tell the observer where they are going and how far the distance will be from their starting point to their destination."

"And a globe is a map, right Papa?" Luka asked her father.

"You are absolutely right. They give you a 360-degree view of what the Earth looks like, where continents lie, how many countries there are on each continent, and the oceans that surround these continents. Can you remember the names of the seven continents from the biggest to the smallest, like we've practised?" He looked at her with a side glance.

She started tentatively, "Asia … Africa, North America, South America …" She stopped and frowned.

Ruben helped her, "Remember that cold one on the South

Pole."

Her face lit up. "Antarctica! Europe, where we live, and Australia." Luka was pleased with herself for remembering.

"Excellent." Ruben took a drawing compass from a shelf next to him and said, "When you draw a circle on a piece of paper using a compass like this, it's important to remember that even though it looks flat, a circle is a two-dimensional shape, meaning you must look at it from above, as well as from the side. In mathematics, this is called an equation. That's a big word to understand, but it will tell you how high and wide your circle is. And even though this globe is a circle, Earth isn't shaped exactly like a circle. It's more of an ellipsoid, which means it's wider at the equator and narrower at the poles. But it's a little tricky to determine the true shape of the Earth since it keeps changing."

"But how does the Earth's shape change, Papa? It looks the same to me every day," Luka asked, baffled.

"That's the tricky part. We don't see it, because it isn't obvious, but there are different things that cause the Earth's shape to change sometimes. Like the moon pulling on the ocean tides, small shifts that take place deep in the Earth's tectonic plates, or sometimes it changes suddenly when there's a big earthquake or a volcanic eruption. Scientists can see this from data they collect—they are able to print out all sorts of information, and they also look at photographs taken of Earth from outer space."

"I like those photographs from outer space, they're pretty," she said.

"Yes, they are indeed," her father said as he started drawing a circle around the middle of the mounted globe.

"Why do you always draw that circle first?" asked Luka.

"Remember when I showed you how you can measure the degree of angles? This line is the equator—the middle of the Earth—and it starts at zero degrees. It divides the northern hemisphere, from the southern hemisphere. From here the circles that I will draw above it, as well as below it, will be indicated in degrees of thirty, sixty and ninety—with ninety being at the poles." He showed her and marked it. "When you look at a map, this will tell you how far a place is from below or above the equator, in degrees."

"And how many longitude lines will there be, Papa?" she asked, as she rested her cheek on her fist.

"The longitude lines, also called meridians, start with the prime meridian in Greenwich, England—at the British Royal Observatory—and it goes all the way from the North Pole to the South Pole. This vertical starting point is zero degrees, just like at the equator. Then there are 180 vertical longitude lines east, and 180 vertical longitude lines west of the prime meridian." Again, he showed her. "Do you know how much a 180 times two is, Lukie?" She shook her head, and he said, "It's 360, the shape of a full circle," and he drew a circle around the globe with his index finger.

Her eyes lit up in understanding, and she gave him a wide smile, revealing the gap where her two top front teeth had been.

"Who made the first map ever, Papa?" Luka asked.

"Nobody can say for certain, but it is believed that the Greek philosopher, Anaximander, created the first map of the world. But there was a man called Claudius Ptolemy who was a brilliant mathematician, music theorist (the part of music Mama would understand) astrologer, astronomer, and geographer—"

Luka interrupted, "A geographer like you, Papa."

Ruben smiled. "Yes, he was also a geographer, like me. In fact, he invented geography. Ptolemy knew the Earth was round, and he wrote a handbook about how to draw maps using latitude and longitude. He also wrote some pretty interesting things about the stars and the planets."

"The sun is Earth's star," said Luka.

"That's right. And is the moon a star?" asked Ruben, glancing down at her.

"No. The moon is Earth's satellite."

"Right again. The moon is our beautiful, bright light at night—"

"And the sun is our daylight, right Papa?" Luka interrupted again.

She loved to show her father how she remembered the things he had taught her about the Earth and the planets and stars.

Ruben nodded.

"Why don't you ever make a globe of the sun, Papa?"

"Well, my dear, it would only be a red, orange, or yellow ball. There would be nothing to paint on top of it—no countries or islands, or even the blue sea. It would be quite plain to look at. But can I tell you a secret?" he asked, and she nodded. "The sun isn't just yellow or orange or red, but a mixture of all the colours."

Luka frowned. "All the colours?"

"The colours we see at sunrise or sunset come from sunlight that passes through the atmosphere: a special layer of gases around the Earth that protects it. Then that light bounces off water vapour, dust particles, and gases, and it scatters in all directions. They are only tiny molecules, but they make big, colourful skies. In the middle of the day, when the sun is high up in the sky, light doesn't have to travel that far through the atmosphere and it causes all the colours of the spectrum to blend, but our eyes see it only as white. So, the sun can look red, orange, or yellow, even white, but really it is many different colours."

"But the sun is much, much bigger than the Earth, and it is full of fiery gases that leap out like dragons' tongues," Luka said with wide eyes as she indicated the scope of it with her arms.

"Can you remember what we call those dragon tongues?"

"Hmm … solar flares," she said triumphantly.

"Yes, and it's very dangerous to be too close to the sun, but the atmosphere luckily protects us against those harmful rays and gases. And you must never look directly into the sun, promise? It would damage your eyes—and I do love your beautiful green eyes so much." He kissed her on the nose, and she gave him another big gapped-teeth smile.

Luka knew she had the best papa in the world.

* * *

"I'm not ready to let you go. You must fight this, Papa, please. We'll help you, Mama and I."

Evi came in and put her hand on Luka's shoulder. "Go grab yourself a cup of coffee, sweetheart. It will do you a world of good. I've spoken to Omoe, and she'll be coming over with Bas in a little while."

"That's good of him to bring her. I'll go have that coffee. See you in a bit, Mama." She kissed Evi on the cheek.

Luka sat staring at the same spot when Bas spoke next to

her, "Hoi. Mind if I join you?" He sat down with a cup of coffee.

She gave a slight smile. "What would you have done if I'd said no?"

He chuckled and looked around. "I suppose I'd have had to find a new friend. How are you?"

"I'm okay. Tired. Thanks for bringing my oma."

"It's my pleasure."

They drank their coffee in silence for a few minutes, then she asked him, "Have you known he was sick?" He nodded. "You and my oma will have to start including me in your little gossip club, Bas."

"It wasn't my place to tell you, Lukie, and I think your grandmother feels the same. Your father only wanted to protect you."

"It's more painful finding out three days before his life-threatening surgery, and you can't hide something as serious as colorectal cancer. How on earth did he think he could keep it from me? Was I supposed to have found out on his death bed? And this could just be that, Bas. I can't even bear the thought." Luka felt a torrent of emotions coming over her and couldn't keep the tears at bay.

Bas got up and pulled her up against him. "Easy now. This is exhaustion and shock speaking," he said as he pressed his lips against the top of her head.

She held on to him. "I'm so scared, Bas. What if he dies?"

"I know you are but try not to think about that. He's receiving excellent care and he's stable. That's what's important right now."

She wiped her eyes and her nose with a tissue and said, "Let's go upstairs. Omoe's waiting for me." He took her hand,

and she held his in a firm grip.

* * *

"Luka, have you decided what you're going to do? I mean, about moving back home or not," Evi asked as they were having coffee at the breakfast nook.

Ruben was home and the nurse was attending to him. She'd told Evi and Luka to take a break.

Luka looked at her mother, taken by surprise. "I haven't made any decisions yet, Mama."

"Perhaps you should, my love. Papa's going to need a lot of care for a long time still, and between him and Oma, I don't know if I'll be able to cope. Physically, I could suck it up, but emotionally I'm not so sure. Forgive me if it sounds selfish." Evi looked out over the garden with sad eyes. "God knows, I'm the last one to make any demands. I've never been there for Papa or for you."

"That's not true," Luka said, and took her mother's hand in hers.

Evi turned to look at Luka again. "Yes, it is true. I was off, doing my thing for years, not really giving a second thought to you and Papa here by yourselves. He's the one who's been a parent to you, not me. But my Rubie has always been supportive of me, even when I had my drama, and it was all about what *I* wanted. The thought of him so sick is unbearable. I love your father, Luka, I do.

"And as for Oma, who is a walking miracle, who knows when her body will have had enough? There can only be so much more grace. I neglected her over the years also, especially when she needed me after Opa died. And you were the one who stood in for me. Fact is, I'm not as strong as you think I am, Luka. Please consider, if not for my sake, for Papa's."

Evi was the one with the zest for life. The bright star Luka always gazed up at in wonder and admiration. She never thought of her mother as weak, nor did she think that now. Before her sat an aging icon admitting to her own sense of failure and limitations. Evi wasn't shying away from it. She simply couldn't carry the full weight of it, and she was asking the only person she could ask, for help.

Luka knew she had an obligation. Her father was gravely ill, and on top of that, her mother felt a daughter's responsibility toward her own elderly mother. Her sweet oma tried hard not to be a burden in this time, but how could she help it that she needed care herself?

Her parents stood by her when Espen died, and they let her go so she could find her independent breath again. But she had been thinking about coming back home for some time. Her father's illness had just brought it front and centre and now she had to confront the reality of making the decision. They were her family and they needed her. And somewhere between these unravelling threads, there was also Bas.

"Don't worry, Mama. I'm there for you and Papa."

She would have to tie up her affairs in Canada fast. There'd be a lot to do, but she could do it. Her father just had to hold on.

She didn't let Evi see her fear.

35

"I need to be here for my parents, Cianán. My father has to undergo more chemotherapy because of the risk that there's still cancer left in him. He may not survive this—he's not a spring chicken anymore—but whether these are his last days, or his road to recovery, I want to be here for him. My mother has asked me to come. I simply have to. I feel as if I'm letting you down. I'm sorry."

Luka had called Cianán a day after her talk with Evi.

"Oh God, please don't feel sorry for me. I am the one who feels sorry for what you have to go through, Luka. This is an awful thing for a family. I remember when my father fell ill—it'd pulled the rug out from underneath me big time. But if there was one consolation, it was being there for my mother, and it's something I will always be glad I did. I'd be disappointed to lose your contribution here at the office, and I'll miss you, but you are right. You need to be with your family."

"And I will miss you too."

"We'll keep in touch. Where there's a will, there's a way, my dear."

Luka smiled. "Yes."

"Do you want me to take care of your things for you, or

how do you want to go about this?"

"I'll fly out to Vancouver in two weeks and settle my affairs. It will also give us a chance to do a transition of the work I've been busy with."

"You know, not to add to your sense of feeling overwhelmed, but you can still do freelance work for me. Not now, of course, but once you have your bearings together," Cianán said.

Luka thought about it. "You'd do that?"

"Absolutely. I have full confidence in your work. But let's not get into the nitty gritty now. Once you're here, we'll have a chat. I do hope things will turn for the better for your father, Luka."

"Thank you. I'll let you know when I'm in Vancouver."

* * *

Bas had asked Luka if she would like him to accompany her to Vancouver, but she'd declined, saying she'd be too busy running around and it'd be no fun for him. He'd said that was beside the point. But it was true, she'd be inundated, and he'd only feel he was in the way. He'd offered to take her to the airport, which she'd accepted. They hadn't spoken more.

Now, two weeks later, she was ready to go to Vancouver to wrap up her things. It felt like her mind was in a permanent fog.

She helped her mother with her father's care. Ruben was weak. The chemotherapy was especially hard on him and caused him to throw up, leaving him shivering, sweating and pale as a ghost. His hair was falling out and he had severe pain and discomfort all over his body. The worst of it, were his eyes, which seemed to apologize for being such a burden on them.

Luka felt utterly helpless seeing him like this, but the anguish in her mother's eyes made her more determined to get through wrapping up her affairs in Vancouver as quickly as possible.

"For how long will you be gone?" Bas asked.

They were having coffee in the living room before he took her to the airport.

"No more than two weeks. I've already given my rental notice to my landlord a couple of weeks ago. I really want to get back here."

Bas nodded. He didn't ask how Ruben was doing. He'd said a quick, hallo, but Ruben wasn't having a good day. Luka wished she didn't have to leave now. Evi's face was taut with worry and her eyes were sunken. The tension was taking its toll on her.

"I'll be back before you know it, Mama. The nurse will be here to help you in the meantime, and I'll call you every day, okay."

"Yes, of course, my love. I hope you get everything done in time—two weeks isn't much," Evi said with concern.

"Don't worry, it will be fine," Luka said, and they embraced.

She kissed her father on the forehead and said, "See you soon, Papa."

"See you soon, Lukie. Don't you go worrying about me now," Ruben said, giving her hand a weak squeeze.

Bas didn't try to make conversation on the way to the airport. He could see Luka wasn't in the mindset to talk.

When she'd checked her luggage, he said, "Hang in there. I'll be here when you get back."

"Thank you, Sebastian." She kissed him and he held her

tight. When she pulled away, she said, "I'll just imagine I'm back in Cat Ba. Time flies when you're having fun."

"Then I'll be waiting for you there," he said with a grin.

* * *

The last of her personal belongings were packed. There wasn't that much. Luka'd decided to sell her furniture and household things, instead of shipping them back to Amsterdam. It wasn't worth the cost, and she was going to live with her parents again, anyway.

She'd advertised on Craig's List, and it had surprised her how quickly everything had sold. The last was her bed, which the buyer had come to pick up half an hour ago. She'd washed the bedsheets and duvet, and put them with the pillows, in bags to donate to charity.

Luka looked through the window with her hands on her hips. This had been her home for nearly two and a half years. It felt like a strange time warp.

She'd called Cianán earlier and confirmed when he'd pick her up. He was already on his way now. She was going to sleep over at his house and tomorrow he would take her to the airport. There were no words for her to express her gratitude for his help and support, but she'd told him she would make it up to him. He'd said he'd hold her to her promise.

Her doorbell rang. Sidney was standing there.

"Hallo," she said, surprised and unsure.

"Good day." She stood looking at him and he asked, "Mind if I come in?"

"Yes, of course. There's nothing to sit on, I'm afraid."

"Don't worry. I won't take up much of your time." He gazed

around at the empty space, then turned to face her. "Were you going to leave without saying goodbye?" She lifted her brow. "Bad joke. I'm sorry about your father, Luka," he said sincerely.

"Thank you."

There was an awkward silence.

He said, "I suppose the saying, sorry often comes too late, is true after all … I'm sorry for how I've handled things between us, Luka. Emotions aren't my strong suit, but in the end it's no excuse." He turned to look through the window. "Thing is, you did matter to me, quite a lot. You still do, but what's done is done now. You are leaving and I have only my wasted chances to contemplate." He looked her straight in the eye. "I hope things will work out for you. And I really hope your father will get better. I'll always remember our conversations, and other things …" He smiled.

Luka didn't know what to say to him. It must have been hard to muster up the courage to come tell her this, but he was right; it wasn't going to change anything between them.

"Thank you, Sidney," she said with a wan smile.

"Cianán's picking you up?"

"Yes, he'll be here soon."

"Then I'll get out of your way. Take care, beautiful lady." He gave her a hug and a kiss on the cheek.

"Take care, Sidney. Thank you for stopping by."

Luka watched through the window as he drove off.

A little while later Cianán's car pulled up. He saw her standing by the window and gave her a quick wave and his cheerful smile.

She thought as she opened the door for him, not everything was worth holding on to, but some things were.

Luka hung the suncatcher in Ruben and Evi's bedroom window.

"I haven't seen that in a while," Ruben said. He was sitting upright in bed, having a compulsory big lunch.

His spirits were up. It had been a few weeks now since his last chemo cycle, but Luka suspected it had something to do with her being back permanently as well.

Evi was sitting next to him on the edge of the bed, having a cup of coffee. "Is that the one Papa bought you when you were a little girl?" she asked.

"Yes. This little spreader of joy did some big-time travelling. I gave it to Espen years ago, when he moved to Utrecht, then it came back to me again. Now it's made its journey from Vancouver back to Amsterdam."

"How wonderful," Evi said with a big smile.

"This is just a loan, Papa, to bring some sun-joy in the room until you're better." Luka smiled and said, "I have a cute story for you. It's by the Tsimshian people of the Pacific Northwest."

Ruben grinned and said, "Let's hear it then."

"The legend goes that there was a chief with two sons. The younger son's name was, One Who Walks All Over The Sky. The older son's name was, Walking About Early.

"The younger son looked up and was saddened by how dark the sky was. So, he decided to make a wooden mask and soaked it in tar and set it alight. From then on, he travelled across the sky as the blazing sun. At night he slept at the edge of the horizon and as he slept, his snores caused embers to fly off his mask, thereby making the stars.

"When his older brother saw this, he became jealous, for he could see how pleased their father was. So he came up with a counter plan: he smeared his face with fat and soot and made his path across the dark sky, and from that day on, he became the moon. And that is how there is day and night."

"Delightful. If only my snores would become sparks that made the stars to distract your poor mother who has to suffer through them," Ruben said and chuckled.

"You don't snore that bad, Rubie," Evi said and mock slapped his leg.

"That part of the world must surely be a paradise," Ruben said, shaking his head as he thought about it.

"That's why British Columbia is called supernatural, Papa." Luka sat down at the foot of the bed.

"Bas had told Omoe how wonderful it had been to see at least some of it," Evi said.

"At least some of it, yes. I lived there a couple of years and had not even scratched the surface."

Luka saw Bas's grey-blue eyes etched against the green of the forest at the base of the Heaven Tree. She could almost feel the hot imprint of his hand holding on to hers. She longed for him.

"How is Bas doing? We've missed having the boy around," said Ruben.

"He says he's doing well. I haven't had a chance to meet up

with him since I got back. I'll give him a call later." Luka made it sound matter-of-factly. She didn't want to let them see just how much she was looking forward to that.

She wondered if her parents knew about her and Bas. What exactly did Bas and her grandmother share? He'd said he was her oma's sounding board, but was that true for Marit as well?

The Feltes-De Cleene club needed another member as the go-between censor. There was much too much discussion of her going on.

* * *

Bas had told her to bring an overnight bag. Luka'd agreed but she was still apprehensive for a couple of reasons. Number one: her father. She felt guilty leaving both her mom and dad while she went out and had a good time.

She'd told Evi and Ruben that Bas had invited her to visit and had suggested that she stay over—she didn't disclose the full nature of it—but she wasn't sure if it was the right thing under the circumstances. Her parents thought the reason for her not wanting to go, the most ridiculous thing they'd heard.

Luka'd said, "Surely not *the* most ridiculous thing. Aren't you both being a little overdramatic about it? You make it sound as if I never go out and that this could be my last chance."

"Who's being overdramatic now?" Evi had rolled her eyes.

"Luka, stop arguing, and just go. Your mother and I will be fine. Your absence for the evening won't cause a medical emergency, my love," Ruben had said.

Secondly—and this was the underlying reason for her apprehension—she was nervous about going to the flat.

Except for the day she'd gone there to speak to Bas, after the funeral, she hadn't been inside since Espen had still been alive.

But this time, she'd be going to Bas. They'd be in his room.

* * *

Luka hesitated before knocking. She took a breath when Bas opened the door.

"Hoi," he said and embraced her.

"Hoi." She took a tentative step inside and couldn't hide her surprise. "You've remodelled."

"Yes, a few years ago. I was afraid too," he said, and she turned her head and looked at him. He had a mysterious smile.

How did he know she'd been afraid? Maybe being clairvoyant was a family trait. Espen used to know everything.

"It looks fresh and modern. I like it."

"It had been due for a remodel, so it worked out well," he replied.

Bas's gaze followed Luka as she walked through and stopped at what was now the guest room. It looked and felt completely different. She turned around and smiled at him, relieved.

"Do you feel like going out for dinner, or shall we grab some take-out and bring it back?" he asked.

"Let's do take-out and have it here."

They walked to an Italian restaurant two blocks away and bought two vegetarian pizzas and stopped at a bakery for chocolate cake—her favourite dessert.

Luka enjoyed being back in Amsterdam. When she'd come home for her father's operation, there hadn't been any time or thought of going out. She'd barely seen Bas.

It had now been a month since she'd moved back permanently. The cool December evening nipped lightly at her fingers as they walked back to the flat, and Bas put his arm around her.

He opened a bottle of red wine while Luka sliced the pizza.

She asked, "Where do you keep the plates now? I'm lost in this fancy kitchen."

He took out two plates from a cupboard behind him and set them on the table.

She smiled when she saw the picture Stijn took from the night she went out with him and Bas for her thirtieth birthday, and she was making her birthday wish with her eyes closed tightly and in full concentration. She looked like a little girl. They named it the trophy shot. It had been up since then, but Bas had changed the frame, and it now hung in a different spot in the new kitchen.

"That was my most fun evening with you two," Luka said.

"I've always wanted to ask you, what was it you so feverishly wished for?"

"Well, it's been a couple of years, and I think it's safe to let the secret out now: I wished that the three of us would always be best friends," she said with a wide smile.

He had a tender look in his eyes. "And so we are. But we have some catching up to do. Luckily Beydaan is tons of fun. We should do something with them soon."

"Stijn is happy with her, isn't he?"

"I've never seen him happier."

Bas handed her a glass of wine. "Proost. It's good to have you here, Lukie." He held his glass against hers and looked into her eyes.

"Proost."

"How's your dad doing?" he asked as they sat down.

"He's had a good week so far, but the next chemo cycle is coming up, and I think he just wants to enjoy not thinking about it right now. He and my mom have been goofing around. It's nice to hear them laughing again."

"Why don't you try to do the same tonight? Don't think, just enjoy."

Luka took a bite of her pizza and said, "The only thing to top pizza and red wine, would be a bubble bath with candles to soak in and enjoy my dessert."

Bas grinned, "I can think of another thing."

After their meal, he poured them more wine. "Let's go sit in the living room. Get comfy, put your feet up."

"This is comfy. Is this … Oude Oom?" She asked in shocked surprise as she ran her hand over the soft, polished leather.

"It's the old man himself. He's had extensive reconstructive surgery."

"He looks and feels amazing!" Luka stood up to have a proper look and sat down again.

"Ironically, it had cost more to have him restored, than two new sofas would have cost me. But I couldn't find it in my heart to part with him. Too many memories."

Luka nodded. "I'm so happy you've kept him. You must have spent quite a bit on your remodelling and refurnishing. Are you sure it's okay to put my feet up?" she asked, although she'd already done so.

Bas indicated with his hand as he said, "Go right ahead. Yes, I had to spend some, but it was worth it. Most of the furniture, as you know, was here from when my parents bought the flat ages ago. This place was due for a deep recycle." He searched for music to listen to. "Do you have a preference?"

"Whatever you feel like." She took a long sip of wine.

He dimmed the lights, came and sat next to her, and lit a reefer he'd produced from somewhere. He inhaled and exhaled slowly, then offered it to her, and she too took a drag, and rested her head back.

It was relaxing just to sit and watch Bas. She couldn't help but think how Espen's energy had been explosive and captivating, and his love had been the same. But Bas's energy was slow and hypnotic, and his love was the same.

He put her feet on his lap and massaged them while she held the joint, passing it to him intermittently. It felt so good, her neck and scalp tingled.

"John Martyn. I haven't heard him in a while," she said, listening to the voice singing in the background.

"Me neither. I like his vibe, though. My parents used to love listening to him when they were younger. It always makes me think of them." He smiled. "It's good to remember sometimes that your parents were young too. When I look at photos of them from back then—boy, they were so good-looking—I become curious about the things they hoped for, and whether they feel they achieved that. And as I measure their overall acceptance to my own life, it makes me want to sulk less about inevitable outcomes." He took a slow pull on the joint again. "John Martyn is a classic, no doubt."

She studied his face. "I can't imagine you sulking about anything. You're the most laid-back person I know, besides Stijn and your father." He chuckled. "How are your parents, Bas?" she asked.

"They're doing well. My mom wants my dad to be more social, so she's organizing events and dragging him along.

36

You know my dad; he's never been big on crowds. I guess I get it from him. They're getting on in years, though. They've had a few rough miles in between."

"Yes, all our parents are getting older. I want to go see them as soon as my dad's next chemo cycle is done."

"They'd like that."

They sat with their heads resting back for a while, listening to the music.

Luka said with a sigh, "Don't you wish we could transport ourselves to Cat Ba right now? How amazing would that be?"

"We can mentally transport ourselves there."

She said with a devious little smile as she poked him in the navel with her big toe, "I won't be able to focus my mind, you're too distracting."

He grabbed her foot. "Let's go take that bubble bath."

"Wait—you have bubble bath?"

"I have candles too." He stubbed out the joint but took it with him. "We'll need this and our wine."

"Don't forget the dessert." She went to the kitchen to get it.

In the tub, Luka covered her breasts with bubbles, and Bas piled more bubbles on them.

"There, temptation hidden from view," he said, and she laughed, causing half of the bubbles to slide down again.

He'd kept the door of the bathroom open so they could continue listening to the music.

"I want to have this kind of bath at least once a week. That way, the relaxation won't have time to wear off," she said, and he nodded as he rested his head against the wall.

Bas'd lit the joint again and was careful not to get it wet before holding it for her to take a drag.

With her own head resting back, she watched him for

a while, then asked, "When did you realize you loved me, Sebastian?"

Thin strands of hair that had become wet clung to the sides of her face and neck. He leaned forward and brushed them away with his fingers, studying her. Luka liked the way he looked at her—lingering, gaze roaming slowly over her face and body. She gently traced his lips with her fingers. He had a sensual mouth.

He kissed her fingers and said, "Long ago."

"What do you mean, long ago?"

"I don't know, perhaps it just feels like long ago."

Luka wondered if it was her imagination that he'd sounded hesitant. Either that or the weed mixed with wine was muddling her perceptions.

She said, "For me, I think it was when we were on Vancouver Island. I've always loved you, but it felt different then. You felt different. I thought I'd heard you say it, that last night on Cat Ba. Did you?"

He nodded. "I'll say it again. I love you." He kissed her.

"I love you too."

They sat back, smoked the last of the weed, sipped on their wine, and ate their dessert. She smacked her lips when he offered her his last bite, grinning at her enjoyment.

Luka washed Bas's body with bubbles, ending by making him a bubble mustache and beard. Then he did the same for her.

"I'm feeling so mellow, I could just stay in here all night," she said with bubbles sliding down her face and neck.

He said with a sly smile, "The bedsheets are silky, although I can't claim that they are genuine silk sheets. But I think you'll like them even better than the bathtub."

He wiped the bubbles off her pink bottom as she stood up. She giggled. "I say, let's give them a try."

37

The last of Ruben's chemotherapy had been at the end of April, and he'd responded favourably to the treatment, although not without some side effects. The scans were showing no signs of cancer and the doctor felt positive about his long-term recovery. It would take a while for his body to bounce back from the damaging effects of the chemo—his lungs were particularly affected—but Ruben's hair was growing again, and he was laughing more.

Evi's mood was also improved, and she sat and played romantic sonatas for Ruben on the piano while he read the newspaper in the mornings, and in the afternoons, they went for walks in the neighbourhood.

Luka had started doing freelance work. Some of the work required that she worked from an office, but most of it she could do from home. Once she'd reconnected with Frits Epperson, who was elated to use her services again, business had picked up quickly, especially with the work Cianán sent her way as well. With her father now out of danger, she was also spending more time with Bas during the week and over weekends, and he'd asked her to consider moving in with him.

Luka found her father in his work shed, setting up his globes.

"Hoi," she said, pausing in the doorway.

"Ah, Luka, hold this for me please," Ruben said standing on a step ladder, trying to adjust the wire hanging from the ceiling while holding a globe in one hand. He held out the globe to her.

She'd brought coffee for them and put the cups down on the worktable.

Holding the globe in both hands above her head she said, "It feels as if I'm about to make a sacrificial offering."

Ruben looked down at her, and they both chuckled.

"Let me have my offering," he said and took if from her.

His body was shaking a little as he struggled to hang it on the hook in the ceiling. Luka imagined that it must be taking an enormous effort for him to perform the task.

"It annoys me so. These eyes are useless, even with the glasses on. And your mother isn't a helpful assistant either. Her eyes are still clear, but her hands are no good to hold anything steady. A fine pair we are," he said, and she helped him dismount.

"You shouldn't be climbing the ladder when you're all by yourself, Papa. What if you fall and there's no one to help you? You must put a wire up from wall to wall at a level where you can easily hang the globes."

"Yes, yes. I know, my love. The body is weak, but the mind is as stubborn as a badger fighting a lion. I'll keep that good idea in mind though."

Luka looked up at the globe. His work was still excellent. "It looks beautiful, Papa."

He put his hands on his hips and sighed as he examined his handiwork. "Not too bad."

He turned to her and asked, "Did you want to talk about

something?"

Either the men in her life had the supernatural ability of knowing everything, or she was indeed as transparent as Espen's Krystallinsk. But was she only transparent to the people she loved, or could strangers also see through her? That would be ironic for someone who was reserved with her emotions, and not a comforting idea at all.

"I do want to talk to you, yes."

Ruben sat down on a stool, and she handed him his coffee, sitting down next to him. He took a careful sip. His taste had not been fully restored from the chemo. He'd battled with painful mouth and throat sores throughout the treatment.

"Good," he said, satisfied. "What's on your mind, Lukie?"

"Bas has asked me to move in with him."

"That seems about right. Were you concerned what I would think?" He looked at her in surprise. "You've taken care of me long enough. It's time for you to go your own way now, and if it's with Bas, then you have my sincerest blessing. You know your mother and I love the boy." He squeezed her hand.

"I know you love Bas. As Omoe would say, who on earth doesn't?" She gave a little laugh and said, "You're my father, and I worry about you, that's all."

"It's a father's prerogative to worry about his only, and dearest daughter. Luka, we've both been through pretty stormy seas these last few years. The cancer nearly had me, but I wake up in the morning and I stretch out my hand in front of me, opening and closing my fist, and then I look down at my feet as I get out of bed. There they are, grounded and ready to carry this battered body around. Such a small, seemingly insignificant act, and yet it is everything. I think, by some kind of grace, I am alive. What a gift this life is. We must take nothing for granted, not waste a second in embracing life fully."

Luka sat watching her father as he looked around his workshop. She was a little girl again, listening to her wise teacher.

Ruben continued, "When I'm making my globes, my mind is filled with the stories about the early people who sailed across the blue waters that cover seventy-five percent of the surface of this earth we inhabit. The human story never ceases to fascinate me.

"Nowadays we have fantastic knowledge at our disposal, and it's right at our fingertips—we merely have to type a word, and a world opens up before our eyes on a computer screen. The ancient people had to discover everything for themselves, and they were incredibly resourceful and clever. But the thing I admire most about them was how much attention they paid to their surroundings and how they lived completely in the moment.

"Take the Polynesians whom you like so much for their sun myths: they navigated thousands of kilometres of the Pacific Sea and were able to do that because they were familiar with the constellations of both hemispheres—that's nothing less than astounding. They recognized landforms, plants, and animals native to distant islands and could read weather patterns almost more accurately than computers today. That speaks of intuition and acute awareness.

"Perhaps if we also live our lives, aware, new constellations will open up for us in our minds, and we will be able to embrace far beyond our eyes' ability to see. Perhaps we will appreciate more." He leaned forward so that their foreheads touched for a moment. "I love you, my Lukie. Be happy."

"I love you, Papa." Luka gave him a kiss on the cheek, and they sat talking, and drinking their coffee.

* * *

"Luka, Stijn tells me you and Bas don't live that far from him and Beydaan," Marit said.

She held her cup and saucer under her chin while she drank her coffee. It was a habit.

As Luka sat looking back at Marit in exactly the same way, she wondered if her own habit was from years of visits at her grandmother's, or if the two of them were just that similar. Thirty-five, and a few months shy of one hundred—but so alike in mannerisms, it was scary.

"Omoe, let me get this straight: you've been sharing confidential information with Bas for years—mostly about me—and now you're doing the same with Stijn. Both are *my* best friends." Luka had a skeptical look.

"Well, Bas is technically no longer your friend, Luka. I thought you'd be happy to know I don't share secrets with him anymore." Marit shrugged and said innocently, as she stared into her coffee cup, "Not that much anyway."

Luka had no doubt she still did. And now she'd added another conspirator to her club. But there wasn't much sense in grilling the loveable old traitor. Besides feeling left out and slightly envious, Luka was happy that her grandmother had something to look forward to in her life.

Marit Feltes didn't stand for anything remotely suggesting that she'd given up on fun. What better way, than having it come to her in the form of young male visitors? It was surely much more exciting than listening to old people comparing all the things that were wrong with them.

"Yes, Omoe, Bas, and Beydaan are close to us. They're in Nieuwe Pijp, though, and we're in Oude Pijp."

"I remember, yes. Bas had spent quite a bit on the remodelling, he said."

"He did. It looks great. If you want, we can come and get you and you can visit with us."

Marit said vaguely, "Yes, we'll see, my sweet."

Luka'd said it to be polite, but the truth was, Marit didn't go out that much anymore. Her eyesight was still fine for short distances, but far-away objects were blurry and made her feel dizzy. Driving in a car wasn't great for her, so she kept it to a minimum.

She was also repeating herself lately and no one could bear to tell her when she'd already said something. Aside from a few memory lapses here and there (and after all, who didn't have them?) her brain was remarkably clear. Luka felt sorry for her grandmother. She just couldn't help being so curious about what was going on in the young people's lives.

But part of the reason for her visit, was that Luka wanted to talk to her grandmother about something Bas had said the evening they were smoking and drinking in the bathtub. She suspected Marit would be able to fill in the gaps for her.

"I feel so lucky that Bas and I have become more than friends. I do love him," Luka began at an angle.

"Yes, it's wonderful how life works sometimes, my dearest."

"He'd mentioned something a while back that's been puzzling me, though. When I asked him how long he'd known he loved me, he said, a long time. I wonder what he meant by that. Do you have an idea, Omoe?"

Marit looked out the window and said in a sympathetic

voice, "It couldn't have been easy for Bas, all those years, Luka."

She did know something.

"All those years?"

"You and Espen had such a great love, and Bas loved his brother also. He had to keep his feelings to himself, the poor dear."

"Did he tell you this, Omoe?" Luka knew Bas must have told her grandmother, or how else would she have known? But she couldn't help feeling shocked. Bas had been in love with her when she and Espen had been together, and she was never aware of it.

"What else could he do? It's not as if he could simply turn off his feelings at will, Luka," Marit said and shook her head. She then said, "I thought you knew by now, my child. I think it's wonderful that you've found your way to each other after what you both had been through. That's all that matters in the end."

Luka sat back in the chair. She didn't have any idea how to respond to this unexpected news.

38

Stijn and Beydaan were living together in a trendy flat he'd bought only a few blocks from Bas's flat. Bas and Luka were over for dinner, and they were having wine.

Luka curiously studied a mug with *World's Best Professor*, written on it, after pouring herself a glass of filtered water from the fridge in the ultra-modern, open-plan kitchen.

"Who has earned the high honour, professors?" she asked both Stijn and Beydaan as she held the mug up.

"That would be Stijn," Beydaan said. "His students gave it to him at the end of the school year. They've also printed and framed an authentic-looking certificate that states the same. That one's in his office and has produced quite a few frowns from some of our older colleagues." They all chuckled.

Beydaan added, "The young people love Stijn because he's a natural teacher and he's nonintimidating. I think he's a great role model and example of how being an academic, doesn't mean you need to be stuck up, boring, and walking around with a huge chip on your shoulder. I'm proud of my best professor in the world." She put her arms around Stijn's waist and gave him a kiss.

"Hmm, I've never thought of myself as a role model. I suppose I am," Stijn said, thinking about it.

"Yes, and you've got the mug and certificate to prove it," said Bas with a grin.

"It takes a special kind of person to teach. It's one of the hardest jobs in the world," Luka said.

"Yes, you certainly need strength and guts at times, or as we Dutch like to say, it takes hair on your teeth. Stijn told me your father had also taught at UvA, Luka," Beydaan said.

"Yes, he was a geography professor for many years, and a natural teacher. I had the privilege of being his student once. That's besides having been his student for my whole childhood," Luka said with a smile.

"Luka has a fantastic imagination. I think much of it can be attributed to Ruben's influence," Bas said.

Luka nodded, "Absolutely. My father used to tell me tremendous stories and legends when I was a little girl, that may have helped shape my imaginary world."

"What kind of legends?" asked Beydaan.

"Suncatcher myths, mostly. You know, like the Polynesian legends, and some interesting North American legends of how the sun had been deliberately caught, and then set free again."

"There was something about that sun appearing and disappearing, that must have intrigued those ancient peoples," Beydaan said and shook her head. "I find it fascinating that their lack of knowledge, drove them to the only logical conclusion, namely that the sun had to be held in one place, where they could see it and control it."

"Exactly. It provided a concept of order. By nature, the human mind and soul needs something solid to focus on, and the idea of catching the sun so that it wouldn't disappear, was a way of making sense of something they didn't understand.

Bas told me something cool: imagination is just another form of reality and helps us make sense of the inexplicable." Luka said.

Beydaan said, looking at Bas, "I love that."

"Tell us one of those stories, Luka," said Stijn with a smile.

"Tell them the one about the little beaver, that's a neat story," Bas said.

Luka looked at him in surprise. "Have I told you that? I'm certain I haven't."

"You told it to Espen, when you were in Ameland."

"Yes, that's also what I recall." She hesitated a moment, but when she saw them, all looking at her in anticipation, she began, "The legend goes that the god, Weese-ke-jak ensnared the sun, but soon realized that everything was at risk of burning to ashes …"

When she'd finished telling the story, Stijn and Beydaan clapped. Luka looked at Bas, then averted her eyes when she saw the slight frown on his face.

Stijn said, "The little guy saves the day. That's a great story."

"It remains one of my favourites," Luka said.

Beydaan said, "Luka, I think you're lucky that your father has bestowed such a wonderful gift to you, the gift of imagination. Einstein said, 'Logic will get you from A to Z; imagination will get you anywhere.'"

"My father's an amazing man. I do feel fortunate that he raised me like that," Luka said.

Stijn asked, "How's he doing now, Luka?"

"He's doing well. He still tires easily and has problems with his breathing that stems from the chemo, but that's getting better. He'll have to go for regular screenings every couple of months, and he'll always need to keep a close watch from here on, but all-in-all, everything's looking good. He's eating healthily, and he and my mom go for walks almost every day. His will to live is strong."

"That must be a great relief to you and your mother," Beydaan said.

"Yes, it is. If there's one thing I'm truly sorry about, it's that my parents never had an opportunity to visit me in Vancouver. I really wanted them to see that part of the world. It's so pristine and, my father in particular, would have loved the geography of the Pacific Northwest."

"Perhaps when he's well enough, he and your mom can still do that," Beydaan said."

"Perhaps they could, I'll nudge them on the idea. It's a great motivator," Luka said.

"I'm sorry I never got around to visiting you, Luka," Stijn said. "And to think, we had such high ambitions too." They both smiled. "Maybe you and I should go there on our next trip," he said to Beydaan, who was keen on the idea.

"You shouldn't miss out on an opportunity to do so. That's a phenomenal place." Bas agreed.

* * *

"What was that all about earlier?" Bas asked when they were walking back to the flat.

"What was what all about?" Luka feigned ignorance.

"You know what I'm talking about. Why did you look at me that way when I mentioned the story about the beaver?"

"I was just surprised that Espen had told you about it."

"Espen and I shared a lot of things, Lukie. He talked about you a lot, in case you didn't know. Does it bother you that he told me the story?"

"No … I just thought it was something between me and Espen. I didn't think he'd tell you, or anyone else."

Bas thought about it for a moment. "I see. This isn't so much about the story, as me, crowding your memory. Is that it?"

Luka was quiet. Her behaviour wasn't fair toward him. He hadn't invaded her privacy. Espen had freely shared a moment with his brother, and Bas, as usual, was spot on. But she couldn't get what her grandmother had told her, out of her head.

"What's really going on here, Lukic?" he asked.

They stopped on the sidewalk outside their building. She didn't look at him, but at the patterns of light and dark on the stretch of sidewalk in their block where the streetlights illuminated spots and in other places, the trees cast dark shadows. She tried to count how many light and dark patches there were but felt Bas's eyes on her.

She looked up at him. "When did you know you were in love with me, Bas?"

"It feels like you already know the answer."

"It's a question I'd like an honest answer to, not a vague one, please."

He hesitated for a moment and said, "Okay. Since the beginning. That day we met in the bookstore. There you were, beautiful and amazing, and holding the book I was looking for." He smiled at the memory. "I've loved you since then."

She had a vivid image of him standing there next to her in the bookstore. He was so handsome and sweet. "Why didn't you tell me?"

"When did you expect me to reveal that? What was I supposed to have said? How about, hey, Espen and Luka, congratulations on having one of history's greatest love stories, and by the way, I'm also in love with you, Luka?" He gave an ironic little laugh. "You gave me your phone number to give to Espen, remember? And I knew there wasn't a chance in hell that he would have said no; that he wouldn't have fallen over his feet to call you.

"He never forgot you after that day at the market; did you know that? When he saw your name on the note, he went nuts. And that was how he felt about you until the day he died. I would never have betrayed my brother, Luka, as much as I loved you, and God knows, I did, and still do."

"What about the fact that I feel betrayed? It makes me feel awful to know that you were carrying around something like that without telling me."

"I'm sorry if you feel betrayed, but I don't expect you to feel sorry for me, Lukie. It was my burden, not yours."

"Did Espen know?"

Bas blew out a long breath. "What will we achieve by talking about this? Can't we just let it go, please?"

"He knew. And here I was, feeling upset that he shared something private between him and me, with you. Meantime you were sharing much more than stories. Everybody seems to have these little cliques where they talk about me, but they withhold it from me. Why is that? Do you think I can't handle hearing the truth? What else is there I should know of Bas?"

She was overreacting, but she couldn't understand the reason behind her stupid behaviour.

"I'm not hiding anything else from you, and neither is everyone else, whoever that may be. Espen suspected I had feelings for you, but I never talked to him about it. He knew me well, but he also knew it wasn't an issue." Bas looked at her with pleading eyes. "I want you to be a part of my life—physically as well as emotionally. I love you, but I can't compete with your ghost, Lukie. I just don't have the heart to."

She closed her eyes momentarily. Espen was gone forever. What did it matter now whether he knew Bas was in love with her? She never knew, and that didn't matter now either. Bas was here, and he still loved her, and she loved him—that mattered.

"I'm sorry. I don't want you to feel as if you have to, Bas. I don't know why I'm acting this way; why I'm so upset."

"You're afraid you will lose the memories of you and Espen. Those are your memories. They will always be your memories. And I won't try to duplicate what you two had. I only want us to have our own amazing love." He pulled her to him, holding her tight.

"Our love is amazing, Sebastian."

He kissed her, then said, against her lips, "I like it when you call me by my full name, it makes me sound smart. You should do it more often; I might start believing it's true."

She chuckled. "Come, let's go upstairs."

* * *

Luka lay on her back and looked at the soft-blue walls and moved her arms and legs around on the bed.

"These sheets do feel silky. I like our cool blue room—it's peaceful; almost transcendent." She turned onto her side to look at Bas. "And I love our life together, I truly do."

He pulled her up against him so that her head rested on his shoulder, and he ran his hand down her shoulder and arm. "Me too."

"I want to tell you something about that beaver story," she said.

"Okay."

"When I told the story to Espen, I thought of him as the brave little beaver, because he was always trying so hard to do the right thing. But later, after his death, I came to think of him as the sun instead, who couldn't be bound but had to be set free. I still like to think of him out there. I think that he's free to shine and move and fill us with his energy."

Bas lay looking up at the ceiling, thinking and nodding his head. "And you, who are you in that story?"

She looked at him, surprised at the question. "I don't know. I haven't thought of myself as a character in it. I'm definitely not the god, Weese-ke-jak."

He chuckled and spoke with his lips against her temple. "No, not Weese-ke-jak. *You* are the brave little beaver, Lukie. The generous, humble one who makes way for others to shine."

She thought about it for a while and sighed, then hugged him tight. "It's ridiculous how much I love you, Sebastian."

39

Cianán met up with Luka at the Van Gogh Museum. He was staying at a hotel close by.

"Look at you, a glowing ball of sunshine. A woman in love, is a sight to behold." He looked her over at arm's length, smiled and gave her a hug.

"Hallo, dear friend. It's good to see you. Are you excited about meeting her in person?"

Luka was referring to her grandmother. Cianán had come to visit Luka, but they were also going to celebrate Marit's hundredth birthday on Saturday evening at a special venue.

"Yes, oh yes. I asked her if there was anything special I could bring her from Vancouver, and she said a Canucks hockey shirt." He laughed in his merry way.

Cianán had also been part of the Marit fan club for a while now. All three of Luka's male friends—she still regarded Bas as part of that category—were close with her grandmother.

Although Marit didn't bake anymore, she had taught her kindly live-in caregiver how to bake the traditional, favourite cookies just the way she'd perfected them over the years with her own special touches here and there, and she supervised the process. For Marit's adopted grandsons, it meant that there was always something sweet to have with their coffee when they visited (Cianán received his share in the mail). Luka thought how much joy and validation it gave her oma.

Cianán paid for their tickets at the entrance to the museum and as they walked through the well-lit foyer, he stared up and around at the glass structure—an architectural wonder with a high, curved, glass ceiling—and then outside over Museumplein.

"This is a marvellous place. I've been here ages ago, before this new glass structure was built. It really creates a lovely mood when you walk in," he said.

Luka nodded. "Museumplein has also been upgraded, and all the other cultural institutions now face the square."

The exhibitions started chronologically on the ground level and moved up to the third floor. Luka'd suggested that they come early before it started getting crowded. They walked through rooms with grey, blue, beige, and teal walls that accentuated the path of Vincent van Gogh's creative processes.

"The piercing introspection of his self-portraits makes you stare, as if unable to tear away your gaze. It's like you become entranced by Van Gogh's moods." Cianán said as he paused, studying one of the artist's self-portraits.

"Vincent was the ultimate suncatcher. He always moved around from place to place so he could be close to sunshine, and then he'd capture it on his canvas—bold and bright—but he painted himself modestly. He was constantly searching for the person within," she said.

"Truly beautiful. He was a tragic figure, though," Cianán said.

Luka roamed her gaze over the painting and said, "He had an exquisitely lovely soul. Look at those eyes. The rarest kind of purity lay behind them. He loved not only the beauty around him, but he saw the beauty in the most unlikely to be loved person. He cared so much that it tormented him to death. His heart was filled with sunshine, and it burst out in his sunflowers and wheat fields and big skies. It is the gift he shares with us eternally."

Cianán turned and looked at her. "I know someone who's full of sunshine. She's particularly dear to me."

When they'd finished walking through, she said, "Let's go have some coffee," hooking her arm in with his, and added, "When you're in the Netherlands, you must have lots of coffee."

They sat down at a café and Cianán remarked, "Although I like my coffee black, I can't get over how you Dutch drink your coffee so black and bitter."

"We're stuck in tradition. Coffee with milk and sugar is called, *koffie verkeerd,* meaning wrong coffee," she explained.

"If you say so, but I do like a bit of sweet in mine," he said, stirring his coffee and taking a sip. "How's Bas?" he asked.

Cianán had met Bas in Vancouver but hadn't seen him since he'd arrived in Amsterdam. Luka, Bas, and Cianán were going out for dinner in the evening with Stijn and Beydaan.

"He's doing well. You know, when we were standing in front of Vincent's self-portraits just now, it struck me how Sebastian is, in many ways the way Vincent painted himself: unassuming, and always honest about who he is. He blends in with the background so that there is harmony between all the colours within himself and his environment. Even so, he is no less dazzling and amazing."

He studied her face for a moment. "You do look happy. Married life suits you," he said.

Luka and Bas had gotten married six months ago, in June,

in a small ceremony. She had found out she was pregnant, and he'd asked her to marry him. She'd told him he didn't have to make her pregnant, for her to marry him, but they were both thrilled at the news of the baby. So were their parents. Marit was simply ecstatic. They'd learned a week ago that it was a boy.

"Yes, I am happy. It turns out Bas was born to be a husband and I know he'll be a phenomenal father," she said with a smile.

"I envy you your joy. It's not for a lack of want that I'm not married, but I still have a week left here in Amsterdam with its beautiful Dutch women and my pocket full of hope." He said after a pause, "I've been asked to send greetings from Sidney."

"Thank you. How's he doing?"

"Not much has changed there, except his hair colour has a little greyer shade." Luka nodded and Cianán added, "It's of no consequence now, but I think you derailed his speed train somewhat. He's not quite been himself ever since."

"The thing about speed trains is that when they become derailed, they get up and run fast again. I prefer a slow train ride through the countryside to appreciate the view."

He chuckled. "True. Anyway, I'm glad to be here in this wonderful city and your delightful company and am thrilled that I'll be sharing in your granny's big occasion."

* * *

Luka had arranged that Stijn and Beydaan pick Cianán up at his hotel. Anton and Adelheid were visiting for the weekend and were driving with Bas and Luka to Marit's birthday dinner.

The venue was a gorgeous property east of the Amstel River that hosted weddings and had a superb restaurant with a cozy private room which Arne and Evi had booked for the evening. The manager had gone to great trouble to alert his staff about the guest of honour, and Marit was greeted with cheers and, "Hoera!" when she walked through the doors.

The guest list included: Marit; two of Marit's surviving circle of friends (whom she called the youngsters because they were still in their eighties) and Arne; Betje; Anouk; Isa and her boyfriend; Ruben and Evi; Bas and Luka; Anton and Adelheid; Stijn and Beydaan; and last but not least, Cianán.

Marit wore an elegant 1950s-style, aquamarine dress. Evi had taken her to the hairdresser to have her hair done and had helped her put a little makeup on.

Cianán was a hit with Luka's family and Marit's friends. Marit was delighted when he gave her the Canucks hockey shirt, which immediately became a topic of conversation with everyone standing by. Marit's green eyes sparkled with excitement and from all the attention.

Luka couldn't help noticing the glances between Cianán and her vivacious cousin, Anouk, who was newly single and taking it in her usual nonchalant stride. She thought, with a smile, that Cianán's pocket full of hope might well produce positive yields for him—if only as a temporary remedy. But then again, maybe it would end up not being transitory.

"How are you feeling, Papa? Are you taking it easy on the treats?" Luka asked her father, whose eyes twinkled. His appetite was back, and he was walking around, inspecting the delicious snacks set out on a table against the wall.

Evi cautioned, "Don't make yourself sick, Rubie.

"I'll pace myself, don't worry, my sweetheart," Ruben said and popped a sweet pastry into his mouth.

Luka looked at the plates of treats with interest, and she too decided to give one a try. Ruben looked at her and asked, "Are you and my grandson having a good time?"

"We're having a great time. Isn't Cianán a hoot? He and Omoe are getting along like a house on fire," she said and ate another puff.

Bas joined them. "Don't fill up on those too much. The food's supposed to be excellent here."

"I won't, but taste this," she said with a mouth full of food, and put a savoury puff into his mouth. He lifted his brow in agreement and grinned as he held her affectionately.

Just before it was time to serve the meal, Evi stood to make a speech (Anouk translated for Cianán).

"It is my heart's joy to celebrate with you tonight, the life of a woman who continues to inspire us all. She is our mother, our grandmother, our friend, to some of you here, the godmother of a secret society …" She looked at Bas, Stijn, and Cianán, who had big smiles. "… and a truly amazing human being: Marit Feltes.

"My brother and I grew up in post Second World War Netherlands. Our parents both survived harsh circumstances, and not only did their spirits endure, but they grew stronger. And it was with this tenacity and purpose we were raised.

"As a physician, our father sacrificed much of his family life—there are a few doctors around the table who will be able to relate to that—and our mother made the decision to raise my brother and me herself, instead of relying on help. That was by no means a small sacrifice for her. She was a career woman and a strong proponent of women's financial independence at a time when it was anything but the norm.

"Yet she did it without complaint, and she was, and still is, a wonderful mother to us." Evi looked at Marit and said, "Mama, I am so proud to be your daughter. Thank you for many, many years of love and joy and friendship." She said to all at the table, "Will you please raise your glasses with me as we say, happy hundredth birthday!"

Luka said to Bas, sitting next to her, "I may not live to be a hundred years old, but if I have just some of Omoe's spirit in me, I shall consider myself a fortunate woman."

"You may consider yourself a fortunate woman then, you have a lot of her spirit in you. You are so alike, you and her," he replied.

"Hmm … perhaps I'll also become the godmother of a secret club, to our son's friends one day."

"You mean our grandson's friends."

"Will you ever tell me some of the things you talk about with her?" she asked.

Bas looked at her and said, "Absolutely not, you get your own club. Don't worry, you only need to wait another sixty years or so to qualify as a godmother." He chuckled when she gave him a pouty look.

As the evening went on, both Marit and Luka started showing signs of fatigue, and Luka was trying to hide her yawns behind her hand.

"I'm sorry," she apologized when a yawn came up halfway through a sentence. "This little one has been bouncing around in here. He's also celebrating Omoe's birthday, and has had a bit too much cake, I think." Luka was sitting next to Marit and squeezed her hand.

Stijn said with a grin, "Maybe that's a good omen, Luka and

you're going to produce the next great star for Oranje." (A nickname meaning, orange, for the Dutch national football team.)

There were encouraging cheers from both the men and women around the table.

Luka laughed, "Well, he's certainly been practising like a soccer star."

"What a marvellous moment this is," Marit said. "My eyes have seen a hundred years go by, like the blink of an eye. But I am not done yet, I still hope in the near future—to see my great grandson soon." Marit touched Luka's belly affectionately, before adding, "Thank you all for being here. My heart is bursting with love. I mean it sincerely."

When they were ready to leave and Bas helped Luka put her ultramarine velvet coat on, he looked into her eyes for a moment, then gave her favourite crooked smile as he said, "You're going to be a killer godmother someday."

"I hope you'll be there with me to show me the ropes, Sebastian," she said as she put her arms around his neck and kissed him.

40

Marit died quietly in her sleep at the age of one hundred and five and a half, after having attended the first piano recital of her five-year-old great grandson, Espen De Cleene.

When he'd finished his performance, Espen had jumped up and applauded himself with a big grin.

Bas had said, "Well, there's the proof: his spirit lives on."

Luka had nodded with a knowing smile.

Marit had said, as she'd held her hands together after her own applause, "Now I've seen it all."

About the Author

Leonora Ross is an artist and fiction writer and lives in Western Canada.

You can connect with me on:
- https://www.leonoraross.com
- https://twitter.com/LeonoraAuthor

Also by Leonora Ross

Leonora Ross is a contemporary and literary fiction writer.

Tess Has a Broken Heart, and Other Comedies Full of Errors
A quirky tale of friendship and longing for love.

Tess, her best friend Zara, and Zara's daughter, Zénnie, move from Los Angeles to Calgary, Alberta and decide to rent an enormous house with beautiful Rocky Mountain views, but they can only afford it by getting subtenants.

Into their lives, enter a kooky English woman and five gorgeous men.

Tess—slightly neurotic, but lovable—has a hard time letting things go and letting change in; especially the love of a younger man who is eager to prove her doubts and fears wrong.

Her girlfriends worry; not that she'd get hurt, but that she would be too afraid to take the chance and miss out on something wonderful.

*Tess Has a Broken Heart, and Other Comedies Full of Error*s, is a story about deep friendships, aging women's never-ending desire to stay relevant through every changing season, and beautiful men with deep souls, who often prove women wrong when they think they are so smart and have all the answers.

www.ingramcontent.com/pod-product-compliance
Lightning Source LLC
Chambersburg PA
CBHW020906060726

47591CB00004B/1115